Praise for the Jane Austen

"Rollicking . . . a witty demonstration of how beautifully the dilemmas of being Jane Austen and a vampire can comport with the tropes of chick lit. You'll thirst for the conclusion of the trilogy."

—*Kirkus Reviews* on *Jane Goes Batty*

"Inventive and funny, and the story progresses with the kind of light touch that compares favorably to the . . . Stephenie Meyer Twilight series. . . . [Ford] consistently delights."

—*Bay Area Reporter* on *Jane Bites Back*

"Fang-tastic."

—*Publishers Weekly* on *Jane Bites Back*

"Hilarious . . . I thoroughly enjoyed reading this book and know you will too!"

—The Vampire Librarian on *Jane Bites Back*

"A fun, humorous weekend read! . . . It [made] me laugh out loud. Ford does a fantastic job capturing the spirit of Jane Austen."

—Vamp Chix on *Jane Goes Batty*

"A rollicking good read . . . Ford is wickedly funny."

—Dirty Laundry on *Jane Bites Back*

"Ford approvingly cites Seth Grahame-Smith's *Pride and Prejudice and Zombies*, but his own mashup is better integrated, more knowledgeable about Austen and considerably funnier."

—*Kirkus Reviews* on *Jane Bites Back*

"Filled with sly humor and fast-paced quips, this [is a] delightful romp. . . . Ford's Jane is as lovely and as ladylike as ever, her vital spirit a perfect reflection of literary heroine chic."

—Curled Up with a Good Book on *Jane Goes Batty*

"Ford delivers an original take with a sharp and well-formed wit. I found myself laughing and groaning in no time at all."

—January Magazine on *Jane Goes Batty*

"A hilarious romp . . . This book is definitely worth picking up and reading and I can't wait to read the third installment in this building series."

—The Obsessive Book Worm on *Jane Goes Batty*

"A funny, smart, well-crafted book that will keep you glued to the pages . . . This book has a little bit for everyone. If you like the classics, you'll enjoy the references. If you like physical comedy, you won't be disappointed. And, if you're enjoying the rapid rise of the vampire genre, *Jane Goes Batty* is your cherry on the top. Pick up your copy today."

—Romance Reviews Today on *Jane Goes Batty*

"[*Jane Goes Batty* is] the kind of book you can start reading late at night and fight off sleep just so you can keep reading. . . . I highly recommend this book and its prequel. It will have you dying to meet your favourite authors."

—Bibliomantics on *Jane Goes Batty*

Also by Michael Thomas Ford

Jane Bites Back
Jane Goes Batty

Jane
Vows
VENGEANCE

Jane
Vows
VENGEANCE

A NOVEL

Michael Thomas Ford

BALLANTINE BOOKS TRADE PAPERBACKS  NEW YORK

A Ballantine Books Trade Paperback Original

Copyright © 2012 by Michael Thomas Ford

Published in the United States by Ballantine Books, an imprint of The Random House Publishing Group, a division of Random House, Inc., New York.

BALLANTINE and colophon are registered trademarks of Random House, Inc.

Library of Congress Cataloging-in-Publication Data
Ford, Michael Thomas.
Jane vows vengeance: a novel / Michael Thomas Ford.
    p.   cm.
ISBN 978-0-345-51367-0
eBook ISBN 978-0-345-52437-9
1. Austen, Jane, 1775–1817—Fiction. 2. Vampires—Fiction. I. Title.
PS3606.O7424J39   2012
813'.6—dc23   2011046722

Printed in the United States of America

www.ballantinebooks.com

2 4 6 8 9 7 5 3 1

Book design by Elizabeth A. D. Eno

This one is for Famous Author Rob Byrnes,
because he told me not to.

Jane
Vows
VENGEANCE

Chapter 1

Brakeston, New York

"WHAT ABOUT THIS ONE?"

Jane glanced at the magazine Lucy was holding up, opened to a picture of a bride standing in a field of daisies. The bride wore a sheath-style dress of ivory silk and a birdcage veil to which was affixed a huge pale yellow gardenia. Not far behind her stood a Holstein cow, gazing at the camera with a disinterested look.

Jane grimaced. "I don't think I have the upper arms for that," she said.

"Of course you do," scoffed Lucy. "Well, with a little work you could."

Jane ignored her best friend. "Why would a bride go tromping around in a field of cows?" she said irritably. "If there's any train at all on that dress, she's going to drag it right through a pile of—"

"It's one cow," Lucy said wearily. "And it's a photo shoot for a fashion magazine, not an article in *National Geographic*. Get a grip."

Jane sighed, closing the magazine she was paging through and tossing it onto the pile of them covering the top of the kitchen table. "It's just that they're all starting to blur together. Cap sleeves. Bateau necklines. Basque waists. Mermaid this and sweetheart that and princess whatever. It's maddening."

Lucy picked up another magazine. *"Victorian Bride,"* she read, looking at the cover. She glanced at Jane. "Really?"

Jane chewed the nail on her left index finger. "I grabbed everything they had," she replied. "I think I have wedding sickness."

Eight months had passed since she'd accepted Walter Fletcher's marriage proposal. Shortly before the Christmas holidays she had moved into Walter's house. It was now February, and although Walter was not pressuring her to pick a date for their wedding, another deadline hung over her head like the ominous clouds of an approaching thunderstorm.

Jane had so far avoided telling her fiancé that she was a vampire. Her undead condition was, however, known to Walter's mother. Miriam Ellenberg, much to Jane's dismay, had turned out to be even more of a challenge than mothers-in-law generally were: Miriam was a vampire hunter. Not surprisingly, she disapproved of her son's choice of a girlfriend, and initially had vowed to dispatch Jane at the earliest convenience. However, after Jane rescued Miriam from almost certain death at the hands of a deranged vampire turned book reviewer, a truce had been declared. With one condition: Jane had a year in which to produce a grandchild. Should she fail, all bets were off and Miriam and she would once again be mortal enemies.

In addition to not having planned a wedding, Jane had not become pregnant. She still wasn't even sure she *could* conceive, which was in itself no small concern. To make matters worse, Miriam had decided to move from Florida to upstate New York so that she could keep an eye on her daughter-in-law-to-be. Thankfully, Walter had not suggested that his mother move into the house with them. However, he had suggested that Miriam buy Jane's former home, since Jane would have no more use for it now that she and Walter were living together. As neither Jane nor Miriam—despite both thinking very hard—had been able to come up with a good reason why this course of action should not be taken, a deal had been struck, and the week after Jane moved herself, her pets, and her possessions into Walter's house, a trio of anxious young men had unloaded Miriam's belongings from a truck under Miriam's scrutinizing supervision.

The matter of Jane's barren state was becoming a greater problem with each passing week. With only four months left in which to become pregnant, she sensed Miriam becoming increasingly impatient. To her credit, Miriam had never once reminded Jane of the looming deadline. She and Jane were cordial enough to each other that Walter had often remarked on how pleased he was that they were getting on so well. Still, Jane knew that she was being watched.

She was not surprised, then, when Miriam made an appearance in the kitchen just moments later. She was dressed in a variation of the peculiar ensemble she'd adopted following the first snowfall of the winter. Unused to cold, she had opted for warmth over fashion, exchanging the lightweight pantsuits that had served her well in Florida's tropical climate for sturdy corduroy trousers and heavy wool sweaters in Irish fisherman and Norwegian ski patterns. At the moment she was wearing moss-green pants and a cream Aran sweater with a rolled neck. Below the knees her pants were tucked into a pair of brown Wellingtons, and on her head was a black-and-red buffalo plaid hunter's cap with earflaps and a shearling lining.

"It's cold enough to freeze a bear's ass," she said as she pulled the cap off and sat down. "I need some coffee."

In addition to her new wardrobe, Miriam had also acquired a collection of sayings generally used only by residents of the New England states. No matter how many times Walter told her that New York—despite its name—was not considered part of New

England, Miriam persisted in behaving as if it were, occasionally even taking on an accent that was more Maine lobsterman than Jewish mother of a certain age.

Jane got up and poured Miriam a cup of coffee, thinking that she really needed to start locking the front door. She handed the cup to Miriam, then refilled Lucy's mug. She herself was drinking hot chocolate. Although her vampire metabolism didn't require that she eat, she still enjoyed the activity, particularly if it involved sweets.

"Still looking at dresses, I see," Miriam remarked, nodding at the magazines.

"Yes," Jane said evenly. "Still looking."

"I really don't see what the problem is," Miriam said. "Choosing a dress shouldn't be any more difficult than choosing a paint color. Just pick the one that's going to hide the problem areas the best. Take you, for example. You've got a wide—"

"I believe I've narrowed it down," Jane said. "The dress choices," she clarified as Miriam started to reply.

Miriam peered at her through the steam from the coffee cup. "And have you set a date?" she asked. "Summer's right around the corner, you know."

Jane was unsure whether Miriam was referring to the approaching anniversary of their agreement or just remarking on the fact that a summer wedding would be lovely. She chose to believe it was the latter, although Miriam's tone could be interpreted either way.

"Why don't you and Walter just elope?" Lucy suggested.

Miriam and Jane both turned their heads to look at her.

"What?" said Lucy, pushing a strand of long curly black hair behind her ear. "It would save a lot of fuss and bother."

"I thought you were excited about being my maid of honor," Jane said.

"I am," Lucy assured her. "I'm just saying, if this is making you so crazy, just get married at the courthouse and go to Tahiti for two weeks or something."

"That would be nice," Jane mused. "We could lie on the beach and have fruit drinks."

"Nonsense," said Miriam. "You're going to be married right here so that I—so that all of your friends can join in the celebration."

Jane looked at Lucy, who rolled her eyes and puffed out her cheeks. "It was just a suggestion," she muttered.

"Walter's first wedding was simply perfect," Miriam informed them. "Evelyn was absolutely stunning."

And now she's dead, Jane thought, immediately mortified that such a thing would pop into her head. But it was true. Besides, it was becoming far too common an occurrence for Miriam to compare Jane to Walter's deceased wife. The week before, when Jane had tried her hand at cooking a brisket because Miriam had mentioned how much she enjoyed one, Miriam's response was to tell her how Evelyn's brisket had been so much moister and how she had served small roasted potatoes with it and not mashed.

"Miriam, what kind of dress do you think Jane should wear?" Lucy asked.

Miriam waved a hand at her. "Oh, you know I don't care. I'm sure whatever she wants is fine."

Jane felt her fangs click into place. She closed her eyes and concentrated on forcing them to retract. *You can't bite her,* she reminded herself.

Miriam raised an eyebrow. "Do you have a headache, Jane?" she asked. "You look tense."

"I'm fine," Jane snapped. She opened her eyes. "I'm fine," she repeated, giving Miriam a tight smile.

She heard the front door open and close. "Jane?" Walter called out. "Where are you?"

"In here," Jane replied. "With Lucy and your mother."

Walter came into the kitchen, brushing snow from his navy blue peacoat. "I have great news," he said as he bent to kiss first his mother and then Jane.

"You got the Thorne-Waxe house job!" Jane said. A restorer of historic houses, Walter had recently been asked to submit a proposal for restoring a run-down Victorian house that had been cut up into four apartments. The new owners wanted to bring it back to its original glory.

"Oh, yes, I did," said Walter. "But that's not the big news." His blue eyes, always sparkling, had an extra twinkle to them.

The three women looked at him. "Well?" Jane said after a long pause.

"I've solved our wedding problem," Walter said, beaming. "Well, not so much the wedding problem, but the honeymoon problem."

"What do you mean, the honeymoon problem?" Miriam asked.

"Jane and I have been trying to decide where to go on our honeymoon," Walter explained.

"What honeymoon?" said Miriam. "You haven't even set a date for the wedding!"

"We'll figure that out," Walter said. "The important thing is, I know where we're going afterward."

"Tahiti?" said Lucy hopefully.

"Europe," said Walter.

"Europe is a big place," Jane reminded him. "Can you narrow it down a bit?"

"That's the best part," said Walter. "We don't have to narrow it down. I've been invited to go on a tour of historic houses with the International Association of Historic Preservationists. They're spending two weeks looking at homes in Ireland, France, Switzerland, Italy, and England. Oh, and Scotland or somewhere. I can't remember the exact details. Doesn't it sound fun?"

"How many other people will be going on our honeymoon with us?" Jane inquired.

"I don't know—two dozen or so, I guess," said Walter. "But we don't have to do everything with the group. There's a lot of free time built into the itinerary. And it's not really our honeymoon. We can add another week on at the end for just the two of us. Anywhere you want to go." He looked at the three women, who sat there saying nothing. "Well?"

"When is this trip?" Jane asked.

"March," said Walter.

"March!" Jane, Lucy, and Miriam shrieked in unison.

"March what?" asked Lucy.

"We leave on the ninth," Walter answered.

"The ninth!" the three women chorused.

"Walter, that's . . . " Jane counted on her fingers.

"Seventeen days from now," said Miriam. "We can't possibly plan a wedding in that short a time."

"Why not?" Walter asked. "You're my only family, and Jane has none."

"Hey!" Lucy exclaimed.

"You know what I mean," said Walter, patting her shoulder kindly. "No parents or cousins or other people who would need to make travel plans. Everyone we want to invite already lives here. All we have to do is get married."

Lucy looked at Jane. "It sounds so simple when he puts it like that," she said.

"It does rather, doesn't it?" Jane agreed.

"See?" said Walter, sounding very pleased with himself. "It's all settled."

Jane looked at Miriam. Her mouth was set in a grim line, and she scowled at Jane with undisguised dislike. *She's been hoping all along that the wedding would never happen,* Jane realized. *She wants me to run out of time. Well, we'll just see about that.*

"I think it's a splendid idea," she said. "Don't you, Miriam?"

Miriam narrowed her eyes. "Just peachy," she said through gritted teeth.

Walter put one arm around Jane's shoulders and the other around his mother's. "I knew you would be thrilled," he said. "Hey, I just thought of something. Once Jane and I are married you'll both be Mrs. Fletcher."

Miriam let out a little yelp, which she covered by pretending to cough. "You know I don't go by that name any—"

"You should take care of that cough, Mom," Walter said, grinning and ignoring her. "You don't want it to turn into something worse."

"I don't think it's possible for it to get worse," said Miriam, reaching for her coffee.

"Well, maybe you should go home and rest," Walter told her. "We want you in fighting shape for the big day. Right, Jane?"

"By all means," Jane said, flashing her teeth at Miriam. "I know I will be."

Chapter 2

New York City, New York

"EXPLAIN TO ME AGAIN HOW YOU'VE LIVED THIS LONG WITHOUT A passport," Byron said to Jane as they walked down a narrow street on New York's Lower East Side. Surprised by a snowstorm that had begun just after midnight, the city was in a state of disarray. The normally bustling thoroughfares were largely empty as cars huddled beneath blankets of white, and the few people out walking did so with hats pulled down over their ears and hands jammed into the pockets of their coats.

Jane and Byron, having arrived on the first train of the morning from Brakeston, took little notice of the cold. They wore coats and scarves not for warmth but to blend in, although Byron wasn't doing a particularly good job of that. The black wool ulster he was wearing gave him the appearance of someone from another era. This impression was intensified by the cane he used to compensate for his limp. Made of cherry wood, it was topped with the head of a rabbit cast in bronze. The ensemble, coupled with Byron's pale skin and dark hair, created an aura of otherworldliness. The fact that he was extraordinarily handsome only made him more noticeable.

"I've never needed one," Jane said, answering Byron's question. "I don't go anywhere."

"Still," said Byron, running his hand across the top of a car as they passed by it and scooping up a handful of snow, "I would think you would want one *just in case.*"

He packed the snow into a tight ball. Then, with a casualness that belied the speed at which the snowball traveled, he hurled it across the street, where it struck the back of a man who was standing and watching his dog, a French bulldog wearing a red-and-white striped sweater, relieve itself on a lamppost. The man whirled around, exclaiming loudly, but saw only the retreating figures of a well-dressed couple walking arm in arm through the snow.

"That was for making that poor dog wear a sweater," Byron explained to Jane. "Oh, and here we are."

They had stopped in front of a narrow brownstone remarkably like all the other brownstones on the block, although the ground floor of this particular building was taken up by a small watch repair shop. The front window was crowded with timepieces, and the faded gold lettering on the glass read TIME OUT OF MIND. Underneath that in smaller black lettering was S. GRUNDY, HOROLOGIST. Bits of paint had long ago fallen off or been chipped away, giving the letters a moth-eaten appearance, and the dust that was gathered in the corners of the window provided additional reason to suppose that the establishment had long ago ceased to do business. Only the faint glow of a light hidden in the recesses of the shop suggested otherwise.

Byron turned the handle of the shop's door and pushed. Protesting, the door opened, and Byron stood aside, motioning for Jane to enter ahead of him. As Jane looked around the small, cluttered room Byron walked to the back and called out, "Solomon! Solomon, are you here?"

"Solomon?" Jane said, glancing at the window. "Solomon Grundy?"

"Indeed," said Byron. "Do you know him? I thought you said—"

"No," Jane interrupted. "I mean, I don't know *this* Solomon Grundy. But there's the rhyme. 'Solomon Grundy, born on a Monday, christened on Tuesday, married on Wednesday, took ill on Thursday, grew worse on Friday—'"

"'Died on Saturday, buried on Sunday,'" said a voice, followed by a violent cough. "'This is the end of Solomon Grundy.'"

Standing before Jane was a very tall, very thin man who if not a century old was very close to it. He had long gray hair that fell in greasy strands to the shoulders of his worn black velvet frock coat, pale gray eyes that peered out at her from behind shockingly thick gold-rimmed spectacles, and a forehead creased like the spine of a well-read book. Most peculiar of all was his nose, which extended from his face almost like a beak and ended in a blunt point that was covered by a gold cap.

"Very good, young lady," he said. "And what is today?"

"Thursday," Jane answered, trying not to stare at his unusual appearance.

"Thursday," the man repeated. "That explains the cough, then. It's a good thing you didn't come a day later, as I would almost certainly be unable to see you. And of course by Saturday I will be dead and of no use whatsoever. So before that happens, perhaps you should tell me why you have come."

"Jane is in need of a passport, Solomon," Byron explained.

"Indeed?" said Solomon. He eyed Jane with curiosity. "And who *are* you? Before, I mean. Not now."

"Oh," Jane said uncomfortably. *Saying* that she was Jane Austen always made her feel as if she were lying. Or boasting.

"Solomon, allow me to introduce you to Miss Jane Austen," Byron said.

Solomon stepped back. "My, my," he said. He bowed toward her. "It's my distinct pleasure."

Jane felt herself blush as much as someone with no beating heart could. "It's lovely to meet you," she said.

Solomon smiled, revealing a row of gleaming gold teeth. "I have long been a fan," he told Jane. His eyes sparkled. "Just a moment," he told her. "I want to show you something."

He retreated to the rear of the shop, where Jane heard him rummaging around. There was a great deal of rustling, a very loud thud, and several rounds of enthusiastic sneezing. Then Solomon reappeared, clutching in one hand a trio of leather-bound volumes. He waved them at Jane, cackling gleefully. "I admit I haven't read them in quite some time," he said. "But here they are."

He handed the books to Jane, who looked at the covers and gasped. "The first edition of *Sense and Sensibility*!" she exclaimed.

Solomon nodded. "I had them bound, of course. Otherwise they're exactly as I bought them from a London bookstall on the day of their publication."

Jane ran her fingertips over the leather, tracing the title of her book. She lifted the cover of the first volume and gazed upon the familiar title page. "Even I don't have the first editions," she said. "I did once upon a time, of course, but I'm afraid I lost them in a move. I believe I mistakenly threw them out along with a stack of old *New Yorker* issues."

"Pity," Solomon said, quickly taking the books back from her and slipping them into one of his coat pockets. Jane stared wistfully at the pocket, wondering if perhaps the watchmaker might be persuaded to part with the novels.

Byron cleared his throat. "Now that introductions have been made, perhaps we can get down to business," he said.

"Ah, yes," said Solomon. "A passport. For Miss Jane Austen."

"Fairfax, actually," Jane said. "It should say Jane Fairfax. That's the name by which I'm now known."

Solomon turned and walked toward the back of the shop. This time Jane followed him, arriving at a large workbench covered with tools and upon which were scattered various gears, faces, crystals, and minute and hour hands that had become detached and now lay disembodied among the corpses of broken watches. A lone stool sat before the table, and a single bare bulb was screwed into the end of an electrical cord that dangled from the ceiling.

Solomon seated himself on the stool, pulled open a drawer in the workbench, and removed several passport books. "Would you like to be English, Canadian, or American?" he asked.

"American, I suppose," Jane answered. She felt a bit as if she were turning her back on her homeland by assuming an American identity, but she knew it was the most practical choice.

"American it is," Solomon said, placing a blue passport on the table and returning the others to the drawer. "Now then, did you bring the photographs?"

Jane fished in her coat pocket and withdrew the small cardboard folder containing the photos she'd had taken the evening before at the copy shop near her bookstore. "I'm afraid they're dreadful," she told Solomon as she handed them to him.

"Nonsense," Solomon assured her as he opened the folder. "I'm sure they're perfectly love—" He hesitated, then looked at Jane. "Well, at least your eyes are nice and open," he said.

Jane watched as Solomon took one of the photos and began trimming it to the correct size. "If you don't mind my asking, do you do a lot of this sort of thing?" she asked.

"Oh, yes," Solomon answered. "Passports. Driver's licenses. Anything you need, I can forge it."

Jane, intrigued, said, "And are all of your clients as we are?"

"Vampires, you mean?" said Solomon. He had removed his glasses and inserted a jeweler's loupe in his left eye. His head was bent over the passport as he did something Jane couldn't quite see. "Most are, but not all."

"And are you . . . " Jane began. She decided the question was indelicate, however, and stopped.

"Am I a vampire?" said Solomon, lifting his head and grinning at her. "No. I'm something . . . different."

He returned to his work. Jane, sensing that he didn't want to be disturbed, went in search of Byron. She found him crouched on the floor, rummaging through a box of old pocket watches.

"How did you say you know Solomon?" she asked Byron.

Byron blew the dust from a watch, looked at the back, then returned it to the box. "I didn't," he replied. "And I really don't remember. But he's proved to be quite useful over the years." He stood up and looked at Jane. "Do you know he once forged me a death certificate from the state of Missouri that was so realistic I almost believed the gentleman in question really had died of cardiac arrest?"

"Why would you need . . . Never mind," Jane said. "I don't want to know. I'm sure he's very good at what he does. But what exactly *is* he?"

"Ahh," Byron purred. "He wouldn't tell you, would he?"

Jane shrugged, feigning disinterest. "I didn't ask," she said. "It only now occurred to me to."

"Did it?" said Byron, smirking. "Well, I suppose there's no harm in telling you. He's a zombie."

"A zombie!" Jane said.

Byron made a shushing sound. "Quiet," he said. "He doesn't like to discuss it."

Jane, chastened, lowered her voice to a whisper. "He doesn't look like a zombie," she said. "Well, not like any I've ever seen, although I'll grant you those have only been in movies."

"Solomon isn't like that," Byron explained. "Not exactly. Remember the rhyme?"

As Jane had only recently recited it to him, she assumed Byron's question to be rhetorical, and said nothing. Byron continued, "He wasn't joking when he said it was lucky we came on a Thursday. By tomorrow he'll be quite ill, and by Saturday night he'll be dead. Sunday he'll—well, I don't really know what becomes of him on Sunday—but on Monday he'll be right as rain and it will start all over again."

Jane made a face. "How awful," she said. "How does a thing like that happen? I mean, surely he wasn't always like this."

"No, he wasn't," Byron agreed. "But I don't know how he became what he is. As far as I know, he's never told anyone, except perhaps his wife."

"His *wife*?" said Jane.

"Yes, his wife," Byron repeated. "'Married on Wednesday,' remember?"

"What's she like?" Jane asked.

"That depends," said Byron. "When she is good, she's very, very good, but when she is bad she is horrid."

Jane snorted. "And I suppose she has a little curl?"

"Yes," said Byron. "Right in the middle of her forehead. I thought you said you didn't know her."

"I don't," Jane said. "I was quoting the rhyme."

"What rhyme?" said Byron, giving her a puzzled look. "Anyway, she runs the boardinghouse upstairs."

Jane glanced at the ceiling. "Up there?"

Byron nodded. "They cater mostly to our community," he said. "Generally the newly turned. They stay here while they adjust. Also, Alice teaches them a thing or two about being undead."

"Alice?" said Jane. "That's Solomon's wife?"

"Now that I think of it, I should have just sent you to Alice," Byron said. "I could have saved myself a great deal of fuss and bother. Not that I haven't enjoyed it," he added quickly.

"There's a school?" said Jane. "How do people find out about it?"

"Oh, they have cards," Byron explained. "The more thoughtful vampires leave them in the pockets of anyone they turn. Otherwise it's mostly blind luck or being fortunate enough to run into someone who knows about this place. Someone like myself, for example."

"Except that you didn't tell me about it," Jane argued.

Byron shook his head. "Well, how *could* I have told you?" he said. "That was two hundred years ago. I didn't know about it then."

"We could have sent Chloe here," said Jane, thinking about the young actress she had been forced to turn the previous summer.

"I did consider that," Byron admitted. "But only briefly. I don't think they take celebrity clients. Anyway, I think we did rather well with her on our own."

"Yes," Jane agreed. "I think we did. Which reminds me, the film will be out this summer."

"Have you decided whether or not you'll see it? I know you weren't at all happy with how things went."

"I think I'm over it. Besides, if I can stomach Greer Garson as Elizabeth Bennett, I can stomach anything."

"All right, here you are."

Solomon's arrival brought Jane's attention back to the moment. She accepted the passport Solomon held out to her and opened it. "It looks perfect," she said after checking that all of the information was correct—or as correct as it could be for a bunch of out-and-out lies.

"With that document you will be able to make your way all over Europe with no difficulties," Solomon assured her.

"Thank you," Jane said.

"And if you get caught and thrown in an Italian prison, I will refund one-half of the purchase price."

Jane looked at Byron, unsure of what to say.

"I'm joking," Solomon told her. "I don't give refunds. All sales are final, and if anyone asks, I've never seen you before. But don't worry, everything will be fine. Go and have a lovely honeymoon."

"I'd almost forgotten that that's why I need this," Jane said as she slipped the passport into her coat pocket.

"Solomon, as always, it's a pleasure doing business with you,"

Byron said, shaking the other man's hand. "Now go have Alice make you some chicken soup. You look terrible."

Solomon laughed heartily, but after a moment it turned into a wet-sounding cough. "Oh, dear," he said. "It seems to be coming on early this week. It must be the weather."

When they were outside again, Byron took a bottle of hand sanitizer from his pocket and squirted some into his palm. He extended the bottle to Jane, who shook her head. "We're already dead," she reminded him. "What's the point?"

"Yes, we're dead," said Byron. "But so are zombies. Do you really want to risk it?"

She held out her hand. "You're right. Explaining to Walter that I'm a vampire is one thing. Trying to explain why I want to eat his brain is quite another."

Chapter 3

Brakeston, New York

"STEPHANOTIS! CASABLANCA LILIES! HYDRANGEAS!"

Jane sat straight up in bed and pointed a finger at Walter, who had pulled the blankets up to his chin and was looking up at her with a puzzled expression.

"But absolutely no baby's breath!" Jane shrieked before collapsing back against the pillows.

Walter sat up slowly, cleared his throat, and said, "I take it you had another wedding dream."

Jane groaned. "It was horrible," she said. "I'd forgotten all about the flowers. For some reason every florist in town was closed, and I had to run to the A&P and buy one of those horrid bouquets of daisies dyed bright blue and wrapped in cellophane. Then when I tried to check out, my club card wouldn't scan and I couldn't remember the fake telephone number I'd given them when I opened the account, so the clerk wouldn't give me the discount. I only had a ten-dollar bill and the bouquet was twelve ninety-nine. The woman behind me was yelling at me to hurry up because her chicken thighs were thawing and she was worried about salmonella, and the bag boy kept shouting, 'Paper or plastic? Paper or plastic? Paper or plastic?'"

She began to cry. Walter reached over and put his arm around her shoulders. Jane leaned against him and sniffed loudly.

"I'm going to have a nervous breakdown," she informed him. "I'll have to be institutionalized, and I'll spend the rest of my life sitting in an uncomfortable chair next to a window, wearing my wedding dress and staring out at the sidewalk, waiting for you to come. And you will at first, because you'll think there's still hope, but after a few years you'll realize that I'm never getting better and you'll stop coming. Then everyone will start calling me the Bitter Bride and torment me by humming the wedding march until I go completely mad and begin mumbling our wedding vows incessantly. Eventually all I'll say is, 'I do, I do, I do,' over and over and over and the other patients will wait until the nurses aren't looking and pelt me with rice." She paused. "Or more likely with rice pudding, because that's what they make you eat in those places."

Walter kissed the top of her head. "Are you done now?"

"For the moment," Jane said.

"First of all," said Walter, "they wouldn't let you wear your wedding dress in a mental institution. Second, you don't need a club card at the A&P anymore. You automatically get the sale price."

"Really?" Jane said. "Well, that just makes it worse. The clerk was deliberately being difficult, and it was obvious I needed those daisies. Who does that to a bride on her wedding day?"

Walter stroked her hair. "I have an idea," he said. "What would you think about postponing the wedding?"

Jane pulled away. "You don't want to marry me," she said. Her lip began to tremble.

"Of course I want to marry you," said Walter. "But not if it's going to put you in an institution. And I'm not talking about postponing the entire wedding. Just this one."

"This one?" Jane said. "I don't understand."

"We could have two weddings," Walter explained. "One would

be just for us. We can do it during our trip. Then, when we come back and we have more time to plan, we can do it again for all of our friends."

Jane considered this plan. "Can we do that?" she asked. "Just get married, I mean."

"I don't see why not," said Walter. "All we really need is the marriage license. It doesn't matter where we have the actual wedding. We can take it with us and have someone marry us wherever we want to."

"You really wouldn't mind?" Jane said.

Walter shook his head. "I don't care where I marry you, or what you wear, or whether you're carrying a bouquet of daisies from the A&P or a bunch of—what did you scream earlier?"

"Casablanca lilies?" said Jane.

"No, the other one," Walter said.

"Stephanotis?" Jane suggested.

"A bouquet of stephanotis," said Walter. "All I care about is marrying you."

"It really would be less stressful," Jane said. Then a horrible thought came to her. "But what about your mother? She won't like this at all."

Walter smiled. "Don't worry about her," he said. "I have a cunning plan. I'll explain it at the war council this morning."

"War council" was what Walter had come to call the daily meeting between Jane, Lucy, and Miriam as they attempted to pull together a wedding in record time. Really, it was just the three of them sitting in the kitchen of Jane and Walter's house as Jane and Miriam quarreled over the details and Lucy played referee and did the bulk of the actual work.

And so at several minutes past eleven in the morning, Walter stood before the three women and announced in a firm voice, "The wedding is off."

"Only temporarily," Jane added as she saw Miriam start to leap to her feet with a triumphant expression.

Miriam remained seated and scowled. "What kind of nonsense is this?" she said. "I thought you wanted to be married before you go on this ridiculous trip of yours."

"We're going to get married in Europe," Walter told her. "In England. That's where Jane's family is from, so it's a way to include them."

"But they're *dead*," Miriam said, looking pointedly at Jane.

"It's symbolic, Mother," said Walter.

"We'll have another wedding when we come back," Jane added. "You know, with a dress and flowers and shrimp puffs."

Miriam snorted. Jane glanced at Lucy and saw that she too looked slightly distraught.

"I knew you'd find some way of cutting me out of the wedding," Miriam said, looking neither at Jane nor Walter but condemning them equally with her tone.

"But we're not," said Walter. "You haven't heard the rest of the plan. You're coming with us."

"What?" Miriam said. "Going with you?"

Walter nodded. "Lucy too," he said. "And Ben and Sarah if they want to come. You're all invited as our guests."

"It would be a kind of traveling wedding party," Jane told them. "We'd follow the itinerary of Walter's house tour."

Miriam sighed. "I'm too old to be traipsing around Europe in the wintertime," she said.

"Nonsense, Mother," said Walter. "Last year you went hiking in Nepal."

"We had Sherpas," Miriam snapped. "And llamas. That's hardly the same thing as wandering around the moors with damp feet. I could get pneumonia."

"With a bit of luck," Jane murmured, just loudly enough for Miriam to hear.

"Well, do as you like," Walter told his mother. "Lucy, will you be coming with us?"

Lucy grinned. "Absolutely," she said.

"What about Ben and Sarah?" asked Jane. "Do you think they'll come?"

"There's only one way to find out," Lucy said. She removed her iPhone from her pocket and tapped the screen three times. "Hi, Rabbi Cohen," she said a moment later. "I have a question for you."

As Lucy spoke with Ben, Miriam resumed her campaign of grousing.

"I don't see why you're abandoning the wedding after everything we've done," she said.

"That's just it," said Jane. "We haven't really accomplished *anything.*"

"Don't be ridiculous," Miriam told her. "There are only a few minor details to iron out."

"That's right," said Jane. "Like the dress, the flowers, the cake, the rings, the reception food, the—"

"Why must you always be so negative?" Miriam interrupted. "We know *where* the reception will be held."

"Only because there was only one place available on such short notice," said Jane. "And now that we're not having it at all, I don't mind telling you that I wasn't terribly thrilled about the idea of having my wedding reception at the Elks Lodge. It's such a dreary place."

"It's a blank canvas," Miriam argued. "We could have done anything we like with it. It would have been marvelous. But no. You had to go and put this wild idea in Walter's head just to spite—"

Walter stopped her. "Mother, this was my idea. Now, Jane and I are going to Europe and we're going to be married while we're there. We'd like you to be there with us, but if you won't come, then you won't come."

Miriam shook her head. "I just don't know. I'm an old woman. My arthritis," she added vaguely. "The croup. Chilblains."

"Ben's in," Lucy announced, returning her phone to her

pocket. "Well, he's in if he can find someone to take care of Sarah. He doesn't want to take her out of school for so long."

Walter looked at Miriam. "Since my mother doesn't want to come, he said, "perhaps she could look after Sarah."

"Who said I'm not coming?" Miriam said defensively.

Jane looked at Lucy. "I think I know someone who might be able to look after Sarah," she said.

"What a delightful idea," Byron said. "I adore children." Then he frowned. "But why am I not invited to come along?"

Jane handed him a mug of coffee. "I think you know the answer to that question," she said as she took a seat.

"But I wouldn't be a bit of trouble," said Byron. "Honestly, what could I *possibly* do?"

"Really?" Jane said, regarding him balefully.

Byron waved a hand at her. "Don't judge," he said. "Besides, I could be enormously useful. I've lived in Europe much more recently than you have. I could be a kind of tour guide."

"You'll be much more helpful by staying here with Sarah."

He sighed. "Very well. What do I have to do?"

"I'll let Ben explain your duties to you," said Jane. "But I will tell you what you will *not* do. You will not teach her how to dematerialize, or how to glamor, or how to summon the red-eyed wolves of the tulgey wood."

"Of course I won't," Byron said. "She'd have to be a vampire for her to be able to . . . " He paused as an expression of delight crossed his face.

"And you will absolutely not do *that!*" Jane said.

"You're right," he said. "I absolutely will not. I was just thinking aloud. Besides, you're the one who brought up the whole tulgey wood thing."

"I was just making examples," Jane replied. "I might just as easily have said 'no playing with matches' or 'no cutting the tails off mice.' I was simply using references to which you could relate."

"I would never cut the tails off mice," he said, a wounded tone to his voice. "Do you take me for a monster?"

"That's settled, then," Jane said, ignoring him. "I think it's best if you stay at Ben's house. Sarah will feel more at home there."

Byron's eyes lit up. "Oh, to be in such close proximity to the rabbi's underwear drawer," he said.

"You may add investigating the rabbi's underwear drawer to the list of things you are forbidden to do," said Jane. "Although I can't blame you for wanting to."

"Do you think he wears boxers or briefs?" Byron mused as he sipped his coffee.

"Boxers," he and Jane said simultaneously.

With the arrangements for Sarah's looking-after taken care of, Jane turned her attention to the matter of Flyleaf Books. Lucy was the manager, and with both of them going away the question of who to leave in command loomed large. That afternoon Jane and Lucy gathered the staff together to address the issue.

"Ted and I have been here the longest," said Ned, one half of the Hawthorne twins. The boys had come to work for Jane at the suggestion of Byron, who had turned one of them (Jane could never remember which one) into a vampire.

"True," Lucy said carefully. "But Shelby has been helping me do the ordering."

Shelby Doolan was a more recent addition. She was the sister of the inept videographer who, the previous summer, had been sent to shoot behind-the-scenes footage for the eventual DVD release of *Constance*, the movie based on Jane's bestselling novel. Shelby had been acting as her brother's assistant, but in reality she had been his savior, again and again rescuing him from his own incompetence. Impressed by the girl's abilities, Jane had offered her a position at the bookstore.

The Hawthorne twins were not quite as pleased with the addition to the staff. Although charming, educated, and handsome, they could also be a bit careless. Furthermore, Jane had yet to entirely forgive the vampire twin (she thought it was Ned, but wasn't certain) for his part in turning one of the actresses in the film. That indiscretion had resulted in not a small amount of bother for everyone, and as the nonvampire twin had colluded in covering up his brother's misstep, he also could not be entirely trusted.

Still, Jane was leaving the final decision to Lucy. She had long ago made Lucy the manager and now spent far less time in the store, supposedly so that she could devote her hours to writing the follow-up to *Constance*. This she had not yet done, though, and standing in the store, surrounded by the books of others, she was reminded of her failure. At the moment, however, she pushed this worry from her mind as she waited with the others to hear Lucy's decision.

"Shelby will be in charge," Lucy said.

Jane sighed with relief.

"Yes!" Shelby said, pumping her fist.

"But she will not make any changes in how things are done," Lucy added. "*And* Ted and Ned will write me a report on how she handled things."

"Yes!" Ned and Ted said as one.

Shelby glared at them, but a smile played at the corners of her mouth.

"Good," Lucy said. "Now get back to work. Go on. Shoo."

When they were gone Lucy turned to Jane. "They'll be fine."

"Of course they will," said Jane. "There's nothing to worry about. It's not like Shelby is going to bring in finger puppets of literary figures."

"Hey, those sold really well," Lucy reminded her. "And as I re-

call, the Jane Austen one was the most popular. That and Charlotte Brontë," she added mischievously.

"I can still fire you, you know," said Jane.

Lucy pretended not to hear her. "I have to say, this is all going
remarkably smoothly," she said. "Sarah is taken care of, the shop
situation is under control, Ben has arranged for someone to take
his services while we're gone. I keep waiting for something to not
work out, but so far, so good. It's as if this is exactly how things
were supposed to go in the first place."

"There's still time," Jane said.

Lucy rolled her eyes. "You're such a pessimist," she said.
"Can't you just relax?"

"I suppose you're right," Jane said. "Things *are* going rather
well. Walter got our marriage license. Ben has agreed to perform
the ceremony. All I have to do is show up."

"See?" Lucy said. "Nothing to worry about. So where is the
ceremony going to take place?"

"That's the best part," Jane said. "Walter has arranged for us
to get married in—"

At that moment the front door of the store opened and Miriam
stormed in. "There you are," she said, coming toward Jane. "I
need to talk to you. We have a problem."

Chapter 4

On a Plane

"I DON'T WANT TO GO IN THE BAG."

Jane closed her eyes and groaned. "For the last time, you don't have a choice," she said. "It's either get in the bag or stay home."

"Then I'll stay home."

"That wasn't an actual choice," Jane said. "You have to get in the bag."

"Do you really think talking to her is going to work?" Walter asked, taking the seat next to Jane's in the airport boarding area.

Jane looked at Lilith. The small brown Chihuahua was sitting in her lap. Because Lilith was missing her right front leg, she had to lean against Jane to remain upright. Neither Jane nor the dog was pleased with this arrangement.

"Oh, I think she knows what I'm saying," Jane told Walter.

In truth, Lilith knew exactly what Jane was saying. The ability to communicate with animals, at least on a limited basis, was one of the powers Jane possessed by virtue of being a vampire. Walter reached over and scratched Lilith's ears. "Who's a good little girl?" he said in a high voice.

"I'm going to bite him," Lilith announced, and Jane felt her straining forward.

"I think she's just a little anxious," said Jane, putting her hand across the little dog's chest to prevent her from lunging.

As it turned out, the pressing problem Miriam had announced in the bookstore was that the airline on which she was flying (Walter had been unable to get additional seats on his and Jane's flight) would not allow her to take Lilith in the main cabin. "They want to put her down below!" she'd wailed. "With the *luggage*."

As a result, Walter and Jane had agreed to take Lilith with them. Having already put Miriam on her flight, they were now waiting to board their own. Lucy and Ben, booked onto yet a third flight because Ben wanted to use his accrued miles, were waiting at their airline's boarding area in another part of the airport.

"Attention, passengers on flight 739 to London. We will begin boarding momentarily." The voice coming over the loudspeaker was overly cheerful. "We remind you that all animals accompanying passengers in the main cabin must be confined to their airline-approved carriers."

Jane picked Lilith up and, before the dog could protest with her teeth, dropped her into the zippered carrying bag in which she was to spend the next eight hours. "There you go, sweetie," she cooed. "Now be good."

Lilith responded by barking loudly.

"Shh," Jane said as some of the other passengers eyed her with irritation.

"I won't," Lilith said. "In fact, I'll keep it up for the entire flight if you don't get me something good to eat."

"Like what?" Jane said.

"I want one of those sausage muffin things," Lilith said.

Jane groaned. "And where am I supposed to find that?" she said.

"I smelled them when we came in," said Lilith. "One of those restaurants we passed must sell them."

Jane looked at the clock. "There's no time," she said.

"Yip! Yip! Yip!" Lilith let loose with a barrage of high-pitched protests.

"Fine!" Jane hissed. "But you promise—not a peep out of you the entire flight."

"I promise," said Lilith. "Now go get me my sausage."

Jane stood up. "Watch her," she said to Walter. "I'll be right back."

Walter, having heard none of the conversation between Jane and Lilith, nodded absentmindedly and returned to the magazine he was looking at.

Jane hurried down the hallway leading from the boarding area to the main concourse, scanning the shops for one that might sell Lilith's requested sausage muffin. Finally, when she had almost reached the end of the corridor, she saw a familiar fast-food restaurant. Rushing up to the counter, she smiled at the bored clerk. "Two sausage muffins, please."

The clerk shook his head. "No more breakfast," he said.

"Please," Jane said sweetly. "My dog—daughter—would very much like two sausage muffins. It's her favorite item on your menu," she added, as if brand loyalty might count for something with the sullen teenager.

"Breakfast ended ten minutes ago," the boy said tonelessly.

Jane smiled. "Perhaps you have one or two muffins still back there," she said.

"Like I said—" the boy began.

Jane fixed him with a stare. "Go back there and get me two sausage muffins," she said, focusing her glamoring powers. "Now!"

As if he were being controlled by invisible strings, the boy turned and moved jerkily toward the back of the restaurant. He returned a moment later with two sausage muffins wrapped in paper. He handed them to Jane, who took them and asked, "How much will that be?"

"On the house," the boy said, smiling stiffly. "Have a nice day."

"Not much chance of that," Jane muttered as she turned and ran down the hallway back to the boarding area.

When she arrived, Walter was standing in line and looking anxiously about. Lilith, in her carrier, sat at his feet.

"I just needed to get a snack," Jane said as she knelt beside Lilith's case and unzipped the door.

"For the dog?" said Walter.

"Yes," Jane said as she unwrapped the sausage muffins and placed them in the carrier. "I read something the other day that said feeding dogs sausage muffins before they fly can help calm their stomachs."

"What?" said Walter, clearly doubtful. "Where did you read that? I can't imagine all that greasy meat is good for them."

As Lilith began devouring the sausage muffins, Jane closed the carrier and stood up. "I don't remember," she answered Walter. "Shall we board?"

Walter had purchased seats in first class, and Jane was astonished at how much space they had. As the coach class passengers filed by her like cattle on the way to the abattoir, she avoided their jealous glances, occupying herself by stowing Lilith's carrier and placing in the various pockets of her seat the things she'd brought to amuse herself during the flight. She thoughtfully waited until the last of the lesser-class passengers had gone by before slipping on the luxuriously soft slippers provided by the airline and leaning back in the equally comfortable seat.

"Did you see this?" Walter asked, pressing a button on the console between their seats and watching as a screen slid from a hiding place in the ceiling and descended until it was in front of his chair. "Individual movie screens."

Jane pressed another of the many buttons and her seat began to gently vibrate. "Oh my," she said as her muscles relaxed. She hit the button again and the vibrations increased.

A flight attendant who was walking down the aisle stopped beside Walter's seat. "Hello," he said, showing off impossibly white teeth as he smiled broadly. "I'm Trey, and I'll be your server for this flight. We're going to be taking off soon, so I'm afraid you'll have to turn off all electronic devices until we're airborne. Also, all onboard amenities will be deactivated until it's safe to restore them to service. I apologize for the inconvenience."

As if on command, Jane's chair ceased vibrating and Walter's screen slid up into the ceiling. "And I was just getting comfortable," Jane told Walter as the plane began to move slowly away from the gate.

"I feel sick." Lilith's voice cut through Jane's thoughts.

"We aren't even in the air yet," Jane said.

"We will be soon," said Walter, who thought she was speaking to him.

"My stomach is gurgling," said Lilith. "I need some air. Let me out."

"I can't do that," Jane thought back, remembering to not use her voice. "You have to stay in your carrier."

Lilith whined unhappily as the plane taxied down the runway and got into position for takeoff. Jane adjusted her seat belt and tried to relax. Although she'd been around long before airplanes were invented, she was still suspicious of them. As far as she could tell, there was absolutely no reason that something so large should be expected to remain aloft without the benefit of sorcery. She closed her eyes and reminded herself that in a matter of hours she would be back in her homeland.

"Uggghhhhhh," Lilith groaned loudly.

"Is she all right?" asked Walter.

Jane, realizing that the little dog's noises of discomfort were audible, opened her eyes. "She's fine," she assured Walter.

"I am *not* fine," Lilith barked. "Now let me out of here."

The plane lurched forward and began to pick up speed. At the same time, Lilith began to paw wildly at the door of her carrier.

"Stop that," Jane said.

"Out!" Lilith said. "Now!"

"I *can't!*" Jane said as the plane, rumbling, rose into the air.

Lilith clawed frantically, and suddenly the carrier opened. The Chihuahua bolted from it and leapt up onto Jane's lap.

"All I needed was some air," she said as she breathed deeply. "I think I'll be okay—"

The airplane chose that precise second to hit an air current and drop momentarily. In response, the contents of Lilith's stomach rose and exited her mouth, covering Jane in a viscous spatter of half-chewed sausage and bits of English muffin. Jane's mouth opened in a soundless shriek as she contemplated the horror that had just befallen her.

"That's better," said Lilith as the stench of the vomit filled Jane's nose and made her own stomach lurch. Sensing imminent danger, Lilith scrambled onto Walter's lap and watched as Jane heaved dryly.

"Oh my," said Walter as he grabbed a handful of napkins from his seat pocket and handed them to Jane. "I told you I didn't think those sausage muffins were a good idea."

Jane used the napkins to clean off the worst of the mess and deposit it into the airsickness bag handily provided by the airline. But her blouse was damp with dog upchuck, and the smell lingered in her nose. As the Fasten Seatbelt sign was still lit, she couldn't get up to use the washroom, so she had to remain seated as the airplane continued to climb. Lilith, on the other hand, had curled herself into a tiny ball on Walter's lap and gone to sleep. He was rubbing her ears.

"This isn't the most auspicious way to begin our wedding trip," Jane said as she kicked the airsickness bag away from her with her foot.

"Oh, I don't know," said Walter. "Getting pooped on by a bird is supposed to bring you good luck. Maybe getting puked on by a Chihuahua is even luckier."

"Doubtful," Jane said. "Anyway, I can't wait to change out of this shirt."

"Did you bring another?" asked Walter.

Jane groaned. "Yes," she said. "Quite a few of them. But they're all in my checked bag."

Just then the seatbelt sign went off and a flight attendant announced that it was now safe to move about the cabin. Walter took the opportunity to press the call button on his console, which summoned Trey.

"How can I be of assistance?" Trey asked.

Before Walter or Jane could answer, the attendant saw Lilith and let out a little squeal of joy. "Isn't she the cutest thing!" he exclaimed. "Technically she shouldn't be out of her carrier, but since she's so well behaved I don't see why she can't stay just where she is."

"Thank you," said Walter. "But you see, she's not feeling very well and—"

"Poor baby," Trey said, looking at Lilith and frowning. "Does she want something for her tummy? I can bring some crackers for her."

"No, thank you," said Walter. "It's just that she's thrown up."

"On me," Jane said as the flight attendant looked at the floor around Walter's feet.

"Oh," Trey said. He regarded Jane's stained blouse with distaste. "She really got you, didn't she?"

"She gave her sausage muffins," said Walter.

"Why would you do that?" Trey asked, casting a suspicious glance in Jane's direction.

"I thought it was odd too," remarked Walter. "But she said—"

"I read it somewhere!" Jane interrupted. "Now Trey, the thing is, I want to get cleaned up. But I didn't anticipate being thrown up on by a Chihuahua when I packed my carry-on bag, and I don't have another blouse. I don't suppose you have any kind of shirt I could borrow?"

Trey looked her up and down, as if taking her measurements. "Just a sec," he said. "I might have something."

"Remember when being a flight attendant was the most glamorous thing a girl could hope to achieve?" Jane mused after he had left. "All of those cute skirts and thigh-high boots."

"That was back when you could smoke on planes and they didn't charge you seven dollars for a soda," Walter said. "But did you ever really want to be a flight attendant?"

"Not really," said Jane. "But it *did* seem glamorous."

Like magic, Trey reappeared and handed Jane a T-shirt wrapped in a plastic bag. "This is all I could find," he told her. "It's from a promotion we ran a few months ago."

"Thank you," Jane said as she stood up to head for the washroom. "I'm sure it will be fine."

She returned five minutes later, having washed up and changed into the T-shirt. When Walter saw her his face immediately contorted into the pained expression of someone trying very hard not to laugh.

"It's not funny," Jane said as she looked down at the 3XL shirt that on her became something of a cross between a muumuu and a nightshirt. It was bright pink, and across the front was written in white lettering: FLY VIRGIN, LAND HAPPY.

"Oh, it's not so bad," Walter said as Jane took her seat. "Besides, you can change the minute we get our bags at Heathrow."

Jane looked at Lilith, who was still sleeping peacefully. *Filthy little beast,* she thought maliciously.

"I heard that," Lilith answered sleepily.

"Whatever," Jane muttered. She rooted around in the seat pocket and pulled out a paperback novel. Opening it, she settled into her seat, pressed the button to start the massage function, and began to read.

But she couldn't concentrate. Her mind kept straying from the story—which involved a detective attempting to solve the theft of a very large statue from the British Museum—to the matter of her impending marriage. She briefly wondered if perhaps this was the perfect opportunity to reveal to Walter that she was really Jane Austen. And a vampire. After all, he was something of a captive audience, and they would have another seven hours to discuss the situation. *And does it really matter where or when I tell him?* she asked herself. *He's not going to believe me anyway.*

She turned her head and looked at Walter. Like Lilith, he had fallen asleep. She watched him for a few moments. *I love him so much,* she thought. *Am I being fair to him?*

This was the question she had been asking herself for months. Was it right that she should marry him when he didn't know the truth about her? When she knew that he would age while she remained forever forty-one? Time and again she'd come to one conclusion, only to change her mind. That Miriam knew the truth only added to the problem. What if she told Walter before Jane told him herself? It was a threat that would hang constantly over Jane's head as long as she continued to keep her secret.

Lilith opened one eye and looked at Jane. "Would you stop thinking so hard?" she said. "I'm trying to sleep."

"Then just stop listening," Jane told her.

"I'm trying," said Lilith. "But you're so *loud.*"

Jane sighed. "Then if you're so smart, why don't you tell me what I should do?" she said.

Lilith yawned. "That's easy," she said. "You should . . . zzzzzz."

"Wake up!" Jane ordered.

But the little dog only put her single front paw over her nose and went on snoring. Jane thought about shaking her awake, but she knew what Lilith was going to say anyway. It was what Jane had known all along that she had to do. And she would. *Soon,* she promised herself as she closed her eyes and tried to rest. *Or at least soonish.*

Chapter 5

Monday: London

"What on earth are you wearing?"

"Don't ask," Jane said to Miriam. She handed over Lilith's carrying case. "Here's your dog."

"How was your flight, Mom?" asked Walter, giving her a kiss on the cheek.

Miriam shrugged. "The plane didn't crash," she said. "I suppose that makes it good."

"That's one opinion," Jane said under her breath. It had taken forever to get through customs and find Miriam. Now all she wanted to do was get to the hotel and take a shower. But they had to wait for Ben and Lucy's flight to arrive.

Fortunately, they had less than an hour to wait. While Miriam took Lilith outside for a walk and a pee, Jane located a souvenir shop and purchased the least offensive T-shirt she could find, a blue one with LONDON EST. AD 43 stenciled across the front in white. She ducked into the women's room and exited a few minutes later, having stuffed the offensive pink tent into the trash. When she returned to where Walter was waiting, Lucy and Ben's flight had landed. Twenty minutes later the two of them emerged from customs.

"You already went shopping?" Lucy asked, looking at Jane's shirt.

"It was either this or the Big Ben pencil case," Jane joked as she hugged her friend. "And speaking of Big Ben," she added, giving Ben a squeeze, "I don't know how you put up with this girl."

"She tells me I have no choice," Ben joked.

Despite having known Ben for almost a year now, Jane still couldn't quite imagine the hunky, dark-haired man as a rabbi. It was easier to imagine him chopping down a tree or wrangling a steer than reading the Torah, although she'd heard him do that and he did it beautifully. She was thrilled that he and Lucy had found each other, and hoped that one day soon the two of them would announce their engagement.

Getting themselves and all of their luggage outside was no small feat, but eventually they managed to secure two taxis and load one of them up with Walter, Miriam, Lilith, and half the bags and the other with Jane, Ben, Lucy, and the other half of the bags. As soon as the door was shut and they were on their way to the hotel, Jane grabbed Lucy's hand.

"I'm so glad you're here," she said. "That woman is going to drive me mad."

"Isn't that what mothers-in-law are supposed to do?" Ben said.

"Yes, well, Miriam goes a bit beyond the call of duty," Jane told him.

"You know, you've never told us where you're getting married," said Lucy.

"Didn't I?" Jane said. "I guess I keep forgetting. It's actually very exciting. Walter had to pull some strings, what with it being such a historic site, but one of the advantages of marrying a man like Walter is—"

"Out with it!" Lucy shrieked. "I'm going crazy here."

Jane feigned being wounded. "Now I don't know if I want to tell you."

"You'd better," said Lucy.

"No," Jane told her. "I don't think I will. I think I'll let it be a surprise."

Lucy gasped. "Horrid cow!" Ben laughed. She turned to him. "Well, she is. Don't you want to know what this amazing place is?"

"I already know where it is," he said. "Walter told—"

"Shut up!" Jane said forcefully. She narrowed her eyes and pointed at Ben. "Not a word out of you."

Lucy grabbed Ben's arm. "Out with it," she ordered.

Ben looked out the window of the cab. "London is really lovely when it's covered with snow, isn't it?"

"Tell me!" Lucy crowed.

"Is that the statue of Lord Nelson?" he asked.

"Not a word," said Jane.

"I don't know anything!" Ben bleated. "I swear."

"Lies!" Lucy exclaimed. "And you a man of the cloth."

"I'm a rabbi," Ben objected. "Not a priest."

"And you a man of the *tallit*," said Lucy. "Shame."

Ben held up his hands. "I promised not to say anything. I can't break my word."

"You didn't promise," Lucy argued. "You're just afraid of *her*." She jerked her head in Jane's direction.

"As well he should be," said Jane. "Ben, not a peep out of you."

Lucy fumed. "Oh, I'll get it out of him," she promised. "Will you at least tell me *when* it's happening?"

"Yes," Jane said agreeably. "On Tuesday."

"That's tomorrow!" said Lucy.

"Smart girl," Jane said, patting her arm. "Indeed it is. So you don't have all that long to wait to find out where it is."

"I still want to know," Lucy said.

Ben turned to her. "Jane's right," he said. "Besides, isn't it kind of fun that it's a surprise?"

"No," said Lucy. "It isn't fun at all. I mean, if *you* didn't know and I did, that would be fun. But I don't like being the only one who doesn't know."

"Miriam doesn't know," Jane informed her.

"Actually, I think Walter is telling her right now," said Ben. "He wanted to prepare her so she wouldn't be shocked."

"Why would she be shocked?" asked Lucy.

"She wouldn't," Ben said.

"You just said she would," countered Lucy.

"Did I?" Ben said. "I don't remember. So Jane, who else is going to be on this trip?"

"What an excellent question," Jane said.

"No it isn't," said Lucy. "It's a stupid question. Now tell me where this wedding is happening."

"We're not entirely sure who our traveling companions will be," Jane said, speaking across Lucy. "The first get-together is this evening. That's when all will be revealed." She waggled her fingers as if casting a spell. "It's all very secretive."

"It will be interesting to see who else is in the group," said Ben.

"I'm rather dreading it," Jane admitted. "I'm all for looking at architecturally significant houses, but honestly, if they go on about flying buttresses this and Ionic that, I'm going to lose my mind."

"Don't worry," Ben reassured her. "You'll have us. If the tours get boring, you can leave them to their house business and go sightseeing with Lucy and me."

"Maybe with *you*," Lucy said darkly. "I haven't decided if I'm going anywhere."

"You and Lucy and Miriam," said Jane.

"Why is Miriam with us?" asked Lucy. "I sort of hoped she'd tag along with you and Walter."

"You'd rather Walter and I spend our first days as a married couple enduring his mother?" Jane asked.

"No!" Lucy said. "I mean, well, yes."

There was a pause before both Jane and Lucy burst out laughing. "Don't worry," Jane said. "I can hardly blame you. The woman is a terror. And I suspect she *will* stay close to me and Walter, if only to ensure we don't run off without her. But I'm still not telling you where the wedding is going to be."

"Come on!" Lucy pleaded.

Ben shook his head. "Listen to you two," he said. "I bet Miriam isn't nearly as bad as you make her out to be."

Lucy and Jane looked at him. "Have you *met* her?" Lucy asked.

"I know she can be . . . bristly," said Ben. "But I bet underneath it all she's just lonely. Most unpleasant people usually are."

"Or perhaps her heart is made of pitch," Jane suggested.

Lucy chuckled. "Tell you what," she said to Ben. "*You* can spend some time with Miriam. I'm sure she'd love that, what with you being a rabbi and all. Then we'll see what you think."

Before Ben could answer, the cab pulled up to the front of the Savoy hotel. They got out and began the elaborate ritual of handing the bags over to the bellman, who had appeared as if out of nowhere with a cart. The cab containing the rest of their party pulled up shortly thereafter, adding to the confusion as Miriam began directing the transfer of the luggage.

Jane escaped both Miriam and the cold March air by entering the hotel lobby through one of the revolving doors. She could still hear Miriam's voice as she crossed the black and white checkerboard tiled floor to the front desk.

"This place is gorgeous," Lucy said, looking around at the grand lobby with its soaring ceiling, polished wood paneling, and Art Deco chandeliers.

"You should have seen it when it opened," Jane told her. "It was 1889. No one had ever seen anything like it. Electricity in all the rooms, hot and cold running water—it was a miracle of the age."

"Did you stay here?" asked Lucy.

"Of course," Jane replied. "Richard Mansfield brought me here for dinner. He was playing Richard III at the time. You know they suspected him of being Jack the Ripper."

"Was he?" Lucy asked.

"I certainly hope so," said Jane as they reached the desk. "How many women can say they dined with the Ripper and lived to tell about it?"

"Welcome to the Savoy," said a pleasant voice.

Jane turned to find a handsome young man looking at her from behind the check-in counter. "Yes," she said. "I believe we have a reservation under Fletcher."

"Jane?" the man said. "Jane Aus . . . " He left the word unfinished. "I'm sorry," he said. "It's just that you remind me of someone I used to know."

Jane stared at the man's face. The wavy blond hair. The aquiline nose. The clear blue eyes. They all seemed very familiar. Then she noticed the thin scar running from the corner of the man's mouth to his chin.

"Gosebourne?" she whispered. "Is it really you?"

The young man beamed. "It *is* you," he said happily. "I knew it the instant I saw your face."

Jane looked at Lucy. "Gosebourne has worked at the Savoy since . . . " She looked at Gosebourne. "Well, since it opened."

"Indeed I have," Gosebourne said, nodding at Lucy. "I dare say I've moved up a bit in rank during that time, but yes, I hold the distinction of being the hotel's longest-serving employee."

Before Jane could ask Gosebourne any of the dozen questions that were buzzing around in her head, Walter and Ben arrived with the bellman and the luggage in tow. Miriam, like some kind of insane border collie, brought up the rear, barking orders at everyone in sight.

"All checked in?" Walter asked.

Jane nodded. "We were just getting to that," she said.

Gosebourne, now all business, typed furiously on his computer's keyboard. "Here we are," he said. "I have you staying for two nights." He looked at Jane. "Is that all?" he said sadly.

"I'm afraid so," Jane answered.

"We're here with the International Association of Historic Preservationists," Walter explained.

"Ah, yes," said Gosebourne. "Many of your party have already checked in. I believe you'll be meeting later this evening in the American Bar for cocktails. Nine o'clock, if I'm not mistaken. There will be more information in your room."

He handed Walter a small envelope containing their passkeys, then repeated the process for Ben and Lucy. Before Miriam could step forward to take her turn, Jane leaned over the counter and whispered to Gosebourne, "Put her next to an elevator."

Once all the rooms were assigned, it was off to the elevators and up to their rooms. Gosebourne, Jane was pleased to see, had indeed placed Miriam in a room right next to the elevator bank. Miriam frowned as she opened her door, and Jane continued down the corridor to her own room with a feeling of satisfaction.

Jane and Walter's room was on one side of the hallway, and Lucy and Ben's was on the other. It was only when Jane was in the room that something occurred to her.

"Did you book a room with one bed or two for Ben and Lucy?" she asked Walter.

"One," Walter said as he went to the window and pulled back the drapes, revealing a spectacular view of the River Thames. "Why?"

"Well, with him being a rabbi, I'm not sure that they're . . . you know."

"Sleeping together?" said Walter.

Jane nodded. "I know that sounds old-fashioned of me," she said.

Walter laughed. "It does," he said. "But don't worry. I'm sure if it's not okay they'll say something." He came over and put his arms around Jane, pulling her close. "Don't you girls talk about these things?"

Jane kissed him. "Of course not. We only talk about raising babies and how to cook for our menfolk."

"And we men only talk about hunting and making fire," Walter said.

Jane laughed. "Speaking of talking, I understand you told Ben where we're getting married."

"I suppose I did," said Walter. "Is that all right?"

"It's fine," Jane told him. "But Lucy is furious because I won't tell her." She hesitated before asking, "Did you tell your mother?"

"I was going to," Walter said. "But then she started complaining about the airline and the snow and all the English accents and I decided not to. Let her be surprised."

"Oh, she'll be surprised all right," said Jane. "I can't wait to see the look on her face."

Walter picked up a folder that was sitting on the room's desk. "This is the packet from the IAHP," he said. He sat down on the bed and opened it while Jane commenced unpacking.

"Here's the welcome letter, itinerary, handy hints for avoiding pickpockets . . . Ah, here we are. The guest list." His eyes scanned the page. "Interesting," he remarked.

"What is?" asked Jane as she hung one of Walter's shirts in the closet.

"Well, I've heard of some of these people," Walter answered. "But I've only met one of them." He looked at the clock on the nightstand. "We're about to, though," he said. "It's almost nine now."

"I'd forgotten about the time difference," said Jane. "What time is it back home?"

Walter glanced at his watch. "A quarter to four," he told her.

"Your mother will be clamoring for dinner," Jane said.

"Maybe she can go with Lucy and Ben and get something," said Walter. "Do you want to go with them? I'm probably going to be tied up with these people for a while."

"I'll come," said Jane. "I want to see the motley crew we'll be sharing the road with for the next two weeks."

"You mean you'd rather do anything else than have dinner with my mother," Walter said, grinning.

"And there's that," said Jane. "Now come on. We don't want to be late for our first get-together."

They knocked on Ben and Lucy's door. When Ben answered, Jane peeked around him to see what the bed situation was. As Walter had told her, there was only one. Lucy was stretched out on it, looking at a guidebook. *I'll have to have a chat with her later,* Jane thought.

"Jane and I have to go to this cocktail hour," Walter explained. "I'm wondering if you would mind taking my mother with you to—"

"I don't need a babysitter, Walter."

Jane jumped at the unexpected sound of Miriam's voice. When she turned she saw Walter's mother approaching, Lilith in her arms. They were wearing matching red sweaters. Lilith, to her credit, did not look particularly pleased.

"Oh, hi, Mom," Walter said. "Nobody said you needed a babysitter. I just thought you would be more comfortable going to dinner with Lucy and Ben than you would be hanging around with Jane and me and a bunch of people into old houses."

"Well, you're right about that," said Miriam. She smiled at Ben. "I'm sure the rabbi will be excellent company."

Ben glanced at Lilith. "I don't know if they allow dogs in restaurants here," he said.

"Nonsense," Miriam replied. "They adore dogs here. You can take them anywhere."

"You're thinking of Paris," Jane remarked before she could think to stop herself.

Miriam pointedly ignored her. "Anyway, I'll just tell them she's a helping dog. She senses when I'm about to have a seizure."

"But you don't have seizures," Walter objected.

Miriam's face suddenly twisted in a rictus of pain. She began to shake, and her tongue protruded from her mouth as a series of groans poured forth.

"Mother!" Walter cried.

Miriam's facial expression returned to normal. "See?" she said. "Seizures."

"Good God, Mother," Walter said. "Don't go doing that in a restaurant, or anywhere for that matter."

"If my seizure dog is with me, I won't," Miriam said. She took Ben's arm. "Now, shall we go find something to eat? I'm famished."

Chapter 6

Monday: London

THE MAN SITTING AT THE PIANO WAS PLAYING "A FOGGY DAY" AS Jane and Walter entered the American Bar. The air was filled with the sound of laughter and murmured conversations and ice tinkling in highballs. The light was flattering and the atmosphere was gay. It was impossible not to feel glamorous in such surroundings.

Which of course meant that Jane did not. For one thing, her shoes pinched. They were new, purchased just days earlier in a frenzy of last-minute shopping. Seeing them on display in the store, Jane had imagined herself wearing them while sharing scintillating conversation with her fellow travelers. This thrilling possibility had blinded her to the reality of the shoes, which was that the heels were entirely too high. They caused her to tip forward, much like the famed Pisa tower, as a result of which she felt as if she were always just about to topple over. But they looked wonderful, and so she'd insisted on wearing them, even though it meant she had to keep a firm hold on Walter's arm or risk a fall.

She was hoping that perhaps she and Walter could take up a position somewhere central, so that the others could circle them like bees around a flower. And so it was with great relief that she

soon found herself seated at one of the tables scattered throughout the room, waiting as Walter ordered a gin and tonic for her
and a Manhattan for himself. She used the time to look about her
and try to put faces to some of the names Walter had rattled off
when reading her the roster of participants.

"Have you identified any of them yet?" Walter asked, handing
Jane her drink and taking a seat.

"I think so," said Jane. "That one over there. I think she must
be Genevieve Prideaux."

She indicated a tall, thin woman of about thirty-five. Her hair
was pulled into a tidy knot at the back of her head, and she was
wearing a chic dark suit with a pale green silk blouse. Jane noted
with some jealousy that Genevieve's heels were higher than her
own and that the woman had no trouble whatsoever walking in
them.

"I think you're right," Walter agreed. "I remember seeing her
picture in one of the trade magazines."

"I'm not surprised you'd remember *that* one," said Jane.
"She's stunning."

She waited for Walter to contradict her, and was oddly pleased
when he didn't. She liked that he didn't try to deny the beauty of
other women simply out of a sense of duty. *Then again*, she
thought, *he could have denied it a* little.

"Ah," said Walter. "I know that fellow. It's Brodie Pittman."

He pointed to a handsome man leaning against one of the
bars. He was very large and very loud, gesturing with a cigar as
he argued some point with his companion, a much smaller and far
less handsome fellow. Brodie Pittman was wearing khaki pants, a
white shirt with the sleeves rolled up past the elbow and the neck
open, and braces that attached to the pants not with horrid metal
clips but with proper buttons. His hair, which was thick and fell
rakishly over one eye, was of a sandy blond color, and he had a
mustache. He was perhaps forty-five, and Jane liked him immediately.

The smaller man had little to recommend him. Dressed fussily in an ill-fitting gray wool suit complete with waistcoat and a dreary, firmly knotted tie that appeared to be strangling him, he had pale skin, fine brown hair that was plastered down with copious amounts of grease, and tiny, sinister eyes that made Jane think he was someone who spent the majority of his time lurking about and the rest of his time plotting and scheming.

Walter waved to Brodie, who bellowed hello and came charging toward them. Regrettably, the other man followed.

"Walter!" Brodie said. "Good to see you again, mate."

Walter shook Brodie's hand. "Brodie, I'd like you to meet my fiancée, Jane Fairfax. Jane, Brodie Pittman."

"How do you do?" said Brodie, engulfing Jane's tiny hand in his enormous paw.

Jane winced instinctively, expecting to feel her hand crushed, and was surprised when Brodie's grip was firm but gentle. "Very well, thank you," she said, not a little relieved. "It's lovely to meet you."

"You say that now," Brodie said, winking at her. "You might change your mind once you've known me a day or two."

"Brodie is an architect," Walter told Jane. "He designed Wexley House."

"Oh," Jane said, having no idea what Wexley House was. "How exciting."

"Not at all," sad Brodie. "It's a monstrosity. But the rich old fool who hired me to design it paid me enough to kill off any sense of guilt I might have felt for my role in bringing it to life." He laughed loudly and drained his drink.

"I think we owe it to the world to give birth only to buildings that speak with strong, clear voices," said the little man standing beside Brodie, his voice as thin and unctuous as his hair. Jane had almost forgotten about him, but now she turned her attention to him. He looked back without blinking.

"Walter, Jane, let me introduce you to Bergen Frost."

"Faust," the little man said. "Bergen *Faust.*"

"Bergen is German," Brodie said, as if that explained everything.

"I have a blog," Bergen added.

Jane looked at Walter, who looked at Brodie.

"Apparently it's read by a bloody lot of people," Brodie said. He cleared his throat. "Shall we order more drinks?"

"None for me," Bergen said. "I'm going to retire now. I want to be rested for the morning."

"What's happening in the morning?" Walter asked, sounding slightly concerned. "I thought tomorrow was a free day."

"Yes," said Bergen.

When no further explanation came, Walter said, "All right, then. Good night."

"Good night," Bergen said. He nodded at Jane before turning and walking away, quickly slipping into the surrounding crowd.

"Rum little fellow, isn't he?" Brodie said as he took a seat. "I have no idea why he's here. Probably a friend of Enid's."

"Enid?" Jane asked.

"Enid Woode," said Walter. "One of the two organizers of this adventure."

"Who's the other?" asked Jane.

"Chumsley Faber-Titting," Brodie said. "Enid's ex-husband."

"How interesting," Jane said. "Well, they must get on well enough to be able to work together."

Brodie guffawed. "Can't stand the sight of each other," he said.

"Then why would they do this?" asked Jane.

"Because they're only good as a pair," said Brodie. "They used to be the most successful design team in the UK. Married right out of school and started their careers together. After they divorced neither of them could design a thing that wasn't crap. They had to get back together, at least as architects. Their offices are in buildings on opposite sides of London. They communicate only through e-mail, and when they're in the same room each pretends the other doesn't exist. Their work is extraordinary."

Jane, intrigued, looked around the bar. "Are they here?" she asked.

"Oh, they're somewhere about," Brodie said. "Neither wants to be the first to arrive, so they're probably both peering around corners waiting for the other one to show up."

"I can't wait to meet them," said Jane. Suddenly the upcoming trip seemed not nearly as dull as it had earlier in the evening.

Brodie pointed his cigar at Walter. "I'm guessing you're on Chumsley's team," he said.

"Team?" Walter said. "What do you mean?"

"Everything Chumsley and Enid do is a competition," Brodie explained. "As I understand it, they've each chosen half the guests for this little expedition of ours. Who invited you?"

"Chumsley," Walter said.

"There you are then," said Brodie. "He invited me as well. Genevieve Prideaux was invited by Enid. Told me so earlier. And as I said, I'm guessing that Bergen fellow is one of hers as well. I was going to ask him, but he started talking about how Cold War Soviet architecture doesn't get the respect it deserves, and then all I wanted to do was kill myself."

"All that concrete and grimness," Jane said, shuddering, and Brodie raised his glass to her.

"Who else is on our . . . team?" asked Walter.

"Orsino Castano," Olivier said.

"I don't think I know him," said Walter.

"Nice fellow," Brodie said. "There he is over there." He indicated a man of average height and slightly more than average weight. His black hair and beard framed a pleasant face, and when he saw Brodie waving at him he smiled warmly and waved back, then returned to the conversation he was having with a woman wearing what looked disconcertingly like a kimono.

"Oh yes," Walter said. "I recognize him now. He won the Krassberg Prize last year." To Jane he added, "For excellence in restoration of historic properties."

"Maybe you'll win that one day," Jane said.

Walter laughed. "I restore houses," he said. "Orsino restores *castles.*"

"What's a castle?" Brodie said. "Just a big house made out of rocks."

"Who's the woman Orsino is talking to?" Jane asked Brodie. "She's very unusual-looking."

"No idea," said Brodie. "But I'm sure we'll find out soon enough. I do know she's one of Enid's, though."

"How do you know?" asked Walter.

"Because there's four to a side, so to speak," Brodie explained. "If I'm right, Enid's got Genevieve, Bergen, that one, and Ryan McGuinness."

"McGuinness?" Walter said, lifting an eyebrow. "That's interesting."

"Why?" asked Jane, sensing a story.

"McGuinness is the reason Chumsley and Enid divorced," said Brodie.

"How scandalous," Jane said, taking a sip of her gin and tonic. She looked at Walter. "How come you never told me your field was so exciting?"

"It never occurred to me," Walter said. "Who's our fourth?" he asked Brodie.

"Old friend of yours," Brodie said. "And another Yank. Sam Wax."

"Sam?" said Walter.

"Do you know him?" Jane asked, detecting something in Walter's voice suggesting familiarity.

"Her," Walter answered. "Sam's a woman. We worked together on a couple of projects when we were both starting out, but I haven't seen her in, oh, fifteen years or so." He looked around, and Jane, to her surprise, felt a pang of jealousy. "I didn't see her name on the list."

"She was a last-minute addition," Brodie told Walter. "But she isn't here yet. Comes in tomorrow."

"Sam Wax," Walter said. "Wow. It will be nice to see her again."

"Too bad we're getting *married* tomorrow," Jane said, rattling the ice in her now empty glass.

"What?" said Walter, looking up. "Oh. Yes. We are."

"Married?" Brodie said.

"Yes," said Walter. "I've arranged for us to be married in the chapel in—"

"Walter Fletcher?" said a woman's voice.

The woman who had been talking with Orsino Castano now stood beside the table. As Jane had thought, she was wearing a kimono. It was made of red silk and embroidered with dragons done in white and yellow thread. The woman's jet-black hair was pulled back into a thick ponytail secured with a circle of leather pierced by a single ivory pin. The delicate bones of her face were covered by flawless skin, and for a moment Jane thought she might be wearing white powder.

"That would be me," Walter said.

"I'm very pleased to meet you," the woman said. "I am Suzu."

"Suzu," Walter repeated. "What a lovely name."

"Thank you," said Suzu. "I just wanted to tell you how much I enjoy your work. I saw the article about you in *Spaces* last year and thought what you did with that house was wonderful."

"I didn't know anybody actually read that magazine," Walter joked.

"I do," Suzu said, her tone so soft that she might have been apologizing.

"If you don't mind my asking, how did you get mixed up with

us lot?" asked Brodie. "Pardon me for saying so, but you don't seem like an architect."

"You mean you've never heard of me," Suzu said, smiling lightly.

"That's precisely what I mean," Brodie admitted. "So who are you?"

"I teach aesthetics at Kumamoto University," said Suzu.

"Ah," Brodie said. "A professor."

"Yes," Suzu said. "Well, good night. I'm sure we'll be seeing more of each other in the days to come."

They said their good nights and watched as Suzu left the bar. When she was out of earshot Brodie looked at Walter and Jane. "I still have no idea why she's here."

"Is it so odd that a professor would be invited?" asked Jane.

"Not if she was a professor of something useful," said Brodie.

"Aesthetics is useful," Walter countered, although he sounded less than convinced himself.

Brodie shot him a look. "Like I said, must be a friend of Enid's."

"Well, she seems sweet enough," said Walter.

"Careful," said Brodie. "She's the enemy."

"Enemy?" Walter said. "Oh, you mean the whole Chumsley-versus-Enid thing." He laughed. "I'll be careful not to share any state secrets with her, then."

More drinks were produced, and Jane listened as Brodie and Walter exchanged stories about people she didn't know doing things she cared little about. Still, she was having a good time. Chumsley and Enid had, she thought, assembled quite an interesting cast of characters. With a bit of luck they would provide entertaining company for the next two weeks.

Suddenly a hush fell over the room. The piano player, who was halfway through "Happiness Is a Thing Called Joe," hit a wrong note and stopped. Even the ice ceased its tinkling. Jane looked around to see what was happening and saw the guests looking in opposite directions—half toward the front of the bar and half toward the back.

At the front stood a short, stout woman, her graying hair cut in an unflattering shag. She wore a plaid skirt that did little to flatter her figure, a bulky sweater of green wool that was equally unhelpful, and heavy black shoes that could only be described as sensible. *That must be Enid,* Jane thought.

Enid—along with half of the guests—was staring at a man who Jane assumed to be Chumsley. He was all that his name implied. As short and stout as his ex-wife, he too had gray hair, although less of it. Curiously, he was dressed in what appeared to be some kind of riding outfit, including brown twill breeches tucked into leather boots, a yellow high-collared shirt beneath a red vest, and a herringbone ivy cap.

"Is he carrying a crop?" Jane whispered to Walter.

"And here we go," Brodie said as Enid and Chumsley advanced on each other. They stopped when they were about a yard apart and as if by some unspoken cue turned so that they were back to back.

"Welcome, friends," they said in unison. Oddly, it was impossible to tell their voices apart.

"We have a terrific trip planned," Chumsley continued.

"We've each selected our favorite homes to show you," said Enid.

"Some of which are more exciting than others," Chumsley added.

"Indeed," said Enid icily.

"Our tour will begin on Wednesday, when I take you to one of the finest homes in all of England," Chumsley announced. "It's one that is seldom visited, as the owner is a reluctant host. But as it happens, he is a good friend of mine and has graciously allowed us a visit. We'll journey by railway to the village of Cripple Minton in Warwickshire and spend the day touring the house.

That evening, following a delightful dinner, we'll board another train, which will take us through the night to arrive the next morning in Pembroke, Wales, where we'll catch a ferry to Rosslare, Ireland."

He said *Ireland* as if he were naming a particularly vile type of pudding, and Jane caught his eyes cutting to a lanky, red-haired man leaning against the wall behind Enid. *That must be Ryan McGuinness,* she thought. *Oh, this will be fun.*

"And *that* is where the tour will truly begin," Enid said loudly. "But enough of what's to come. Let us enjoy the rest of the evening together."

She and Chumsley exchanged curt nods and walked to separate parts of the room. Chumsley, seeing Walter and Brodie, came over to their table.

"Gentlemen," he said expansively. "So good to see you."

"And you, Chumsley," said Walter, shaking the man's hand.

"Chumsley," said Brodie, "you appear to have lost your horse."

Chumsley tapped him on the shoulder with his crop. "Enough out of you, you cheeky bastard," he said. "You know I wear this only to annoy Enid." He looked at Walter and Jane. "My ex-wife is deeply afraid of horses," he explained. "As a child she was nipped quite badly by an Icelandic fjord pony, and ever since has harbored a fear that she might be eaten by one. If you want to give her a good fright, sneak up behind her and give a little whinny. She'll likely soil her knickers."

Jane laughed despite herself, earning a smile from Chumsley. "A lady with a wicked sense of humor," he said. "I like you already."

"That fine young lady is soon to be Walter's wife," Brodie informed him. "Tomorrow, to be exact."

"A lucky man he is, then," said Chumsley. "I'll drink your health as soon as I can find someone to give me a whiskey. Will you all join me?"

Walter glanced at his watch. "I'm afraid we should be getting to bed," he said. "We have a big day tomorrow."

"Tomorrow night, then," said Chumsley. "Once you're properly married. We'll have dinner at the Lord and Lamb."

"I look forward to it," said Walter.

"As do I," Jane said.

"And I," said Brodie.

Chumsley looked at him. "Who said you were invited?"

"I suppose I could always go with Enid's group," said Brodie. "They seem like a jolly bunch."

"Like hell you will," said Chumsley. "Now you two lovebirds run along. This degenerate and I have some drinking to do."

Walter stood, as did Jane, and they exchanged good nights all around. Jane, now even less stable on her feet thanks to the gin and tonics, took Walter's arm. "Should we say hello to Enid?" she asked, glancing toward the back of the bar.

"Best not to start a civil war on our first night," said Walter. "There will be plenty of time for that."

As they waited for the elevator to arrive Jane happened to glance toward the reception desk and saw that Gosebourne was standing behind it. Seeing her, he looked around and then waved her over.

"I'll be right up," Jane told Walter. "You go on ahead."

"Are you sure?" asked Walter. "I can wait."

"It's fine," said Jane. "I'm just going to get some . . . mints. At the gift shop."

Walter gave her a peculiar look. "Mints?"

Jane nodded. "I have gin breath," she said.

The elevator came and Walter stepped inside. Jane began walking toward Gosebourne when suddenly Miriam came walking briskly past her.

"Hold the doors!" Miriam yelled, ignoring Jane.

Jane turned and watched as Miriam entered the elevator.

"Mother," she heard Walter say, "I thought you were with Ben and Lucy."

"I was," Miriam snapped. "But I wanted to talk to you. I can't believe you want to have your wedding at—"

The elevator doors shut, cutting off the end of her remark.

"Bloody old vampire hunter," Jane muttered as she went to see what Gosebourne wanted. When she reached him he seemed slightly agitated. "Is something wrong?" Jane asked.

"No," Gosebourne said. "Not wrong. In fact, it might be something very good. I wanted to mention it earlier, but thought it best to wait until we could speak privately."

"Something good?" said Jane. She leaned in and whispered. "Is it something about our kind?"

Gosebourne nodded. "I think it may be of particular interest to *you*," he said. "Given your . . . situation."

"Which situation might that be?" Jane asked. "There are several."

"The man you're marrying, he's mortal?" asked Gosebourne. Jane nodded.

"And you don't wish to turn him?" Gosebourne continued.

"I'd prefer not to," said Jane.

Gosebourne licked his lips. "Then I might know of a way," he said.

"A way to what?" Jane asked. "I don't understand."

"A way to turn you back," said Gosebourne.

Chapter 7

Tuesday: London

"Is this where Anne Boleyn is buried?" Lucy asked, looking around the room.

"No," said Walter. "She's buried downstairs in the Chapel Royal of St. Peter ad Vincula. So are a lot of other people, most of them executed for one thing or another. This is the Chapel of St. Paul the Evangelist. It was used primarily in private services for the royal family, and occasionally by the condemned before they went out to meet the axe. Prisoners were housed upstairs."

"It's so beautiful for a place that has such a bloody history," Ben remarked.

"Isn't it?" said Walter. "It's one of the finest examples of Norman-period architecture we have. See the groin vaulting above the aisles? And look at the scallop and leaf designs on the capitals—so simple, but so beautiful. The proportions here are absolutely perfect."

"How about looking at the bride for a minute?" said Jane.

Walter turned and his mouth dropped open. Her dress was amazing. Unsure what she wanted, Jane had started looking through photographs for inspiration. Somehow she had stumbled upon a series of images of Paris in the 1950s, photographs of people at cocktail parties. There was something glamorous about them—about the highballs and cigarettes, the furniture with its modern shapes, the suits on the men and the dresses on the women—that appealed to her. One dress in particular had caught her eye, and she had gotten a local seamstress to make her a version of it.

Made from lightweight pearl-pink silk taffeta jacquard with a muted pattern of roses and swirls, the dress had a sweetheart décolletage with bolero-style bodice and *manches-cape*. Fitted tightly at the waist, the fuller A-line skirt fell below the knee, and Jane had found the perfect pale pink pumps to pair with it. That morning she'd had her hair done at the hotel's salon. It was now in a low chignon, perfectly set and polished. On her ears were a pair of vintage diamond and pearl earrings, an unexpected gift from Walter, featuring numerous small diamonds in an intricate white gold star-shaped setting with pearls between each arm of the star. It was her only jewelry. Her makeup was similarly low-key, and she carried a simple bouquet of pale pink roses and white hydrangeas.

"Well?" Jane asked when no one spoke.

"You look beautiful," said Lucy, putting her hand to her mouth as if she might cry.

"You look like you're freezing," Miriam said. She herself was wearing a heavy wool fisherman's sweater and a knitted hat, looking more like a Maine sea captain than the mother of the groom.

In truth it *was* cold. Eleventh-century castles are not the warmest places in early March, and the snow outside did little to create an air of cheer. But Jane didn't notice, and not just because being undead made her fairly immune to cold. She was too focused on finally becoming Walter's wife to care about anything else, even her intractable mother-in-law-to-be.

"Walter?" she said when he'd stared at her for a full minute without making a sound.

He smiled. "I've never seen anything so wonderful," he said, his voice cracking.

"It is a nice dress, isn't it?" said Jane.

"It's not the dress," Walter said. "It's you."

Jane felt her breath catch in her throat. She thought she might cry. But she couldn't look away from Walter. He was so handsome in his dark suit, white shirt, and pale pink tie (she'd told him that much about her dress, so that they would match) that she felt as if she'd never seen him before. *He's going to be my husband in a few minutes,* she thought, walking toward him.

Ben was standing in front of the altar at the east end of the chapel. Jane and Walter stood in front of him. Behind him snow fell gently past the stained-glass window, which glowed faintly in the midmorning light.

"She's much prettier than Catherine Howard."

A boy's voice cut through the morning stillness. Jane, wondering if someone had crept into the chapel unannounced, turned around.

"What is it?" Walter asked.

"Didn't you hear that?" said Jane.

Lucy and Miriam, seated on opposite sides of the narrow aisle, looked at her, puzzled.

"Yes, but not as pretty as Lady Jane Grey," argued a second voice, also male and also young.

Jane looked up, wondering if the boys had snuck into the triforium and were playing a prank, but no small faces peered back at her. *Perhaps they're hiding behind one of the pillars,* she thought.

"Do you think she can hear us?" said the first voice.

"Don't be daft," the second answered. "Of course she can't."

"I bloody well can!" Jane called out. "Now come out, whoever you are."

"I think she's drunk," Miriam said. "Smell her breath."

"I am *not* drunk," said Jane testily. "Really, can none of you hear the two boys talking?"

Lucy shook her head. Ben did the same. Jane ignored Miriam, who was shaking her head so forcefully it looked as if she was trying to unscrew it, and turned to Walter. "Seriously, you don't hear anything?"

"Not a thing," he said. "Maybe it's voices coming up the stairs from below. I'm sure there are all kinds of weird things going on with the acoustics in this place."

"Maybe," Jane said, but she sounded doubtful.

"Shall we begin?" asked Ben.

"Absolutely," Walter said. "We only have the place to ourselves for another twenty minutes."

"This won't take that long," said Ben. He smiled at Jane. "Deep breath," he joked. "It will all be over before you know it."

"That's what the executioner said to Thomas More," said one of the voices. This was followed by mad giggling.

Jane ignored them and listened as Ben began the ceremony. Although he was a rabbi, they had decided to perform just a simple ceremony now and hold the more traditional Jewish wedding when they returned home to Brakeston.

"We are gathered today in this place of deep history to witness the joining of Walter Aaron Fletcher and Elizabeth Jane Fairfax."

"Getting married in the White Tower," said one of the boys. "Seems bad luck to me."

Jane gritted her teeth, forcing herself to not look around or say anything. She didn't know why she was the only one who could hear the boys, but this was not the time to try to figure it out. *I'm going to enjoy my wedding if it kills me,* she thought as she squeezed Walter's hand.

"Ow," he yelped.

"Sorry," Jane whispered, loosening her grip.

Ben continued. "Before I join them together as man and wife, if anyone present can show just cause as to why these two should not be joined together in holy matrimony, let him—or her—speak now."

Jane half expected Miriam to stand up and object. However, it was a male voice that said, loudly and clearly, "I declare the existence of an impediment!"

That's from a book, Jane thought vaguely as she turned to see who had spoken.

Standing in the middle of the aisle, halfway between the altar and the chapel entrance, was a man. Of average height and build, he had a handsome face with wide, dark eyes and a neatly trimmed ginger beard. His dress was old-fashioned, the black suit something that might have been worn by a man in the time of King Edward VII. Yet he wore it with such comfort that he gave no indication of pretense or theatrics, as if his entire closet were full of similar garments that were worn on a daily basis.

"I'm sorry to interrupt," the man said, advancing toward the altar. "I was only recently made aware of the impending nuptials, and got here as quickly as I could. Thankfully, I am in time to prevent a great tragedy."

Jane, watching the man approach, felt herself begin to shake. Walter, standing beside her, put his hand on her shoulder. "Jane, do you know this man?"

The man stopped and smiled broadly, one corner of his mouth lifting up in a rakish smirk. "Yes, Jane, do you know this man?"

Walter was looking at Jane, who was looking at the intruder and trying to convince herself that he wasn't who she knew him to be. She tried to speak, but found that her throat was dry.

"I'm afraid this is a bit of a shock for her, poor thing," the man said. He stepped forward. "Allow me to introduce myself. My name is Joshua Mobley."

Jane groaned and closed her eyes. *This isn't happening,* she told herself.

"I don't think she was expecting this," the voice of one of the boys cut through the thoughts in her head.

"Who are you?" Jane yelled, throwing her bouquet to the floor.

"You mean you don't remember me?" Joshua sounded wounded.

"Not you, Joshua," said Jane. "The other ones."

"What other ones?" he asked.

Jane was turning around, glaring at the stone walls. "The ones that keep talking," she said. "The two boys."

"Wait a minute," said Walter. "So you *do* know this man?"

"Of course I do," Jane said, still trying to ferret out the source of the voices. "He's my husband. Now where are you?"

"Husband?" Walter said.

"Husband?" Miriam said.

"Husband?" Lucy said.

"Husband," Joshua said.

Jane, realizing what she'd just done, stopped searching and turned around. "I mean he *was* my husband," she said. "He's not anymore."

"Well now, see, that's the problem," Joshua said. "Technically, we never got divorced."

"Joshua, it was almost two hundred—a very long time ago," Jane said, exasperated. "And we were married for all of a week."

"Nine days," said Joshua.

"Nine days," Jane said. "I don't even think that counts."

"Lady Jane Grey reigned for only nine days and yet her name is listed alongside those of England's other queens," Joshua said.

"Unless one of us is a queen, it isn't the same thing," Jane said.

For a moment Joshua seemed to consider saying something, then he waved a hand dramatically and continued. "There was a minister," he said. He looked at Ben. "That means it counts, right, Father?"

"I'm a rabbi," Ben said. "And I'm staying out of this."

"Well, I'm not," said Miriam, standing up. She marched over

to Joshua, Lilith in her arms. The little dog took one sniff of Joshua and bared her teeth. "Just as I suspected." She glanced at Jane. "Another one," she said, shaking her head.

Walter took both of Jane's hands in his. "Jane, are you really married to this man?"

Jane shook her head. "No. I mean, I don't know. I don't think so. I *didn't* think so."

Walter let go of her. "How could you not mention this?" he said, his voice angry. "You have a husband and it never occurred to you to tell me?"

"It was a *very* long time ago," Jane said. "Honestly, I'd forgotten all about him until a few moments ago."

"You wound me," said Joshua, placing his palm against his chest.

"Oh, shut up," Jane snapped. "Who put you up to this anyway?"

Joshua's eyes grew wide, like a very sad spaniel's. "Whatever do you mean?"

"Someone told you to come here," said Jane. "Who was it?"

"It was my heart," Joshua said. "You called out to it and I came. I've missed you, Jane."

"Nonsense," Jane said. She turned to her fiancé, who was looking from her to Joshua and back again. "Walter, listen to me. I married Joshua when I was very young."

"Not that young," said Joshua. "Actually, many people thought of you as a spinster."

Jane stopped him with a glance. "I was very young," she repeated. "It was only for a few days and I *thought* it was taken care of."

Walter looked at her. "I don't know what to say, Jane. You want me to believe that you completely forgot about marrying him? I know you can be forgetful sometimes, but I find it difficult to believe that even you could forget having a husband."

Jane desperately wanted to tell him that the marriage was

almost two centuries in the past, that she'd married Joshua only because she feared she would otherwise be alone forever. But she couldn't. She couldn't because she'd never been truthful with him about who—and what—she really was.

"Yes," she said weakly. "That's what I want you to believe."

"Well, *I* don't believe it," Miriam said, snorting.

"I don't care what you think!" Jane shouted. She advanced on Miriam. "You've done nothing but try to come between us since the day you heard about me. Well, I've had enough."

She felt her fangs click into place, and she opened her mouth. Because her back was to everyone else, only Miriam saw.

"You wouldn't," she said, taking a step back.

"She's a vampire!" cried a boy's voice. "That's how come she can hear us."

"She's probably come looking for Crispin's Needle," said the other.

Jane's fangs retracted and she whirled around. "What did you say?" she said.

"Who? Me?" Joshua and Walter said simultaneously.

"Not you two," she said. "The other ones."

"Us?" said Lucy and Ben in tandem.

Jane waved them away. "Shh," she said. "I'm waiting for them to answer me."

"She's lost her mind," said Miriam. "She's hearing voices. I knew she was unstable." She pointed at Walter. "I *told* you."

Jane looked at Joshua. "You can hear them too, can't you?"

"I don't hear anything," Joshua replied.

Jane didn't know whether she believed him or not. His face gave nothing away. *I suppose it's possible he's as bad at being a vampire as I am,* she thought.

"Jane, we have to talk about this," Walter said.

Jane focused her attention on him. "I know," she said. "And we will. I just have to sort some things out and then it will all be fine. We're still getting married. Just perhaps not today."

Walter shook his head. "No," he said. "Not today. And maybe not ever."

Jane couldn't believe what she was hearing. Walter's voice sounded not only sad, but cold, as if he'd reluctantly come to a decision he didn't want to make.

"Please, Walter," she said. "Just trust me. This"—she indicated Joshua—"is nothing."

"I am not nothing," Joshua said, sniffing.

Jane ignored him. "Walter, why don't you and your *mother* go back to the hotel. I need to speak to Joshua and see if we can clear this up. I promise I'll be back as soon as I can."

"She's going to run off with him," Miriam declared. "Mark my words."

"No, she won't," Lucy said, giving Miriam a stern look. She began herding everyone ahead of her and out of the chapel. "Now come on. Let's go get a drink. For some reason I feel like a Bloody Mary." She looked at Jane. "Are you going to be okay?"

Jane nodded. "Try to talk to Walter for me," she said.

When Jane and Joshua were alone Jane said, "First, what are you doing here? Second, what do you know about Crispin's Needle?"

"Working back to front," said Joshua, "nothing, and I couldn't let another man have you."

"Don't be stupid," Jane said. "We haven't laid eyes on each other in almost two hundred years."

"That doesn't mean I can't still be in love with you," said Joshua. "Remember, you're the one who left me without so much as a goodbye."

"You know as well as I do that it was a foolish mistake," Jane told him. "We were never going to be suited to each other. Why, we never even . . . you know," she said.

"Walked in the garden of love?" leered Joshua.

Jane made a face. "Now I remember why I couldn't go through with it. You're a lovely man, but then you start to talk and it all goes to pieces. What was it you said to me on our wedding night? Oh, yes, it's all coming back to me now." She cleared her throat and in an obvious imitation of Joshua said, "'Let my key unlock your treasure chest and I will string for you a necklace of rarest pearls.'"

"That's sublime!" Joshua exclaimed.

"It's filthy!" Jane countered.

"You just don't appreciate poetry," said Joshua. "You never did. Now *I'm* starting to remember a few things about *you*. You never were supportive of my poems."

"Because they were terrible," Jane said. "I only fell for you because you reminded me a bit of Byron."

"You're a cruel woman, Jane Austen," Joshua said. "Your heart is cold as winter's breath."

"Don't call me that!" Jane barked. "And stop it with the metaphors. They're unnecessary. Everyone knows what cold is."

"Yes, but it's the *degree* of coldness," Joshua argued.

Jane rolled her eyes. "I'm not having this argument again," she said. "The point is, after two hundred years we can't be married. I mean technically yes, we can be, but surely there's a statute of limitations on these things. It's not as if we can apply for a divorce after all this time. They'll think we're insane."

"Then I suppose we'll just have to stay married," said Joshua. "Tough break for you and that Walter fellow. He seems nice, by the way."

"He is," Jane said. "And I love him. That's why we're going to figure a way out of this. But right now I want to talk about Crispin's Needle."

"I told you, I don't know what it is," Joshua said.

"But *they* do," said Jane, looking around.

"Who?" Joshua asked.

"The boys," said Jane. She cleared her throat. "All right, boys. You can come out now. I just want to talk to you. I promise I won't hurt you."

The sound of giggling filled the chapel. A moment later the figures of two boys appeared before Jane. One appeared to be about ten years old, the other slightly older. Both were thin, with flowing blond curls and angelic faces. They were dressed alike in black velvet tunics, black hose, and black shoes.

"That explains it," Jane said. "Ghosts." She looked at the boys more carefully. "I've seen you somewhere before."

The boys struck a pose so that the smaller one clutched the larger's right hand with his left. Turning his hips to the side, he placed his right hand on his brother's shoulder while the taller boy held in his left hand a velvet cap. Both boys opened their eyes wide so that they took on the appearance of frightened angels.

"The painting!" Jane exclaimed. "The one by Millais. You're—" She tried very hard to remember, but the names escaped her.

"Prince Edward the Fifth of England," said the taller boy, shaking his head.

"And—" began the second.

"Richard of Shrewsbury!" Joshua cried out. "First Duke of York."

"That is correct," said the smaller boy, bowing.

"I would have gotten it in a moment," said Jane when they gave her dirty looks. "I was just a little bit flustered." She turned to Joshua. "So you can see them, then?"

"Yes, yes," said Joshua. "And they do look remarkably like the painting."

"We should," said Edward.

"We posed for it," Richard explained.

"Millais could see ghosts?" Jane asked. "How novel."

"To be truthful, he thought we were hallucinations brought on by laudanum," said Edward. "He never could get used to seeing spirits."

"I must say, this is rather exciting, isn't it?" Jane remarked to Joshua. "So Gothic. I feel just like Catherine Morland, only this is real and I'm not a fool. Oh, I have so many questions. First off, who murdered—"

"We thought you wanted to know about Crispin's Needle," Richard interrupted.

"Can't I ask about both?" Jane asked.

"It depends on our mood," said Edward. "Best ask the most important question first."

Jane sighed. "Very well," she said. "What can you tell me about Crispin's Needle?"

Chapter 8

Tuesday: London

JANE COULD HARDLY BLAME WALTER FOR BEING A LITTLE STAND-offish. After all, discovering that she had once been married—however briefly—was a shock, and that she had forgotten all about it was difficult to believe, particularly when he remained unaware of her condition. Then too there was the necessity of once again postponing their wedding.

To Jane's surprise, and thanks largely to Lucy's intervention, he was handling it rather well. There had been some terse words back at the hotel, but in the end Walter had accepted Jane's sincere apologies. She in turn assured him that she would remedy the situation as quickly as possible and that Joshua would be no more than a momentary nuisance.

Unsurprisingly, Miriam was not as forgiving. She had apparently spent the hour between leaving the Tower and Jane's return to the hotel trying to convince her son to sever the engagement and return immediately to America, where, she'd assured Walter, they could find a nice woman who would give him not a minute's trouble. A nice Jewish woman. A nice Jewish woman who wasn't insane, at least not beyond the boundaries of reason.

Now, seated at one end of a large table in the Lord and Lamb, Jane saw Miriam glaring at her from the other end. Miriam, catching her eye, picked up a steak knife and mimed plunging it into the table. Jane in turn picked up a roll and slowly bit into it. Unfortunately, she choked on the dry bread and began to cough. Lucy thrust a glass of water into her hand and Jane drank, avoiding Miriam's mocking stare.

"Tell me again about the rhyme," Lucy said when Jane had composed herself. Ben and Walter had gone to the bar to order some pints, and the two women were alone at their end of the table. Chumsley Faber-Titting was regaling Miriam and Orsino Castano with a seemingly endless story, and so it was an opportunity to discuss Jane's encounter with the princes in the Tower.

Given how they'd gone on about it, Jane had expected the ghostly boys to tell her all about Crispin's Needle. However, their knowledge of it had proved to be disappointingly limited, confined primarily to the sharing of a rhyme. Jane repeated it for Lucy.

> Cursed creature of the night,
> foul fiend with no soul,
> pierce your heart with Crispin's Nail
> and be once more made whole.

Lucy selected a piece of Irish soda bread from the basket on the table and liberally applied butter to it. "That's not much to go on," she said. "I suppose you're the foul fiend."

"No doubt," Jane agreed.

"And you're supposed to pierce your heart with Crispin's Needle, whatever that is."

"Gosebourne had a bit more information about that," Jane told her. "Apparently Crispin was a medieval monk. He dabbled in alchemy and was a bit obsessed with the occult. Somehow or other he got the idea that he could reverse the process that turns one into a vampire."

"Unmake you, in other words," said Lucy.

Jane nodded. "Exactly."

"How would that work?" Lucy asked.

"That's the problem," Jane said. "Nobody really knows. The legend says that he invented an object of some kind—"

"Crispin's Needle," said Lucy.

"Yes," Jane said. "And supposedly it's capable of restoring the human soul."

Lucy wiped her fingers on her napkin. "So you're supposed to drive this so-called needle through your heart?"

"I'm guessing that's the idea," said Jane. "Only instead of killing you it gives you back your soul. A reverse staking, if you will."

"No offense," Lucy said, "but it sounds like a load of crap. My guess is that it's a trick to get unhappy vampires to kill themselves."

"Possibly," Jane agreed. "But Gosebourne doesn't think so."

"If this thing has been around since the Middle Ages, why are you only just now finding out about it?" Lucy asked.

"Apparently it's something of a vampire urban legend," said Jane. "I gather that believing in it is looked upon a bit like believing in Santa Claus is. No one wants to admit they think it's real, but at the same time there's this fascination with it. Still, it seems that one doesn't admit to believing in it if one runs in educated circles."

"Good thing you don't run in educated circles," Lucy said.

"Indeed," said Jane. "I was hoping the princes could tell me exactly how it works. But they don't know."

"Where did they learn the rhyme?" Lucy asked.

"They say they learned it from another vampire," said Jane. "But of course they can't remember who it was. Between us, I think they're a little mad."

"Did you find out how they died?" Lucy said.

Jane shook her head. "They were asleep when it happened.

But there are no knife marks on their throats, so they weren't slit. I'm guessing they were smothered."

"So we still don't know who did it?" said Lucy.

"Sadly, no," Jane said. "They have some guesses, but they're the same ones people have been making since their deaths. Again, a bit of a disappointment."

"May I join you ladies?"

Jane looked up to see Orsino standing beside them. "By all means," she said, indicating the seat beside her.

Orsino sat. "Thank you," he said. "I had to get away from Chumsley. If I had to listen to one more story about what a cow Enid is, I was going to scream."

"You like Enid, then?" asked Jane.

"Heavens, no," said Orsino. "She's horrible. Which is exactly why I don't want to hear about her." He took a sip from the glass of wine he'd carried over with him. "I prefer to discuss pleasant topics."

Well then, you came to the wrong end of the table, Jane thought.

"I like your name," Lucy said to Orsino. "It's from *Twelfth Night*, right?"

Orsino nodded. "Indeed it is. My mother was a professor of literature at the Università degli Studi di Firenze. She adored Shakespeare."

"It's one of my favorites of his plays," said Lucy.

"I've never read it," Orsino told her.

"Really?" Jane said, shocked. "How extraordinary."

Orsino laughed. "I suppose it seems so," he said. "The truth is, I haven't read it because I fear I won't like my namesake. How awful to go through life named after someone you don't care for." He turned to Jane. "For instance, suppose your mother adored Charlotte Brontë and you had been named after Jane Eyre, yet you found the character stupid and tedious."

"Doesn't everyone?" said Jane, earning her a stern look from Lucy.

"Of course, there are many Janes in literature," Orsino mused. "You could always choose one of the others and pretend that she was the inspiration. There are not so many Orsinos."

"Just the one, as far as I know," Lucy said. "But just so you know, Orsino is a very likeable character."

"I'm pleased to hear it," Orsino said. "I sometimes tell people that my mother named me Orsino because in Italian it means 'little bear.' As you can see, I do in fact resemble the animal." He stroked his beard and held up his hands, the backs of which were covered in the same black hair.

"Very clever," Jane said. "I think that's what I will call you. Little Bear."

"Most of my lovers do," said Orsino.

"Are you suggesting we become lovers?" Jane teased.

Orsino laughed. "I'm afraid my inclinations lie elsewhere," he said. "I prefer the company of other bears."

"Ah," Jane said. "I understand. And I'm sure there are a great many of them who prefer your company as well."

"A few," Orsino said, smiling.

"Are you trying to steal my fiancée?"

Walter appeared, carrying in each hand a glass of ale. Ben, likewise encumbered, took the seat beside Lucy and handed her a glass. "Boddington's Ale," he said. "The cream of Manchester."

"You will be happy to know that your fiancée has deflected all of my attempts to make her fall in love with me," Orsino told Walter. "I am utterly defeated." He winked at Jane, who hid her smile in her beer.

"I'm relieved to hear it," Walter said. Jane detected a note of anger in his voice, and her heart sank as she was reminded that despite appearances he was deeply hurt.

"This beer is amazing," said Lucy, changing the subject, for which Jane was thankful.

"Brodie recommended it," said Ben.

"Where is our Australian friend?" Orsino asked.

"Still at the bar," said Walter. "He ran into some other Aussies and they're having a drink."

"Then I'm certain he'll be in a fine mood when he arrives," Orsino said.

As if on cue, Brodie's voice boomed through the air. "Walter!" he called out. "Look who I found!"

Jane looked up to see the Australian approaching with his arm around a woman. She was about Jane's height, with curly brown hair that was cut short and a pug nose that gave her a boyish look. She was dressed in jeans and a red shirt that Jane was almost certain came from the most recent L.L.Bean catalog.

"Sam!" Walter cried. He got up and walked around the table to give the woman a hug. "It's good to see you again."

"You too," said Sam in a husky but pleasant voice. "It's been a long time."

Lucy leaned across the table. "I don't think you have anything to worry about," she whispered to Jane.

Walter turned around. "Jane, this is Sam," he said.

"It's good to finally meet you," said Jane. "I've heard so much about you." This of course was a lie, but if Walter caught it, he showed no indication of it.

"Brodie tells me the two of you got married today," Sam said, looking between Walter and Jane. "Congratulations."

An uncomfortable silence settled over the table. Jane had assumed that Walter had told everyone about the interruption to their wedding. Apparently he had not. Jane, not knowing how to respond, waited anxiously as the seconds ticked by.

"Thank you," Walter said. He didn't look at Jane as he smiled broadly and added, "We're thrilled to be able to celebrate it with good friends."

Jane, who had never known Walter to be deceitful in any way whatsoever, couldn't decide if she was horrified or proud. Mostly she felt ashamed. Walter would never have had to lie if she hadn't made a mess of things. *If Joshua hadn't made a mess of things*, she corrected herself. Not that it mattered who exactly was to blame. The end result was the same.

Orsino, sensing that Walter probably wanted to sit beside his supposed wife, returned to his original seat on Chumsley's right. Sam sat next to him, with Walter and Jane filling the rest of that side of the table. Brodie took the end seat, facing Chumsley across the table, with Ben and Lucy to his right. That left a seat between Lucy and Miriam. This was occupied by Lilith, whom Miriam had once again presented as a helping dog to a dubious but ultimately acquiescent hostess. The little dog was curled up, asleep but snoring loudly.

A waiter appeared not long after and took their orders. Jane, with feelings of nostalgia, ordered bangers and mash. She hadn't had it in years, and although she of course didn't have to eat due to her undead digestive system, she enjoyed the ritual of it. As she waited for the food to arrive, she listened to the conversations going on around her. Walter, busy catching up with Sam, was turned away from her, and she felt the urge to reach beneath the table and hold his hand. She resisted it, afraid he would pull away.

"Nasty little bugger," she heard Brodie say.

"Who is?" she asked.

"McGuinness," Brodie replied. "Man's a right berk."

Jane was intrigued. The previous night Brodie had seemed more or less indifferent to McGuinness. Now she detected a distinct note of dislike in his voice. She wondered if he'd had enough drinks to let his true feelings for the man show.

"Did I tell you we went to school together?" Brodie asked.

"No," Jane said.

"We did," Brodie continued. "Dalhousie University in Halifax. Wonderful school. I don't know how the hell McGuinness got in. His designs were shit."

"If he was so incompetent, how did he get a degree?" Lucy asked.

Brodie held up one thick finger. "A very good question," he said. "The way he gets everything he gets—by cheating."

"It seems to me it would be rather difficult to cheat at designing a building," Ben remarked.

"Not if you steal other people's designs," said Brodie. "Thieving bastard."

The tone of his voice suggested a personal experience with McGuinness's treachery, and Jane couldn't help asking, "Did he ever steal from you?"

Brodie snorted, sounding not unlike an angry rhino. "Course he did," he said. "Stole one of my best ideas. It was my own fault for telling him about it in the first place, but I didn't know then what a sly one he is. Clever as a shithouse rat. Pardon the expression, ladies."

"Surely you told the professor what he'd done," Lucy said.

"Wouldn't have done a bit of good," he said. "He was having a naughty with her every afternoon while her husband was off teaching the history of Canada to undergrads. No way she would believe me over him." He took a long pull on his ale. "Anyway, that's all in the past. Still, I wouldn't mind if someone kicked him down a flight of stairs."

At that point several servers arrived carrying plates of food, and for the next half an hour Jane focused on her bangers and mash. They were just as wonderful as she remembered, and for the time it took to finish them she forgot all about her unfortunate predicament. Walter too seemed to forget, chatting with her amiably about his fish and chips and exchanging bites with her.

Then, as the empty dishes were being taken away and the waiter was suggesting sticky toffee pudding for dessert, Jane felt a twinge in her stomach. At first she thought it was merely a reaction to the onion gravy (onions had had this effect on her ever since she was a child). But when another cramp came, much stronger than the first, she knew it was something else. She needed to feed. And this time bangers wouldn't do the job. She needed blood.

Chapter 9

Wednesday: Cripple Minton

A TRAIN AT EIGHT-TWENTY IN THE MORNING IS A SLEEPY THING. Jane, having not yet had an opportunity to feed, was particularly lethargic, and the gentle *whump-whump-whump* of the train passing over the tracks made her even more so. Her hunger made it impossible to sleep, however, and so she planned on spending the hour and a half it would take to travel from London to Warwick staring out the window. Walter, who could fall asleep anywhere, had done so within five minutes of the train leaving Marylebone station. His head was against Jane's shoulder and his breath was hot in her ear, which was irritating.

She felt guilty being irritated about Walter's close proximity. She knew she should be grateful that he hadn't broken things off. But when she was hungry she hated to be touched, not least of all because she could feel the blood coursing beneath the surface of the skin of the person touching her and it took enormous force of will not to bite. At the moment she was grinding her teeth, trying to keep her fangs locked in place.

"Good morning."

Jane turned her head. "Oh, good grief," she said. "What are you doing here?"

Joshua, dressed in the same dark suit he'd been wearing the previous day, sat down in the seat across from Jane and Walter. Jane glanced anxiously at Walter, afraid he would wake up.

"Don't worry about him," Joshua said, scratching idly at his beard. "If he wakes up, I'll glamor him and he'll think it was all a dream."

"Why do *you* have to glamor him?" Jane asked. "What makes you think I can't do it?"

Joshua ignored her, which was annoying. *Byron does the same thing,* she thought. *They really are very much alike.* "I did some asking around about Crispin's Needle," he said.

"And?"

"Nobody's entirely sure it exists," said Joshua. "Some vampires think it's a legend. Others think it exists but that it doesn't really work. And some believe in it."

"That isn't terribly helpful," Jane remarked.

"No," Joshua agreed. "It isn't. However, I did find out one useful piece of information. Have you heard of the Tedious Three?"

Jane shook her head. The movement jostled Walter, who opened his eyes and yawned. "Are we there?"

Joshua placed his hand in front of Walter's eyes. "Back to sleep," he said, and Walter's head fell against Jane's neck.

"How did you do that?" she asked.

"You mean you can't?" Joshua said, lifting an eyebrow. "Interesting. So, have you heard of the Tedious Three?"

"No," Jane snapped. *One more vampire trick I don't know about,* she thought, irritated.

"Librarians," Joshua explained. "Names of Zenodotus, Callimachus, and Eratosthenes. Each was at one time a librarian at the Library of Alexandria. Since being turned they've dedicated their lives to recording the history of the vampires."

"How interesting," Jane said.

"You'd think so," said Joshua. "But they manage to make it

boring. Nobody can stand them. For one thing, they're forever correcting your grammar."

"One's grammar," Jane said under her breath.

"If anyone knows about Crispin's Needle, it's them."

"They," said Jane. "I mean, where do we find them?"

"That's the tricky bit," Joshua replied. "They're so annoying that no one wants to spend time with them. Nobody I spoke to can remember where they live."

"Why is everything so difficult?" said Jane. "What good is having vampire librarians if you can't ask them anything?"

"That's where you're lucky," Joshua said. "Their last known whereabouts happen to be in Warwickshire. If you can find some-one there who knew them then—"

"And just how am I supposed to do that?" Jane interrupted. "Is there a vampire directory? Can I just stop in at the visitors' center and ask them to point me to the nearest vampire?"

"You're in a foul mood this morning," Joshua said.

"And whose fault is that?" said Jane. "If you hadn't shown up, I would be married right now and very, very happy. By the way, how did you know I was getting married anyway?"

"Word gets around," Joshua said. "But let's focus on the task at hand. You need to find a vampire."

"You'll help me, of course," said Jane.

Joshua shook his head. "I'm heading straight back to the city," he said. "I'm having lunch with my publisher."

"Your publisher?" Jane said. "You mean someone is actually publishing your poems?"

"I'll have you know I'm quite popular with the undead," Joshua said proudly.

"We have our own *publisher*?" Jane said. "You mean I didn't have to wait almost two hundred years to be published again?"

Joshua looked sheepish. "Actually, he doesn't much care for your work," he said. "He finds it all a bit twee."

Jane, incensed, started to reply, but just then Chumsley passed through the car. "We'll be arriving in five minutes," he called out. "Warwick station in five minutes."

"Just find a vampire," Joshua told Jane as he got up. "It won't be difficult."

"You don't know me very well," said Jane.

"If you're meant to find Crispin's Needle, you'll find the way," Joshua said. "Now farewell, my sweet. Until we meet again."

Jane exhaled loudly. "Stupid Romantic poets," she muttered. "Always blathering on about fate and destiny. Moony dreamers, the lot of them."

"What?" said Walter, who had woken up and was stretching.

"I said we're here," Jane replied.

As the train came to a stop they gathered up their things and walked to the door. Most of the others were already there, all looking less than awake. Jane realized that Joshua had probably glamored the entire car to make sure no one remembered seeing him. *Perhaps he's not as stupid as I think he is,* she mused.

As they exited the train they were herded toward a small bus into which their luggage was also being loaded. Chumsley, after three or four pints the night before, had offered to allow Miriam, Lucy, and Ben to travel with the rest of the group whenever there was room, thereby saving them a great deal of trouble, not to mention taxi fares. Now they all piled into the bus and took their seats. Jane couldn't help but notice that Enid's guests—and Miriam—all sat on one side, while Chumsley's sat on the other.

The first destination being of Chumsley's choosing, he was in charge, and as the bus made its way toward the hamlet of Cripple Minton he briefed them on the site.

"We're going to be touring Pitstone Vicarage," he said. "As the name suggests, it was once home to the presiding vicar of the neighboring church, which is also owned by the family and no longer used for services. However, the church is of little interest to us. It's the vicarage we've come to see. It is, I do not hesitate to say, one of the hidden gems of British architecture."

Lucy, who was sitting behind Jane, leaned forward. "Can we go look at the church anyway?" she asked. "I don't think I can stand a tour this early in the morning."

"I agree," Jane said. "Besides, I suspect they don't really want us tagging along."

She conferred with Walter, who seemed a little disappointed that she didn't want to see the vicarage but didn't try to get her to change her mind, which Jane interpreted as his way of agreeing that it would probably not interest her very much. She was equally relieved when, as the bus arrived in Cripple Minton and pulled to the side of the narrow road on which Pitstone Vicarage was situated, Miriam announced that she and Lilith would be staying with the group. This left Jane, Lucy, and Ben free to investigate the church.

As Chumsley had noted, the church was not particularly distinctive, although it was charming in the way that all English churches of a certain age are. The stones out of which the walls were built were cunningly composed so that no other supports were needed. The wooden pews glowed with a soft shine created by the behinds of the faithful polishing them year upon year. And the stained glass that filled the windows glowed faintly in the winter morning light.

Jane went to the nearest window and looked more closely. The scene depicted showed a group of three women being menaced by two men. Two of the women knelt on the ground, their hands lifted to heaven. The third woman stood defiant, pointing an accusing finger at the men. A small plaque beneath the window read: ST. APOLLONIA THE BLESSED REFUSES TO RENOUNCE HER FAITH.

The next window was most unusual. The woman Jane now knew to be St. Apollonia had her arms held behind her by two men. Her mouth was open and a third man was reaching inside with a pliers-like instrument. It gripped one of Apollonia's teeth. The saint's lips were bloody, and at her feet were scattered a dozen small white objects also dotted with blood. The identifying plaque read: ST. APOLLONIA THE BLESSED HAS HER TEETH REMOVED BY HER TORMENTORS.

"That seems an odd thing to do," Jane said to Ben, who had come to stand beside her and was peering at the window.

"Not really," Ben told her. "They did all kinds of weird things to the martyrs. Well, allegedly. I suspect most of these stories are made up out of whole cloth."

"That may be true," said a woman's voice. "But we do have several of St. Apollonia's teeth in a reliquary."

Jane and Ben turned to see a very pretty young woman standing behind them. Her age was difficult to determine, but Jane put her at no more than thirty. Her long blond hair fell loosely about her shoulders. She was wearing a deep blue cashmere turtleneck sweater and black pants.

"I'm Clare Marlowe," the woman said. "My family owns the house your group is touring, as well as the church."

"It's lovely to meet you," said Jane. She introduced herself, as well as Lucy and Ben.

"How did your family come to own a church?" Lucy asked.

"The church dates from the eighteenth century," Clare said. "The first vicar was Bartholomew Marlowe. His family—our family—was very wealthy. But Bartholomew wasn't interested in money. He was more of a scholar, with a particular interest in religion. When he was twenty his parents and only sister were killed in a boating accident. Bartholomew inherited a fortune, which he used to build this church and the vicarage. Since then a Marlowe has always lived in the house."

"Was the church ever used for services?" asked Ben. "Or has it always been private?"

"At first it was used by the public," Clare said. "Bartholomew liked the idea of being a country vicar. But his son, Tallway Marlowe, wasn't interested in it at all, and after his father's death he closed the church to the public and it's been closed ever since. Occasionally people come to see it, but I'm afraid it's mostly been forgotten."

"That's a pity," Jane said. "It's so lovely. These windows are particularly beautiful, although I confess I've never heard of St. Apollonia."

Clare laughed. "Not many people have," she said. "She's a bit obscure. She lived in the third century, in Alexandria. According to church history, she was a virgin dedicated to the service of God."

"Aren't they always?" Lucy said. "Virgins, I mean."

"It does seem to come with the territory," said Clare. "Apollonia was of course a convert to Christianity, which annoyed her pagan neighbors. One day a group of men rounded up Apollonia and several other Christian women and ordered them to recant or be burned alive. That's what you see in the first window. When Apollonia refused, they tortured her by pulling out all of her teeth."

Clare moved on to the third window and continued the story. "Seeing what was done to Apollonia, the other women threw themselves into the water in order to drown," she said.

Indeed, the window showed two women bobbing in what could only be the ocean, their raised hands clasped in prayer. Their captors stood on the shore, looking on angrily and shaking their fists.

"The men threw Apollonia in after them," Clare said. "But she didn't drown." She indicated the fourth window, in which a very much alive Apollonia was being lifted from the water by what appeared to be an angel. "Although the other women perished, Apollonia was delivered from death."

"Why just her?" Ben asked. "That doesn't seem fair."

"I suppose it depends on how you look at it," said Clare. "Apollonia was willing to suffer for God. The other two killed themselves rather than go through that. Perhaps God didn't think they were worthy."

"And they say *our* God was harsh," Ben remarked.

"The story continues on the other side," said Clare, leading them across the nave to another set of windows. "Since water didn't work, Apollonia's captors decided to try fire."

"Wait," Jane said. "Didn't the angel take her away?"

"She asked to be returned to them," Clare answered. "Remember, she was a martyr."

"Of course," said Jane. "Go on."

"As you can see, they threw Apollonia into a pile of burning sticks," Clare said. "I think the fire is particularly well rendered."

"The glasswork is gorgeous," Lucy remarked.

"Apollonia, of course, did not burn," said Clare as she walked on. "Once again the angel came and saved her, which is what you see in window number six. And now we get to the really good stuff."

The seventh window depicted Apollonia on the ground. One man held her feet while another held her arms stretched out behind her head. A third man knelt beside her, a spike in his hand. It was pressed to Apollonia's chest, just over her heart, and the man was in the process of bringing a hammer down toward it.

"This is unusual in the history of the saints," Clare informed them. "The martyrdom of Apollonia is the only example of a saint being killed in this manner. Supposedly the spike used to pierce her heart was made from the nails that were used to crucify Christ."

"And what's happening here?" asked Ben, moving to the eighth and last window as Jane continued to stare at the seventh.

"St. Apollonia redeemed from death," Clare said. "See how she's rising toward heaven while her executioners fall to their knees? Allegedly they were so frightened by her ascension that all the blood drained from their bodies."

Jane turned to Lucy, who had remained with her in front of

the seventh window. "Don't you find this all a bit strange?" she murmured.

"Christianity?" said Lucy. "Of course I do."

"I mean St. Apollonia specifically," Jane said. "First there's the matter of her teeth, which for some reason they felt the need to remove. Then she couldn't be killed either by water or by fire. And finally they do her in with a spike through the heart, yet she rises from the dead and her killers are drained of their blood. Sound familiar?"

"I admit it's a bit vampire-esque," Lucy admitted.

"A bit?" said Jane. "The only thing they've left out is her turning into a bat."

"I thought you said you couldn't really do that," Lucy said. "Have you been holding out on me?"

"No," said Jane. "I can't. But that's not the point. The point is that this is clearly some kind of allegory about vampirism."

Lucy considered this for a moment. "If that's true, then why didn't the spike kill her?" she asked.

"Maybe it was Crispin's Needle," Jane suggested, keeping her voice low. "The final window shows her with her soul returned to her body."

"And the dead guys?" Lucy asked. "If she's not a vampire anymore, who drained them?"

"Good question," Jane said. "Perhaps God has a more refined sense of humor than we think he does."

"Too bad we can't get a look at those teeth Clare mentioned," said Lucy. "It would be interesting to see if any of them are fangs."

"It certainly explains why the Tedious Three would have spent time here," Jane said. "If this story is true, it would definitely qualify as vampire history."

"The who?" Lucy asked.

"Oh, I haven't told you about them yet," said Jane. "Vampire historians, apparently. Joshua told me about them this morning."

"You saw Joshua again?" Lucy said.

"Not so much saw as was visited by," Jane explained. "A bit like the Ghost of Christmas Annoying. But he did say that the Three have been looking for the Needle for some time."

"So you think the Needle really does exist, then?"

Jane sighed. "I don't know," she said.

"But you want it to, don't you?" said Lucy.

"It would make things easier," Jane said.

Lucy shrugged. "You'd be human again," she said. "Not that you're inhuman or anything," she added quickly.

"I know what you meant," Jane said, leaning against her for a moment. She was quiet as she looked over at the figure of Apollonia ascending. "I could grow old with Walter," she said softly.

"Did you guys see the rose window behind the altar?" Ben appeared beside them.

"No," Lucy said. "Why? Is it as weird as these are?"

"See for yourself," said Ben.

Jane and Lucy followed him to the center aisle of the nave. Behind the altar the rose window hovered like a full moon. When they'd entered the church the light had not been strong enough to illuminate it. Now sunlight poured through the glass, and when Jane saw the image depicted there, she gasped.

A large heart occupied the center of the window. Piercing it was a long, thin needle very much like the one in the scene from the seventh window. The tip of the needle protruded from the bottom of the heart, a single drop of blood hanging down from it. Rays of light emanated from all around the heart, filling the window.

"It's beautiful," Jane said.

"The pierced heart of St. Apollonia the Blessed," said Clare, who had come up behind them. "There's only one other window like it in the world."

"Where?" Jane and Lucy asked simultaneously.

"France," Clare said. "Paris, to be exact. In a private chapel in a house that once belonged to a courtesan named Eloise Babineaux."

"You don't happen to have the address, do you?" Jane asked.

Clare nodded. "I do," she said. "I wrote an article about the windows last year and corresponded a bit with the current owner of the house. But may I ask why you're so interested in the window?"

Jane thought quickly. "I'm very interested in religious iconography," she said. "I've never seen anything like this before." She hesitated a moment before asking her next question. "You mentioned that you have some of Apollonia's teeth," she said. "I don't suppose anyone knows what became of the spike they used to kill her?"

"Not that I know of," Clare answered. "But it's funny you should mention that. Several years ago three men came here and asked that very same question. No one else ever has."

"Three men?" said Lucy. "Did they say who they were?"

Clare shook her head. "They didn't say much at all. Just that they were compiling information about various churches. For a book, maybe. To be honest, I'd forgotten all about them until just now, when you asked about the spike." She paused. "Oh, I do remember one thing. They kept referring to the spike as a needle. In fact, they corrected me when I called it a spike. It reminded me of when my teachers used to correct my grammar."

"Teachers," Lucy said, looking at Jane.

"Or librarians," Jane said.

"That's it," said Clare. "Librarians. They reminded me of fussy old librarians. I kept expecting them to shush me." She laughed.

"Did you tell them about Eloise Babineaux?" Jane asked.

"Now that you mention it, I don't think I did," said Clare. "In fact, I'm sure I didn't. And since we're talking about it I'm remembering more. They weren't just fussy, they were . . . spooky. I can't think of any other word to describe it. I was glad when they left."

"Well, thank you for giving *us* the address," Lucy said meaningfully.

"Of course," said Clare. "Oh. Right. I'll just go get that."

She scurried off to the house, leaving Jane and Lucy to keep looking at the rose window. Ben, having grown bored with the whole thing, had wandered outside.

"It must have been the Tedious Three," Lucy said.

"They certainly fit the description," Jane agreed.

"Eloise Babineaux's house is in Paris," said Lucy. "When do we get to Paris?"

"Sunday, I believe."

Lucy looked at the glowing heart, then at Jane. "Hopefully whoever lives in Eloise's house will be accepting visitors."

Chapter 10

Wednesday: On a Train to Wales

"TRAINS ARE SEXY, DON'T YOU THINK?" WALTER SAT ON THE EDGE of the mattress covering the lower of the compartment's bunk beds. "Except for the sleeping arrangements, that is."

Jane, busy flossing her teeth to remove a bit of mutton stuck there from dinner, mumbled a reply. Despite having eaten, she was still famished, the food having done nothing to ease her more sinister hunger. She hadn't had an opportunity to feed on any of the locals at the pub, and she was running out of time. If she didn't get blood, and soon, there was going to be a problem. It was at times like these that she wished she weren't so conscientious about not feeding on her friends and loved ones. It would make things much easier for her. But one has to have principles, she reminded herself. *Even if one is a bloodsucking fiend.*

Walter was in a very good mood, which was a relief. He'd thoroughly enjoyed the tour of Pitstone Vicarage, as well as the meal taken at the local pub before boarding the overnight train bound for Pembroke. He'd had several pints before and during dinner and, as a result, was more gregarious than usual. Jane wished he would shut up, as his incessant chattering was making her headache worse.

"Oh, and you should have seen the look Enid gave Chumsley when he corrected her about the style of the moldings in the drawing room," he said. "I thought for sure she was going to start a fire with her mind. You know, like that girl in the Stephen King book."

"Carrie or Charlie?" Jane asked, inspecting her teeth in the mirror. She let her fangs click into place momentarily and ran the floss between them.

"What?" said Walter.

"Stephen King wrote two books about a girl who could start fires with her mind," Jane said. "*Carrie* and *Firestarter.*"

"Oh," said Walter. "Um, well, I guess it doesn't really matter which one, does it?"

Jane dropped the soiled floss into the trash can beneath the compartment's tiny sink. "I suppose not," she said.

Walter reclined on the bed, his hands behind his head and his feet crossed at the ankles. "I love you very much," he said. "I hope you know that."

Jane turned and looked at him. "Of course I do," she said, puzzled by the abrupt shift in the tone of the conversation.

"Good," Walter said. "Sometimes I think I don't tell you often enough."

Immediately Jane felt guilty for wishing he would be quiet. If anyone should be apologizing, she thought, it should be she. She was the one who had failed to mention that she had a husband. She was the one who had turned Walter down time after time for years before agreeing to go out with him. She was the one who still hadn't mentioned the minor detail of her being immortal.

She went and sat beside him on the bunk. There really was very little room, and Walter had to turn sideways to accommodate her. It was an awkward position for both of them, but Jane made the best of it.

"I love you too," she said. "I know the past few days have been just slightly peculiar, but I assure you I never intentionally kept Joshua from you."

Walter smiled. "Eighteen months ago I would have thought you were lying through your teeth," he said. "But I know you well enough now to know that you don't exactly think like other women."

"I really don't," Jane agreed.

"Not that I don't think it's odd that his name never came up," Walter continued. "But I don't think you were deliberately trying to keep him a secret."

"I don't think like other women?" said Jane.

"Absolutely not," Walter answered.

"I think that's the nicest thing anyone has ever said to me," Jane told him.

Her stomach rumbled loudly.

"Tummy trouble?" asked Walter. "Something you ate at dinner?"

Something I didn't *eat,* Jane thought.

"Just a little indigestion," she said. "I think I'll go to the dining car and see if I can get some milk. Do you want anything?"

"A bottled water would be nice," Walter said.

Jane stood up. "I'll be right back," she said.

Leaving the compartment, she shut the door and looked for the sign indicating the direction of the dining car. It was already ten o'clock. She hoped it would still be open.

The doors all along the corridor were closed. As Jane walked by she heard voices coming from several of them. A bark came from behind a door on her right: Miriam and Lilith. She bared her teeth at the door and growled.

I heard that! Lilith's voice came through clearly. Jane ignored her, hurrying on to the next car.

In order to reach the dining car she had to pass through several coach cars. Here the passengers who had not booked compartments made themselves as comfortable as possible in the cramped seats. Many of them had simply fallen asleep sitting up, while others had attempted to make beds of a sort by stretching out across two seats. Jane avoided looking at them, finding it odd to be seeing people in public at their most vulnerable, when they were unaware of being watched.

She passed through the door at the far end of the car and found herself in the dining car. A handful of people occupied the tables along either side of the car, and another half dozen were lined up to purchase items from the to-go counter. Jane joined the queue.

"I find railway travel induces insomnia," said a monotone voice.

Jane turned to see Bergen Faust standing behind her, dressed in the same dark suit she'd seen him in at each of the tour group's gatherings. His hands were behind his back, and he peered at her with unblinking eyes.

"Do you?" Jane said. "I'm sorry to hear it."

"I never have been able to sleep in moving vehicles," Bergen continued. "The motion interferes with the workings of the inner ear."

"It sounds terrible," said Jane. "Tell me, did you enjoy the tour this morning?"

"It was very educational," Bergen replied. "I learned a great many things I had not known about the heraldic ornamentation of Georgian-period andirons."

"That does sound . . . marvelous," Jane said.

"It is a fascinating subject," Bergen told her. "I understand you visited the Church of St. Apollonia."

"Yes," Jane answered, surprised that Bergen would pay her comings and goings any mind. "It's really quite lovely, although I'm sure not as interesting as the andirons."

"Few things are," Bergen agreed. "I believe it's your turn."

"Excuse me?" said Jane.

"Your turn," Bergen repeated, nodding slightly and looking past her.

Jane turned around to see that while they'd been talking the line had moved forward. The girl behind the counter smiled wanly. "What may I get for you?" she asked.

"A bottled water," Jane said.

"Will that be all?" the girl asked.

"Yes," said Jane, taking some money from the pocket of her pants.

She accepted the water from the girl, and when she'd received her change she turned to go. "Well, good night," she said to Bergen.

"I'll walk with you as far as your compartment," Bergen said.

"Aren't you going to get anything?" Jane asked, looking back at the bored girl behind the counter.

"No," Bergen said. "Why?"

"I just thought . . . " She let the remainder of the thought die unspoken. "Never mind."

There was no polite way to rid herself of Bergen. Now she could think of no plausible excuse for not returning to Walter. As if to emphasize the predicament, her stomach growled again. She and Bergen walked in silence until they reached the door to her room.

"Here I am," Jane said.

Bergen tipped his head. "Until tomorrow," he said, then continued on.

Jane opened the door and slipped inside. Walter was still on the lower bunk, reading a book. She handed him the bottle of water. "I understand you saw some exquisite andirons on your house tour this morning," she said.

Walter took a sip of water. "Ran into Bergen, did you?"

Jane laughed. "Such an odd little man."

"He reminds me a bit of Dwight Frye," said Walter. "The actor who played Renfield in *Dracula* opposite Lugosi. I'll never forget the scene in the asylum when he's trying to eat a spider and the orderly takes it away from him." He widened his eyes and held his hands up, fingers wiggling. "'Flies! Flies! Who wants to eat flies? Not when I can get nice, fat spiders!'" He shuddered. "That completely creeped me out when I was a kid. The whole movie did. But of course once my mother told me I couldn't see it, I had to."

"Miriam forbade you to see *Dracula*?" Jane asked.

Walter nodded. "Not just *Dracula*," he said. "Any vampire movie. She had a real thing about vampires. I don't know why. I guess they freaked her out or something. I wonder if she's still spooked by them."

I think it's the other way around, Jane thought.

"Anyway, that's who Bergen reminds me of," said Walter. "Renfield. Do you suppose he eats spiders?"

"No, but he ordered black pudding at supper, and that's just as bad," Jane said.

Her stomach clenched. *I'd eat a spider right now if I had one,* she thought grimly. She had to feed soon, but she'd run out of excuses for leaving the room. Besides, until the other passengers were asleep it would be difficult to find somewhere—and someone—suitable for her needs.

With much difficulty she climbed into the top bunk and tried to read. She'd brought with her for the trip a battered paperback copy of Mikhail Bulgakov's *The Master and Margarita.* For years she had been trying to get through it, and had begun and abandoned it at least a dozen times. Each time she got a little further into the book than she had on the previous attempt, and now she was up to page 239. She was determined to finish it once and for all, even if it killed her.

She made a valiant effort but fell asleep after reading fewer than six pages. When she next woke up, the compartment was dark and Walter was snoring below her. A glance at the small travel clock Walter had set on the narrow shelf beside the beds read 1:37.

Jane got down from the bunk as quietly as she could, found her shoes, and slipped them on. She opened the compartment door and went out into the hallway.

The lights in the corridor had been dimmed for the night, but Jane had no trouble finding her way to the coach car. There the overhead lights had also been turned down, and the car was bathed in shadows. Here and there the glow of an e-book reader or the screen of a laptop cast light on the face of its user, but mostly the passengers slept as the train raced through the night.

Jane walked the length of the car, looking for a suitable candidate. With the majority of the people asleep, she allowed herself more time than she usually did when hunting to look at the possibilities. It felt a bit like perusing the produce section in search of the juiciest peach. This thought amused her, and she had to stifle a giggle. *So inappropriate*, she admonished herself.

Not seeing anything she liked, she walked into the next car. This one was less crowded, and there were far fewer lights on. In fact, there was only one, and it belonged to a girl who had fallen asleep while listening to her iPod. Encouraged, Jane went from seat to seat, examining the occupants.

She found him in the middle of the car. He was young—she guessed not yet twenty-five. On the seat beside him was a backpack, and open on his lap was a copy of the Lonely Planet guide to Ireland. He looked to be in good shape, and Jane guessed he wouldn't miss the little bit of blood she was going to take from him.

She moved the backpack from the seat and placed it in the

aisle. Then she took the seat beside the boy. Breathing deeply, she focused her mind so that in the event the boy woke up she would be prepared to glamor him. Then she leaned over as if she were asleep beside him, her face nuzzled in his neck.

His blood was delicious. This was not a thought she often had when feeding. It was an activity she loathed, and ordinarily she just wanted to get it over with. But the boy's blood was undeniably pleasant, sweet and salty at the same time. *Like taffy,* Jane thought vaguely as she drank.

When she'd had enough, she retracted her fangs and sat up. Her headache had disappeared and her stomach was no longer aching. She sighed deeply and opened her eyes.

Suzu was standing in the aisle, not ten feet away, looking down at her. She was dressed in a black robe embroidered in cream with cranes, which caused her to look like a shadow dappled with moonlight. At first Jane, who couldn't recall even having seen the woman since the opening night reception, thought she must be imagining it. But then Suzu blinked. Jane froze, her mind racing. How long had Suzu been there? How much had she seen? Was there blood on her face?

She thought quickly. How could she explain what she was doing there? Then, to make matters worse, the young man beside her stirred. He moaned and twisted his face toward her. Before she knew what she was doing, Jane kissed him passionately on the lips. The boy, slowly coming awake, kissed her back.

Jane pulled her mouth away and laughed lightly. "Oh, Esteban," she said. "You're so naughty."

She pretended to see Suzu for the first time. Her hand flew to her mouth in feigned shock. "Suzu!" she said. "This . . . this . . . isn't what it looks like."

Suzu looked at the boy, who was making kissing movements with his lips as he sought out Jane's mouth. Jane fended him off, pushing against his chest with her hands.

"Esteban! You wicked thing!" she said.

Suzu tipped her head. "Good night, Mrs. Fletcher," she said and walked past.

Suzu's use of what would have been Jane's married name had she and Walter actually completed the ceremony jarred her. It would have been bad enough had Suzu thought Jane was cheating on her fiancé; to be caught cheating on her husband was even worse.

"No," she called after Suzu, trying to keep her voice low. "It's not what you think."

Suzu disappeared through the door into the next car, leaving Jane alone with the now half-awake boy. He was sitting up, mumbling and kissing the air. His eyes opened and, seeing Jane, he gave her a lopsided smile. "Who are you?" he asked. "And who's Esteban?"

Jane focused her attention on him. "Go back to sleep," she commanded. "And don't remember any of this."

The boy sank back against the window and began snoring. Jane got up, replaced the backpack on the seat beside him, and followed after Suzu. When she entered the next car, Suzu was nowhere to be seen. *She's certainly a speedy little thing,* she thought, quickening her pace.

When she entered the sleeper car she saw a door to one of the compartments opening. Not knowing which room was Suzu's, she waited to see if she would emerge. Instead, Chumsley exited. He turned around and spoke to someone inside the room.

"Don't say I didn't warn you," he said angrily.

"Your warning is duly noted," a man's voice replied. There was an Irish lilt to it, and Jane immediately thought of Ryan McGuinness.

The door shut and Chumsley turned around. Seeing Jane, he gave a start. "Look at us both up at this ungodly hour," he said.

"It is quite late," said Jane.

After an awkward silence of a few seconds Chumsley said, "Well, good night then. See you in the morning."

"Good night," Jane said as Chumsley moved quickly past her. She watched him go to the other end of the sleeper and open a door there.

She'd forgotten all about Suzu. Now she found herself wondering what Chumsley had been doing in the compartment of his ex-wife's lover. And what had Chumsley warned Ryan about?

Perhaps I'm not the only one with a secret, she thought.

≈≈≈

Chapter 11

Thursday: Ireland

FORTUNATELY FOR JANE, SHE WAS TOO BUSY RUBBING WALTER'S back and speaking to him in soothing tones to worry about what Suzu thought about their encounter the night before. Walter, for his part, was leaning over the railing on the upper deck of the *Isle of Inishmore* and heaving his breakfast into the choppy waters of St. George's Channel.

The ferry was only forty-five minutes into its four-hour crossing between Pembroke, Wales, and Rosslare, Ireland. A strong winter storm was causing larger-than-usual waves, and despite the *Inishmore*'s impressive size the sea was moving her up and down like a toy boat.

Jane was doing her best to be nurturing, but the sound of Walter's retching, not to mention the scent of vomit, made her feel a bit queasy herself. The scrambled eggs and rashers she'd consumed shortly before boarding were now protesting loudly. Matters were not helped by the fact that Walter was not alone among their party in his misery. Arranged along the rail at polite intervals, Genevieve, Orsino, Enid, and Sam were also delivering up to the gods of the sea offerings of barely digested breakfasts. The remaining guests were huddled in the downstairs lounge.

Brodie was one of the few unaffected by the rough crossing. Strolling along the deck, he sipped from a cup of coffee and whistled "Bollocky Bill the Sailor" in such a cheerful way that those he passed might have shoved him over the rail had they not been otherwise engaged. His gait remained leisurely and smooth, and whenever a swell sent the ferry lurching he corrected himself so that not a single drop of coffee escaped the cup.

"Fine weather we're having," he remarked to Jane. Looking down at Walter, whose head was between his arms as he waited for the next bout of nausea to hit, he said, "Don't worry, mate. Once you've got it all out you'll feel right as rain."

"You're handling it rather well," said Jane as Walter made a choking sound.

"I come from pirate stock," Brodie said. "Great-great-great-great-grandmother or some such was Auckland Annie. Might be missing a *great* in there somewhere," he added, counting on the fingers of his left hand. "Any which way, she sailed with this captain and that captain, until one day the British captured the ship she was on and tossed her in the nick. That's where she met Captain Brodie Banks. Handsome fellow. Went to the gallows not long after, but not before old Annie was in the pudding club. Couldn't hang her in her condition, so they waited nine months until she popped out her little one, gave her a couple of minutes to name the boy, and *then* showed her the noose. That little boy was my great-great-great-grandfather Brodie Banks."

Jane, fascinated by the story, forgot all about her own seasickness. "You made that up," she said.

"God's honest truth," said Brodie. "There's been a Brodie in the family ever since. Or an Olive if there's no boy in a generation. My mother's an Olive. That's why I'm a Pittman and not a Banks." He paused. "Pity, really. Banks is a much better pirate name."

"Rawuuublahhh," said Walter, bringing Jane's attention back to the matter at hand.

"I see McGuinness has joined the party," Brodie remarked.

Jane looked over to see Ryan running to the railing, where he positioned himself between Enid and Orsino. His red hair was a bright spot against the dirty gray sky as he leaned over and gagged.

"Serves the cheating bugger right," said Brodie, chuckling. He looked at Jane. "Pity we can't just give him a little help over the side the next time she rolls," he said. "Let old St. George have him with his morning tea."

Jane, only half listening to him, made a vague noise.

"I leave you to it, then," said Brodie. "Think I'll see if there's any more grilled tomatoes to be had."

Jane and Walter spent another forty-five minutes at the railing as one by one the other seasick guests departed. Finally Walter felt well enough to walk, and Jane led him through the door and into the warmth of the lounge. There they found Lucy, Ben, and Miriam (with Lilith on her lap). They all looked a bit green in the face, and when a particularly large swell lifted the prow of the ship a collective groan rolled across the room.

"Are we almost there?" Lucy asked.

"Another two and a half hours," Ben informed her.

"I hate Ireland," Lucy announced. "I hate Wales. And I really, truly hate St. George and his blasted channel."

They settled into an uneasy silence as the ferry continued toward Ireland. Eventually the seas grew calmer, and although the sailing wasn't precisely smooth, it was much better than it had been. When she felt fairly certain he could keep something in his stomach, Jane fetched Walter a ginger ale and some biscuits. He ate the biscuits slowly, taking tiny sips of ginger ale between bites, and when he was finished he looked a great deal more alive than he had all morning.

The skies cleared and the sun came out, and when the *Isle of Inishmore* finally docked at the port in Rosslare the party was in good spirits. Their luggage was loaded onto a waiting tour bus, and then they were on their way to their destination.

As the day's site had been chosen by Enid, it was she who briefed them on it. She stood at the front of the bus, her sturdy legs planted firmly and a hand gripping the back of the seat on either side of the aisle. Her hair, thanks to the blustery weather at sea and the fact that she had yet to comb it back into submission, stuck out around her head.

"She looks like something out of *Macbeth,*" Jane murmured to Lucy.

"Although yesterday's tour was perhaps mildly interesting to those of you who haven't seen any of the thousands of homes in Britain exactly like the vicarage at Cripple Minton," Enid began, looking pointedly at Chumsley, who was painstakingly removing the cellophane from a butterscotch candy, "today you will see something utterly unique."

Crinkle—crinkle-crinkle went the wrapper on the butterscotch.

"Swichninny Castle is a medieval castle," said Enid. "In that respect it looks very much like most medieval castles."

Chumsley popped the butterscotch into his mouth and bit down with a loud crunch. "Pardon," he said loudly. "Didn't mean to be rude."

Enid narrowed her eyes. "What distinguishes Swichninny from other castles of its kind is its unusually fine barbican, complete with murder holes and arrow slits, as well as the tallest keep of any castle in Ireland."

"How tall is it?" Chumsley asked, sucking loudly on the butterscotch.

She glared at him. "I don't know precisely," she said through clenched teeth.

"I'm only wondering," said Chumsley, "because I've always been of the impression that at fifty-two meters the donjon of Château de Vincennes is the tallest keep."

"I believe you are correct about the height of the donjon of

Château de Vincennes," Enid said. "However, as Château de Vincennes is in France, it can hardly have the tallest keep in all of Ireland."

Chumsley crunched the butterscotch. "I beg your pardon," he said. "I must have misunderstood you."

"You usually do," said Enid. "Now as I was saying . . . "

The rest of her speech was a blur to Jane: moat this and curtain wall that, machicolations and lower baileys and main baileys and hoardings and battered plinths, on and on and on until the words meant absolutely nothing. Jane was far more interested in the back of Suzu's head. The woman was seated three rows ahead of Walter and Jane, next to Sam Wax. She and Jane had said nothing more than good morning to each other all day, and Jane was going mad wondering if she should attempt to discuss the matter with the woman. Of course there really was nothing *to* discuss, at least nothing that would in any way portray Jane as anything other than a wanton. She could hardly deny kissing the young man, as she had made such a show of it, and telling the truth was out of the question. She supposed she could claim to have been drunk (which was no better, really) or out of her mind on cold medication (she practiced sniffling, but knew it was hopeless). Ultimately, however, she had to accept that Suzu now had something on her—even if what she thought she knew was much less disturbing than the actual truth—and behave accordingly.

In short, she would have to take pains not to commit any further offense to Suzu's sensibilities. She had no reason to think the woman would mention what she'd seen to Walter, but she *had* been deferential to him on that first night and there was no telling what designs she might have on him. Thinking about it, Jane decided that *she* should be offended at Suzu's behavior. *Flirting with him right in front of me!* she thought, attempting to work up a bit of self-righteous indignation. But it was no good. She was just going to have to hope that Suzu kept quiet.

When the bus arrived at Swichninny, Miriam took Lilith for a walk along the moat that encircled the castle while the others clustered around Enid to begin the guided tour. Ben, Lucy, and Jane joined them, as by this point everyone was treating them as if they were part of the group anyway. Jane took Walter's hand, feeling only slightly guilty that the affection was in part designed to show Suzu that there was nothing fragile about their relationship.

Enid proved to be quite a good guide, explaining in great detail the workings of the portcullis and drawbridge yet managing to nimbly skirt the line between interesting and tedious. She plumbed the depths of her knowledge of medieval stonecutting while describing the construction of the walls, and even entertained them with a bit of scatological trivia when explaining that in the days of the castle's occupation its inhabitants would have hung some of their garments in the primitive toilets—or garderobes—because the stench kept moths away from the finery.

Because Enid was such a veritable encyclopedia of knowledge on the castle and its charms, Jane was almost, but not quite, saddened when the official tour ended and they were allowed to go exploring on their own. She found it most interesting that the majority of participants headed immediately for the castle's dungeon, where Enid assured them all manner of cruelties had been committed against prisoners of war. Jane herself, loath to encounter any vengeful or peevish spirits that might still be lingering there, chose instead to climb with Walter the 299 stone steps that led to the top of the castle's notoriously tall keep.

The view from atop the tower really was spectacular, although Jane wished they were visiting a little later in the year, when the surrounding countryside would no doubt be swathed in emerald splendor instead of looking as if someone had tossed a brown wool blanket over it. Still, the beauty all around them was undeniable. The sky was blue and cloudless, there was no wind, and Jane could easily imagine herself standing there searching the hills for her returning love, who of course would be riding a white stallion, its mighty hooves churning up the grass as it brought her man home to her.

"Look," Walter said, pointing. "There's my mother. She looks like a bug from up here."

"And there goes *that* fantasy," Jane said under her breath as her stallion turned into a three-legged Chihuahua and her knight raced off to see what his mother wanted.

They were not alone on top of the keep. Several other people, including Sam, Orsino, and Ryan, were there. Suzu too was up there, taking pictures with what looked to be an original Kodak Brownie camera. Fortunately, the space was quite large, and because the central part was taken up by the rounded covering of the stairwell, it was possible to be on any side of the keep and be invisible to all the other sides. Occasionally Jane and Walter would encounter someone while taking a walk around all four sides of the tower, but never did they feel crowded.

On their second time around they ran into Sam. "Hey," she said. "This place is something, isn't it? All it needs is some flying monkeys and a wicked witch."

Walter laughed. "I'll get you, my pretty," he said in a very bad imitation of Margaret Hamilton's famous character. "And your little dog too."

This time it was Sam who laughed. Jane, feeling left out, heard herself say, "Maybe the Wizard can give me a soul."

Walter and Sam looked at her as she realized what she'd said. "I mean a brain," she said. "Ha ha!"

"Anyway," Sam said, "I was thinking about going down to take a look at the armory. "Any interest?"

"Sure," said Walter. "Jane, do you want to come?"

Jane thought for a moment. Although she no longer feared that there were any romantic feelings between Walter and Sam, she envied their ease with each other. There was a past there that she wasn't a part of, and although Sam had been nothing but friendly to her, she still found herself a little bit jealous.

As if you have any room to talk, she argued with herself. *You have entire lifetimes Walter doesn't know about and wasn't part of.*

"You two go on," she said. "I'll be down in a bit."

She welcomed the time to herself to enjoy the solitude the keep provided and think about all that had happened over the past few days. The appearance of Joshua, the revelation of Crispin's Needle, the church at Cripple Minton, and the martyr-dom of St. Apollonia—it was all terribly thrilling. Even the thought of the Tedious Three filled her with excitement. They were all pieces of a puzzle, one she was fitting together bit by bit. What it would look like when, or if, it was ever completed she didn't know. But it was undeniably intriguing. If Crispin's Needle *did* exist, and if she *did* find it, she would have an enormous deci-sion to make.

It's probably all just legend anyway, she told herself. *One of those vampire stories meant to make us seem far more interest-ing than we are.*

Suddenly a scream filled the air, startling her. Turning to her right she was just in time to see Ryan McGuinness leap from the wall of the tower. He hung in the air for a moment, more or less horizontal, his arms and legs moving as if he were trying to fly, or perhaps swim. Then he fell. Jane leaned over the edge of the keep and watched as he plummeted, still screaming and flailing, the two hundred and something (at that moment she couldn't recall the exact number) feet to the ground. Being as how the fall was a great one, and being as how the ground was more like a courtyard made of cobblestones, Ryan's arrival at the bottom did little to allay his anxiety. Rather, it resulted in a satisfying *thwack* and the creation of a bit of a mess in the form of a pool of blood that formed beneath his head.

Jane had only a moment in which to reflect on the peculiar and disturbing beauty of a dead body sprawled across the stones of a three-hundred-year-old castle before the sound of numerous voices raised in alarm reached her ears. This caused her to regain her senses and, now properly distressed, she raced down the 299 steps and out the tower door. There she found herself standing on one side of Ryan McGuinness's lifeless body while the other members of the tour group stared at her.

The first to speak was Brodie. "What happened?" he asked.

"I . . . I don't know," Jane said.

"But you were up there with him," Genevieve said.

"No," said Jane. "I mean yes, I was up there, but we weren't there together, if you see what I mean. And there were others there as well."

Genevieve looked around, her mouth moving silently as she used one long finger to count heads. When she was done she returned her gaze to Jane. "Actually," she said, "it was only the two of you up there. The rest of us were down here."

"Then he must have jumped," Jane said, her voice sounding more defensive than she intended. "You all saw him fall."

"He didn't jump." Enid, who until now had been staring at the crumpled body of her lover, looked up at Jane. "He was afraid of heights. It took everything in him just to go up there, and I assure you he stayed as far way from the edge as possible."

"Apparently not," Jane said, returning Enid's steely gaze.

Someone cleared his throat. Then Bergen spoke in his monotone voice. "I'm afraid I must agree with Ms. Woode's evaluation of the situation," he said. "The angle of fall is inconsistent, suggesting greater force than could be achieved by merely jumping."

"See!" Enid cried. "He was pushed!"

Bergen nudged his glasses up his nose. "That is not quite correct either," he said. Jane thought perhaps she detected just the merest hint of a smile on his face as he looked at her. "He was thrown."

Chapter 12

Thursday: Ireland

INSPECTOR CLOONEY NESBITT SAT ON THE SOFA IN THE FRONT PAR-lor of the Inn of the White Roses and scribbled on the pad in his hand. His pen had stopped writing, and he was trying to get the ink flowing again. Jane sat in an armchair across from him. In be-tween them, on a low table covered with a pretty lace cloth, sat a pot of tea, two cups on saucers, and a plate of digestive biscuits. Jane looked longingly at the biscuits but didn't dare take one, afraid that doing so might suggest an air of frivolity. She was, she felt, in enough trouble as it was.

The inspector had already interviewed the other members of the party. That he had saved Jane for last struck her as a bit pe-culiar. If it had been she who was conducting the investigation into Ryan McGuinness's death, she would have begun with the most likely suspect, which even she had to acknowledge was her-self. It would, she thought, give her less time to concoct an expla-nation for how Ryan might have been launched from the top of the keep without her assistance. As it was, nearly two hours had passed, which was more than enough time for her to have made up a story should she have needed one.

"Now then," said the inspector when his pen resumed working properly. "Why don't you tell me about your relationship to the deceased."

Clooney Nesbitt was not a young man. He had gray hair that was cut short so as to minimize the appearance of his bald spot, a fine, thick mustache that at the moment wanted a little trimming, and bright blue eyes that Jane, if she had conjured him as a character in one of her novels, would have described as the sort of eyes that tended to put innocent people at ease and make guilty people believe that he was not as smart as he really was. In both instances, she imagined, those at whom he directed his gaze were inclined to tell him more than they had expected to.

Jane might have found herself influenced by his eyes as well were she not focused on the digestive biscuits. As it was she found herself saying, "I'm sorry, could you repeat the question?"

Nesbitt did so, making a notation on his pad at the same time. Jane, knowing full well that whatever he was writing was about her, wished she could see what else was on the yellow pad. What, for instance, had Inspector Nesbitt written down about Walter, or Lucy, or Ben, all of whom he had interviewed? And what had he made of Miriam and her three-legged dog? *That would be most interesting,* she thought.

"Miss Fairfax?"

The inspector's voice reminded Jane that she still had not answered his question. "None whatsoever," she said.

"Begging your pardon?" he said.

"My relationship to the deceased," Jane said. "There was none whatsoever. I hadn't even heard of him before this trip."

The inspector made another notation. "And what was your opinion of the gentleman?"

Jane considered the question. Inspector Nesbitt was looking at her with those clear blue eyes. *He's trying to trick me,* she told herself. *Well, we'll just see about that.*

"I really haven't known him long enough to form an opinion," she replied. "*Hadn't* known him long enough, I mean. Being that the deceased is . . . deceased."

"Indeed," said Nesbitt. "But surely you had some interactions with Mr. McGuinness before his death."

"No," Jane said. "As I keep telling people, I was nowhere near him when he jumped. Or fell. Or whatever it is that he did."

"Actually, I was referring to interactions that might have occurred in the previous few days," said the inspector. "Since you first made his acquaintance. However, we will return to the moments before the incident shortly."

Jane coughed anxiously. *Why, he's got me feeling guilty!* she thought. *How rude!*

"Honestly, I don't think Mr. McGuinness and I exchanged more than half a dozen words before today," she said calmly. "Including today," she added.

Inspector Nesbitt wrote on his pad. "You were, however, aware of his relationship with Enid Woode," he said, stating it as fact rather than as a question.

Jane nodded. "I was aware of that, yes," she said.

"And how were you made aware of it?"

"I believe it was Mr. Pittman who informed me," Jane answered. "The first night. In the American Bar."

"Do you know anyone who might have reason to harbor ill-will toward Mr. McGuinness?" asked Nesbitt.

Jane thought for a moment. Now that she considered it, she *did* know a few people who had reason to dislike Ryan McGuinness. Chief among them, of course, was Chumsley Faber-Titting. But there was also Brodie, whose work McGuinness had stolen when they were students. *But Brodie is a perfectly delightful man,* she thought. *I can't imagine him doing such a thing.*

Then she remembered seeing Chumsley emerging from McGuinness's compartment on the train. She remembered too the words of warning Chumsley had uttered. Had they been a precursor to the day's murderous events? It certainly seemed possible. *But Chumsley knows you heard him,* she reminded herself. *He knows that if asked you would likely provide that information.*

Chumsley seemed too clever a man to be tripped up so easily. Also, had he not been on the ground when Ryan McGuinness went over the side? Once again she was reminded that she and she alone had been on top of the keep. *And so we're back where we began,* she thought grimly.

"No," she said to Nesbitt, who had been patiently awaiting her answer. "I really can't think of anyone who would want to kill Mr. McGuinness."

The inspector wrote on his pad, then looked up and expressed the very thought Jane had just had herself. "It seems that everyone in the party was on the ground and accounted for at the time of the incident," he said. "Except for you."

Jane cleared her throat. "I've heard that," she said.

"And yet you say you were nowhere near Mr. McGuinness at the time that he . . . exited the tower unexpectedly," said Nesbitt.

"That's right," Jane said. "I was on the—I believe it was the north-facing side, and Mr. McGuinness fell from the west-facing side."

"Right around the corner from where you were standing," the inspector pointed out.

"Well, yes," said Jane. "Regardless, I hardly have the strength to *throw* a man the size of Mr. McGuinness over a four-foot-high wall."

"Did someone mention throwing?" asked Nesbitt.

"Not you," said Jane. "But the others did. Bergen did."

A small smile played at the corners of the inspector's mouth. "The German fellow," he said. "Yes, he was quite insistent on it."

He flipped through the pages of the notepad. "Something about the 'angle of fall,' I believe he said. Very interesting. And you're correct. I don't think you have the strength to throw a man over a wall."

"Thank you," Jane said, wondering if that was the proper response to such a statement.

"You could, however, have pushed him," Nesbitt continued. "Had he been already standing on the wall, for instance."

"But he wasn't," said Jane. "And I didn't."

"How do you know he wasn't if you couldn't see him?" asked the inspector.

"I don't," Jane admitted. "But I would think someone from below would have noticed if he had been."

"Only if they were looking up," Nesbitt countered.

Jane was becoming annoyed. These were all very good points. *But I* didn't *kill him,* she thought.

"You're a writer, aren't you, Miss Fairfax?"

"Yes," said Jane, eager to be going down a new avenue of discussion.

"I believe my wife has read your novel," Nesbitt said. "She quite enjoyed it. I tend to stick to the likes of Patrick O'Brian myself. I enjoy a good sea battle." He folded his notepad and tucked it into his jacket pocket. "Well, I think that will be all. Thank you for your time."

Jane, perplexed, said, "That's it? Don't you have more questions for me?"

The inspector reached for his notepad. "Would you like me to ask you some more questions?"

Jane flushed. "No," she said. "It's just that the conversation ended so abruptly."

Nesbitt stood up. "I've been an inspector for a great many years, Miss Fairfax," he said. "I've seen many a guilty person and listened to many a fanciful tale designed to cover up the truth. I don't find either here in this room this evening."

"I see," Jane said. "Then may I ask, what *do* you think happened to Mr. McGuinness?"

"I don't know for certain," said Nesbitt. "If I were pressed for an explanation, I would say that he jumped."

"But the angle of fall," Jane said.

"Indeed," said the inspector. "The angle of fall. And we will have to look into that. But you're asking what my gut tells me, and my gut tells me the gentleman jumped to his death. Why, I don't know. Perhaps I will never know. Perhaps no one will ever know save for him and God. In the absence of a likely suspect, however, all I can do is eliminate the people I think *did not* do it, and at this moment that includes everyone who was present at Swichninny Castle this morning."

Jane walked with Nesbitt to the front door. This required passing through yet another sitting room, in which were assembled all of the other tour participants, as well as Ben, Lucy, and Miriam. As Jane and the inspector entered, all eyes turned to her.

"Are you all right?" Walter asked, putting his arm around Jane.

"I'm fine," she assured him.

"Well?" Enid demanded of the inspector. "What have you concluded?"

Nesbitt put on his hat. "Nothing conclusively," he said. "But you are all free to go about your business. If I have further need of you, I will be in contact."

Enid's eyes—and the eyes of several other people—darted to Jane. "So you've cleared everyone of suspicion, then?"

The inspector buttoned his coat. "As I said, if I have further need of any of you, I will be in contact. In the meantime, I thank you all for your cooperation."

After he'd gone, the mood in the room changed perceptibly. Jane sensed a distinct chill in the air, most of it emanating from Enid. No one spoke for a long while, until finally Chumsley said, "Well, we need to decide where we go from here."

"You know very well that our next town is Clonakilty," Enid said.

Chumsley nodded. "I wasn't referring to the location of our next stop," he said. "I meant, should we continue with the tour in light of today's tragic events?"

Enid snorted. "What do you care? You hated him anyway. If she hadn't been the only one up there with him"—she cocked her head in Jane's direction—"you'd be the primary suspect."

"You can't seriously suspect Jane had anything to do with it!" Walter said. "That's ridiculous."

"She *was* the only one up there," said Miriam.

"Nonsense," said Lucy. "We all know Jane could never do something like that."

Jane gave her a thankful look. *Although she knows full well I could do it,* she thought. *If I wanted to.*

"No, we don't all know that," said Genevieve. "Some of us don't know her at all. All we do know is that she was alone with Ryan on top of the keep."

"Jane isn't on trial here," Brodie reminded them all. "If the inspector thought she had something to do with McGuinness taking flight, he would have taken her in."

"I agree," Sam said. "Let's not be pointing fingers."

"Which brings me back to my original question," said Chumsley. "Are we going to continue, or are we going to end the tour here?"

"I know *you* have no problem going on," Enid said. "And neither do I. What about the rest of you?"

"Let's do a show of hands," said Chumsley. "All for continuing the tour?"

Very slowly, hands went into the air. Jane looked around and saw that in addition to Chumsley and Enid, Brodie, Bergen, Sam, Genevieve, and Suzu had their hands raised. A moment later Walter added his agreement.

"Then it's settled," said Chumsley. "We continue on. Now, who'll be joining me down the pub for a drink to the memory of Ryan McGuinness?"

Brodie, Sam, and Orsino got ready to leave with Chumsley, while Enid, Suzu, Bergen, and Genevieve retired to their rooms. Miriam announced that she was taking Lilith for a walk.

"What do you want to do?" Walter asked Jane.

"I'd like to go for a drink," Jane said. "But I'm afraid Enid and her gang will accuse me of dancing on Ryan's grave."

"Don't pay any attention to them," said Walter. "They're going to think what they want to. We know the truth."

"That's right," Ben said. "And given that not one of them voted to end the tour, I think it's safe to say they're not all that choked up about his death."

"I was thinking the same thing," said Lucy. "So come on, let's go drinking!"

"Maybe you shouldn't be quite so enthusiastic," Ben suggested, kissing her on the cheek.

"All right," said Jane. "Let me just go upstairs and change my shoes."

"I'll come with you," Lucy said.

"You don't have—" Jane began, but Lucy took her by the arm and rushed her out of the room. "What's the matter?" she asked when they were on the stairs.

"Something occurred to me," said Lucy, dragging Jane into her room and shutting the door. "You know how we've been saying that you're not strong enough to have picked Ryan up and thrown him over the wall? Well, you and I know that's not true."

"You think I did it!" Jane exclaimed.

"Keep it down," said Lucy. "I do not think you did it. But it got me thinking—maybe another vampire did."

Jane stopped and looked at her. "That would also explain why no one saw anyone else come out of the tower," Jane said. "A vampire could make himself invisible."

"Or herself," said Lucy.

Jane gasped. "You don't think it could be . . . " She stopped herself before speaking the name of her nemesis, an author whose fan base rivaled her own.

"Our Gloomy Friend," said Lucy. "Or some other vampire. But who else do we know who might want to make you look like a murderer?"

"Well, there's Joshua," Jane suggested. "He might do it to drive Walter away. And of course there's Miriam. She's not a vampire, but I wouldn't put it past her to get one to do it for her. Or it could be someone who knows I've been told about Crispin's Needle and doesn't want me to find it." She sighed. "Really, it could be any number of people."

"I hadn't considered any of them," said Lucy, sounding disappointed.

"Also, there's something I haven't told you," Jane said.

She proceeded to tell Lucy about seeing Chumsley coming out of Ryan's compartment. She also, reluctantly, told her about Suzu seeing her feeding on the young man.

"Esteban?" Lucy said. "And you call yourself a writer."

"I was under pressure," said Jane.

"Well, this adds another possible twist to the mystery then," Lucy said. "And here I thought I had it all figured out."

"Our Gloomy Friend is still a distinct possibility," Jane said. "It's exactly the kind of thing she *would* do."

"If she is responsible, who knows what she'll try next," said Lucy. "She might start picking people off one by one, like in that Agatha Christie novel."

"*Ten Little Indians,*" Jane said. "One of my favorites."

"Oh, and there *are* ten of them," said Lucy. "Not counting you, me, Ben, and Miriam, but we aren't really part of the tour anyway."

"And now there are nine," Jane said.

The door opened and Walter stuck his head in. "Are you two coming?" he asked.

"Of course we are," Jane said, taking up her coat. As she and Lucy left she leaned in and whispered, "Keep your eyes and ears open. I don't want my little Indian to be next."

Chapter 13

Friday: Ireland

FRIDAY DAWNED WET AND GRAY, WORDS THAT COULD ALSO BE USED to describe Jane's mood. As she lay on her side in bed and looked at the rain spattering against the windows, she couldn't help but wish that she were back home in Brakeston, a town she'd chosen because it reminded her of the peaceful life she'd enjoyed in Chawton. *People there don't go flying off towers for no reason,* she thought darkly.

Lucy's suggestion that perhaps Charlotte (she could think her name as long as she didn't speak it) might be responsible for Ryan McGuinness's death had unnerved her a bit. If true, it meant that Charlotte had more in mind than just simple revenge. *Trying to kill me is one thing,* Jane thought. *Killing other people to make me look guilty is going too far, even for a Brontë.*

Beside her Walter grunted softly, turned on his side, and put his arm around her. Holding her close, he kissed her neck gently and immediately started snoring. He always snored when he'd had too much to drink, and as they had lingered at the pub until well after two in morning, Jane didn't expect him to be fully functioning until after lunch.

She would have been content to stay in bed all day and not have to face those she knew still suspected her of committing foul play, but they were due on the bus shortly after eight o'clock and it was already seven. Gently freeing herself from Walter's arm, she slipped out of bed and went into the bathroom to shower. She knew Walter would need all of fifteen minutes to get himself ready, so she let him remain asleep.

The hot water went out only five minutes into her shower, before Jane had even begun to rinse the shampoo from her hair. She damned the inn's ancient plumbing, as well as everyone who had risen before her and therefore probably had much more pleasant bathing experiences. She finished under a cold trickle and got out feeling less awake and more peevish than she had before getting in. After towel-drying her hair, she went into the bedroom to wake Walter up and found him already dressed.

"Good morning," he said brightly.

"You're awfully cheerful for someone who nearly drowned himself in whiskey last night," she said as she got dressed.

"I'm operating under the principle that if I *act* happy, I'll *be* happy. The truth is, my head feels as if an army of woodpeckers has taken up residence in it. What time are we leaving?"

Jane glanced at the clock. "Half an hour. Why don't you go get some breakfast and I'll pack up the bags?"

Walter groaned. "I don't even want to think about food."

"Have some porridge," said Jane. "It will do your stomach good."

Walter sighed. "All right," he said. "But don't you want anything?"

She shook her head. "Save me a scone," she said. "And not one of those nasty ones with fruit in it."

Walter left. A minute or two later there was a knock on the door.

"Come in," Jane called out.

She was surprised when Miriam entered. Miriam set Lilith on the bed, where the dog immediately curled up and went to sleep.

"We need to talk," Miriam said. "Did you throw that man off the tower?"

"I did not," said Jane. "Did you have someone do it in order to frame me?"

Miriam snorted. "Why should I hire someone to do anything?" she said. "If I wanted to do you in, I would just stake you myself."

"In your dreams," said Jane, shutting the suitcase she'd been packing.

"Then if you didn't do it and I didn't do it, who did?" Miriam asked.

"Lucy thinks maybe it was Our Gloomy Friend," Jane told her.

"Who the hell is that?" said Miriam.

Jane found a piece of paper and wrote down Charlotte's name. She handed it to Miriam.

"Charlotte Bron—"

"Shh!" Jane hissed. "We don't say her name. Why do you think I wrote it down?"

Miriam crumpled up the paper and tossed it on the floor. "Not this nonsense again," she said.

Although Miriam had almost been killed by Charlotte during Jane's last encounter with her nemesis, she refused to believe that Charlotte was who Jane said she was. Jane had given up on trying to convince her—and had of course never revealed her own true identity to Miriam.

"Regardless of who you think she is or is not, Our Gloomy Friend is a very real danger," Jane said.

Miriam sighed. "All vampires are a danger and need to be destroyed," she said. "This one is no worse than the rest. I can handle her."

"Yes, you did so well against her last time," Jane remarked.

Before Miriam could start an argument the door opened and Walter came in. He was carrying a cup of coffee on top of which was balanced a scone. When he saw his mother he said, "My two favorite people in one place."

"I was just leaving," said Miriam, picking up Lilith. "I have to finish packing."

"Well then, I guess we'll see you on the bus," Walter said, setting the coffee on the dresser and handing Jane the scone.

When his mother was gone Walter asked, "What was that about?"

Jane sat down in the room's one armchair and took a bite of the scone. "Nothing," she said. "She just wanted to borrow some hand cream. This weather is hard on old skin."

Walter chuckled. "I'm glad to see the two of you are getting along better," he said, more than a hint of sarcasm in his tone.

Jane finished the scone and drank the coffee while Walter gathered up the last of their things. Then they went downstairs and out to the waiting bus. Lucy and Ben were already there, and Jane and Walter took the seats beside theirs. The other members of the group were scattered throughout the bus. No one was particularly talkative, which only added to the gloomy mood of the morning.

When the last person—Orsino, looking very much like a grumpy bear who had been awakened a month too early from hibernation—was on the bus, they left. This time there was no briefing from either Chumsley or Enid. Only when the bus passed a sign reading CLONAKILTY did Jane remember where they were headed.

Chumsley stood up. "Clonakilty is not our final destination," he said. "We'll be visiting a house a bit beyond the town limits. However, you might be interested to know that in 1999 Clonakilty won the Tidy Towns competition for the neatest town in all of Ireland."

Jane, looking out the window at the rows of gaily painted houses, said, "It really is very clean."

"Like Disneyland," Ben said.

"Or Singapore," said Walter.

Thus awed by the cleanliness of Clonakilty, they passed out of it and into the countryside. A quarter of an hour later they turned onto a narrow lane, and five minutes after that they passed through a stand of trees and exited the other side to find themselves looking at a manor house.

"Ah," said Brodie in a booming voice. "Gloxhall House. I recognize it from my textbook back at Dalhousie."

"Brodie is exactly right," Chumsley announced. "We are indeed at Gloxhall House. While it's now generally overlooked in favor of more showy homes, Gloxhall is one of Ireland's hidden gems. It is important not least of all because it was designed and built by Fiona Byrne, one of the few female architects of her time. Not that anyone knew she was female," he added. "Fiona disguised herself as a man and attended school under the name Kevin McCready. It wasn't until her death at age eighty-six that her true identity was discovered."

"Just another tragic example of the way in which women are overlooked in the profession," Enid said.

"I'm sorry, dear. Did you say something?" Chumsley asked, grinning broadly. "Another interesting fact about Fiona," he continued, "is that she is widely believed to have been a witch. Among her possessions was found a diary in which she recounted numerous encounters with demonic beings in the house."

"More nonsense perpetrated by misogynists!" said Enid.

"In particular, she is believed to have had as her familiar a creature called a red cap," Chumsley said as Enid fumed. "Red caps are notoriously bloodthirsty sprites who get their name from knocking their victims on the head with rocks and then dyeing their caps in the blood. Fiona's red cap was called Squish. Very appropriate that, what with the rock dropping and all."

"Enough of this twaddle," Enid said, standing up and opening the bus door. "Everybody into the house."

They all exited, with Chumsley bringing up the rear. As Enid marched briskly up the path to the house, Chumsley sauntered along next to Jane and Walter.

"Is it true about the red cap?" Jane asked. "Meaning, is it true Fiona wrote about him in her diary?"

"Yes," said Chumsley. "Of course, it's all the ramblings of a madwoman, but she wrote it."

"How very interesting," Jane said. "I should like to have known her, I think."

"Pity she died in 1888, then," said Chumsley.

"That *is* a pity," Jane agreed. *I could have easily come to know her,* she added to herself. She tried to remember where she'd been in 1888. *Oh, yes,* she thought. *Moscow. The circus.* Well, *that* had been an adventure worth having, and you couldn't do everything.

The inside of Gloxhall House was indeed impressive, all marble floors and grand staircases and pictures of horses in gilt frames. The group wandered through its three grand living rooms, thirteen bedrooms, and two libraries marveling at the woodwork and ceiling construction, the joinery and ingenious layout. Mostly the tour was narrated by Chumsley, although Enid added the occasional caustic comment here and there regarding Fiona Byrne's oppression at the hands of men.

At one point, while touring the west wing of the house, Jane felt the need to visit the toilet and excused herself for a moment. Certain she had seen a bathroom down a particular hallway, she went down it again. Only now it seemed unfamiliar to her, and when she turned the knob on the room she believed would be the one she sought, she was surprised to find instead a bedroom she had not yet visited.

She stepped inside and without knowing why shut the door behind her. The bedroom was not particularly large, and the furniture in it was plain but well constructed. A four-poster bed took up most of the room, curtains of dark red silk hanging from the tester. A washstand with a pitcher and bowl stood to one side of a small dresser over which was set an oval-shaped mirror. On the wall closest to the door there hung a painting. It was to this that Jane gravitated.

The painting was perhaps two feet wide and half again as tall. Done in oils, it depicted a woman with red hair wearing a white dress in the artistic style. She was standing in a garden of roses, in front of a stone wall. On the wall stood a small man, perhaps a foot high, wearing a pointed red cap. The woman had her right hand on his shoulder, and he looked out at the viewer with an expression of unconcealed malice.

"You would be Squish, I imagine," Jane said.

"I would," said a voice with a heavy Scottish accent. "An joost how did ye find this room?"

Jane started, then looked toward the bed. Seated on the edge was the little man from the painting. "You're much uglier in person," she said.

"Thank ye," said Squish. "Now answer ma question afore I bash ye on the head with a rock."

"My name is Jane Fairfax," she said. "I am a vampire."

A grin appeared on Squish's face. "A fellow bloodbeast," he said happily.

"I wouldn't call myself that. But I suppose you could."

"Ya drink it. I dye ma cap in it. The person ends up dead one way or t'other," said Squish.

"I don't kill them," Jane protested. "I just drink from them a little."

Squish spat on the floor. "What good are ya then?" he asked.

Jane pointed at the painting. "I take it that's Fiona," she said. Squish nodded.

"Then the stories are true," said Jane. "About her being a witch."

Squish snorted. "She weren't nae witch," he said. "Joost had second sight is all. Could see those of us from the other side, so to speak."

He jumped down from the bed and walked over to where Jane stood. His pointed hat reached just above her knee. It was very red, and Jane wondered how recently it had been dyed. Squish looked up at the painting and sighed deeply. "I dae miss her," he said. Then he turned his gaze to Jane. "I still da nae know what you're doin' here, though."

"I was looking for the bathroom. I came in here by mistake."

"No one comes in here by mistake. There's a spell on this room. Only ones who find it are ones what get stuck in the enchantment, and them's the ones whose heads I stave in."

"Well, I certainly hope that won't be the case," said Jane. "But honestly, I don't know why I'm here."

Squish stared at her for a long time. "Said yer a vampire, did ya?"

She nodded.

"Nae a very good one, I don't think."

"Why do you say that?" Jane asked, wounded.

"The other ones that come through here, they knew just what they wanted."

"Other ones," said Jane. "What other ones?"

"The three," said Squish. "Can nae recall their names. Very tiresome, they were."

"Tedious," Jane said.

"Whit?" asked Squish.

"They were tedious. The Tedious Three. At least, I'm guessing they were. Were they looking for Crispin's Needle?"

The red cap brightened. "That was it!" he said. "Mibbie yer lookin' for the same thing?"

"Actually, I am," said Jane. "Did you give it to them?"

Squish shook his head. "Could nae give them what I do nae have," he replied. "Naw idea what they were talkin' aboot. Care to fill me in?"

Jane explained what the Needle did, or was supposed to do. When she was done Squish nodded. "Now I see," he said. "Fiona, she knew a lot of strange folk. Vampires, some of 'em. Probably these three thought one of them may have given it to her or told her where 'twas."

"But she never mentioned it to you?" Jane asked.

"Nae that I can recall," said Squish. "And I ken recall a lot."

Jane sighed. "Well then, I guess there's nothing you can do for me either."

"Who said I was goin' to do anything for ye? Yer lucky I did nae bash yer head with a rock. I think that's doin' enough."

"Yes, you would," said Jane irritably. "But it seems to me that if there's a spell on this room and only people who have second sight can find it, there should be some reason. Do you see what I mean?"

Squish rubbed his chin. "Ye may have a point. Almost makes me feel bad for bashin' in the heads of so many what come here."

"You didn't bash the heads of the Tedious Three, did you?" Jane asked.

"That I did nae," said Squish. He reached in his pocket. "Nicked this from one of them, though," he said, pulling out a gold key about four inches long.

"What's it for?" she asked.

"I've nae idea," said Squish. "I joost like stealin' things. Think it might be important?"

"I don't know," Jane said. "It looks like an ordinary old-fashioned door key. It could be to anything really."

"Then ye might as well have it," he said, holding it out to Jane.

"What will I do with it?"

"How am I supposed to know that? Yer the one goin' on aboot there bein' some reason ye came here, and I've got nothin' to give ye save this key or a rock to yer head, so choose which it'll be."

"I choose the key," Jane said, taking it from him and slipping it into her pocket.

"I thought ye might," said the red cap, sounding disappointed. Jane turned and put her hand on the doorknob. Then she looked at Squish, who was once again sitting on the bed, staring at the painting of Fiona.

"Thank you," she said.

Squish looked at her and frowned. "Be gone with ye," he said. "I've no time for foolishness." He hesitated. "But mibbie if that key turns out to be somethin', ye kin come back and tell me aboot it. If ye can find yer way, that is, and not get lost in a toilet."

Jane smiled, but just a little. "I'll do my best," she said, and opened the door.

Chapter 14

Friday: Edinburgh

As the plane bounced around, first dropping and then rising as the winds carried it like a leaf, Jane fingered the key in her hand and wondered what it would be like to die in a crash. Would the plane drop out of the sky like a stone, or would it somehow glide down before eventually landing in the sea and coming apart? She considered asking Walter to explain to her once more the principles of flight. Walter, however, was too busy throwing up into an airsickness bag to answer any questions.

"First the ferry, now the plane," he said as he rested his head against the back of the seat in front of him. "I hate traveling. I'm never leaving home again."

The plane dipped precipitously. A collective groan went up from the passengers, and Walter added to the contents of the bag. Jane took the bag from her seat pocket and handed it to him. He took it without comment, rolling up the full one and placing it on the floor between his feet.

Just in case, Jane looked at the laminated safety card helpfully provided to each passenger. The nearest exit was a few rows ahead of her, and in the event of a water landing she was fairly confident that she could get to the door without too much bother.

And my seat cushion becomes a flotation device, she noted. *How clever. Although I would be more impressed if the plane could become a ship.*

She tucked the card back into the seat pocket, put her hand on Walter's back, and went back to wondering what the key Squish had given her might be for. The fact was, she had absolutely no idea, and any guess she might make would be just that, a guess. But she supposed that should she ever come across the door or chest or gigantic egg to which the key fit, she would know to use it. *That's always how it is in the fairy tales,* she thought.

"Ladies and gentlemen, we are beginning our descent into Edinburgh," a pleasant woman's voice came over the PA system, her calmness belying the shaking of the plane. "Please be sure your seatbelts are fastened securely and that all carry-on items are stored to prevent them from flying about."

The plane's nose dipped noticeably and Walter wailed. "We're going to die, aren't we?" he asked Jane, squeezing her hand.

"We're fine," Jane said. "Just keep breathing."

Ten minutes later, as the plane taxied to the gate, Walter gratefully accepted the bottle of water Jane handed him and drank deeply. Outside the storm continued, and when a flash of lightning lit up the sky Walter gave a little shriek. Jane pulled the plastic window shield down so that he wouldn't see any further bolts.

"Have I mentioned how much I hate airplanes?" Walter asked.

"And boats," Jane said.

"Trains are fine, though," said Walter. "We can take as many trains as we have to. As long as they don't go in the air or in the water."

Jane refrained from reminding him that they were now in Scotland, and that should they want to reach any of the remaining destinations on their tour they would have to once again board one or the other of his despised forms of transport. Instead, she helped him locate their carry-on bags and line up to disembark, a process that was slowed considerably by the fact that most of the plane's occupants were trying very hard not to throw up.

The requisite post-flight bathroom visits took a bit longer than usual. But eventually they all were gathered together again and Enid led them through baggage claim to a waiting bus. Perhaps because she was in her homeland, Enid seemed even more efficient than usual, and Jane watched from the bus window as bags were located and loaded into the hold with impressive quickness. The storm showed no sign of letting up, and in fact the rain fell more fiercely now. Walter, curled up in the seat beside Jane, had closed his eyes and was breathing evenly.

To Jane's surprise they were taken not to some quaint inn housed in a centuries-old building, but to a sleek, modern hotel in the city's downtown. It was all glass and sparkle and sophistication, and although she was slightly disappointed that they weren't staying somewhere more atmospheric, Jane had to admit that it was nice to stay in a place that didn't smell quite so much of cabbage and Persil.

Because the plane had arrived rather late, it was now past ten o'clock. Walter, his stomach still unsettled from the turbulent flight, was in no state to go out to dinner. Ben and Lucy were content to perhaps just order something from room service and go to bed, and when Miriam announced that she was going to take Lilith for a walk and then settle in with a book and a can of sugared almonds from the minibar, Jane was relieved. She told Walter that she would come back with something for him to eat, then rode the elevator down to the hotel's restaurant level.

She was pleased to discover that the restaurant served until eleven. After looking over the menu, she ordered a roast beef sandwich for herself and a chicken Caesar salad for Walter. Then she sat down at the bar to wait. The nightly news was showing on the television and she watched as the headlines scrolled by, pleased to see that apart from the occasional natural disaster and spot of political upheaval, the world was fairly peaceful.

"May I join you?"

She turned to see Orsino Castano standing beside her. He was dressed in jeans and a black polo shirt with the Rugby Viadana emblem on it.

"I won't be here long," Jane said. "I'm just ordering food to take back to the room."

"I'm doing the same," said Orsino. "It seems no one is in the mood for socializing tonight."

"I think the flight was a little rough for most of them," Jane said.

Orsino took a peanut from the bowl on the counter and popped it into his mouth. "Understandable," he said. "Fortunately, I have never suffered from airsickness."

"Neither have I," said Jane. "Although I admit that when I was on top of the keep at Swichninny Castle I had a moment when I felt a little dizzy while looking down."

There was an awkward silence as Jane realized what she'd said. "That probably sounds very cold of me," she said.

To her surprise, Orsino chuckled. "It sounds very truthful to me," he said. "Hardly the thing one would say if one had thrown a man off that tower, am I right?"

Jane smiled. "Yes," she said. "You're right."

"Besides, I do not think any of them seriously believe that you are responsible for McGuinness's death."

"Now *that* I'm not so sure about," Jane said. "I think Enid might have a few opinions on the matter that aren't quite so favorable."

"Enid," Orsino said, snorting. "What does she know? Please, the woman can't even buy a pair of shoes that don't look like orthopedic devices."

Jane giggled. "They really are awful," she agreed. "I must say, I don't see how she managed to attract not one, but *two* men."

Orsino ate another peanut. "She was not so unattractive when she was young," he said. "I've seen pictures. Not that I'm saying she was a beauty, but she had a certain rough appeal. Also, I believe her talent was very attractive to Chumsley."

"What about McGuinness?" Jane said. "How do you explain that?"

Orsino was quiet, watching the television as he ate some more peanuts. Jane thought perhaps he hadn't heard her question, and was about to repeat it when Orsino spoke. "Ryan McGuinness was a man of opportunity," he said. "And he did not care who offered the opportunity."

"You mean he was using Enid?" said Jane.

"They were using each other," Orsino said. "Ryan was using her for his career, and Enid was using him for, let us say, entertainment."

"A familiar story," said Jane. "Although usually it's the man bedding the beautiful girl who hopes he'll make her a star."

"Enid is many things," Orsino said. "Stupid is not one of them. Ryan too was many things. Honorable was not one of them."

"You didn't like him much, did you?" said Jane.

"On the contrary," Orsino replied. "I loved him very much. When I found out he was leaving me for Enid, I could have killed them both."

Jane, surprised, wasn't sure she'd heard correctly. "You and Ryan were lovers?" she said.

Orsino nodded. "Briefly," he said. "Less than a year. Then I found out about Enid. Even then I begged him to stay with me." He waved his hand. "It's all in the past."

"Does Enid know?" Jane asked him.

Orsino shrugged. "Who knows? Ryan was very secretive. And an exquisite liar. He could make Satan himself believe that he was in love with him."

Jane hesitated before speaking again. "Enid didn't seem all that distraught over Ryan's death," she said.

Orsino shrugged. "I think things were mostly over between

them," he said. "There were rumors that he'd found someone else."

Suddenly Jane remembered something. "A man, or a woman?"

"I don't know," said Orsino. "I didn't care enough to find out." He spoke brusquely, but Jane sensed a note of untruth in his voice.

Before she could ask any additional questions, the waiter arrived with Orsino's food. He accepted it and stood up.

"Good night," he said. "I hope you will excuse me, but there's a game I would like to watch."

"Football?" Jane asked, knowing the Italians' fondness for the game.

"Rugby," said Orsino, pointing at his shirt with his free hand. "I played at university. It was one time when being heavy and low to the ground was an advantage. Now I just watch."

Jane bid him good night. As he walked away, Jane imagined him on a rugby pitch. She knew a bit about the game, at least enough to know that a man built like Orsino would likely be very good at hitting his opponents. *Or tossing them,* she thought.

Yes, it was entirely possible that Orsino, if so moved, could lift a man off his feet and throw him some distance. *Over a wall, for example.* True, Orsino had not been seen on top of the keep, but could he not have very quickly run down the stairs and pretended to have been on the ground all along?

It was possible, but unlikely. Still, he had reason to want Ryan McGuinness dead. Their relationship might have been brief and ended years earlier, but revenge, as was so often said, was a dish best served cold. Perhaps Orsino had waited for the occasion. Or perhaps seeing Ryan with Enid had been too much to take. *Although I think it would be harder on Chumsley,* she thought.

This brought her back to the question she'd been about to ask Orsino. Chumsley. The night she'd seen him coming out of Ryan's compartment, she'd assumed that Chumsley was angry with

McGuinness because of his relationship with Enid. But was it possible that something else was going on? Was it possible that Chumsley too had fallen for Ryan, and had been threatening to reveal their affair to Enid?

The more she discovered about the members of the party, the more questions she had. So far there were at least four people who might have wanted Ryan dead. In fact, the only person she could think of who might have cared if he remained alive was McGuinness himself.

"Here's your dinner, miss," said the waiter, interrupting her thoughts.

"Thank you," Jane said, taking the bag with the food in it. As she walked back to the elevator and rode it up to her floor, she reflected some more on her situation. Truthfully, the death of Ryan McGuinness was the least of her concerns. She was far more interested in finding Crispin's Needle and in marrying Walter. But she could do nothing about either of those things at the moment, and so the mystery occupied her thoughts.

She was passing the twenty-first floor and on her way to the twenty-second when the elevator suddenly came to a stop. No alarm went off, so she assumed there was nothing to worry about and that the elevator would begin working again in a moment. When it didn't, she told herself not to panic. Instead she pressed the button for her floor again, even though it was still lit. When nothing happened, she pressed it again several more times, with the same result.

"That's not going to work," came a voice from the speaker on the elevator's panel. "So you might as well stop."

Jane stared at the speaker. "Who is this?" she asked. "Are you a custodian? Is there something wrong with the lift?"

The voice laughed. "There's nothing wrong with the lift," it said. "I just want to have a word with you."

Jane couldn't tell if the voice was male or female. This was disconcerting, but not as much as the fact that whoever the voice belonged to was able to stop the elevator at will.

"Don't worry," the voice said. "I'm a friend."

"Then why won't you tell me who you are?" Jane asked.

"Because it's not important," said the voice. "I have just one thing to say, and not a lot of time."

"Which is?" Jane said.

"The Needle is real. And it works."

"How do you know this?" said Jane, her heart beginning to race.

A kind of static burst from the speaker, as if someone was trying to talk. The fuzzy words were indecipherable.

"What?" Jane said, leaning down and putting her ear next to the speaker.

"Find . . . key . . . choice." The words were faint beneath the buzzing.

"Find what?" Jane cried. "Where?"

The speaker went silent. A moment later the elevator began rising. Then she was on the twenty-second floor and the doors opened, revealing two elderly women.

"Thank heavens," one of them said. "We thought it would never come."

Chapter 15

Saturday: Edinburgh

"DOES IT EVER NOT RAIN IN SCOTLAND?"

Jane looked up at the sky, which was filled with dark clouds. She was wearing a blue raincoat and red rain hat purchased minutes ago from the shop outside which she stood with Walter, Lucy, and Ben. Somehow she had forgotten her rain gear in Ireland, and so had been forced to buy new things. The hat was a bit too large for her, and the brim hung down all the way around. She felt ridiculous, but at least she was dry.

"You look like Paddington bear," Ben remarked. "Sarah has one, and he's wearing the same getup."

"All you need is a tag that says PLEASE LOOK AFTER THIS JANE," Lucy joked.

"Very funny," Jane snapped, although secretly she rather liked the idea of resembling Paddington. *I ought to get some red Wellies,* she thought. *I wonder if they have them in my size.*

The sound of laughter caught her attention and she turned to see Miriam exiting the shop with Lilith. The Chihuahua was wearing a tiny blue raincoat very similar to Jane's. A little red hat was perched on her head, and on her three paws were wee red booties.

"Oh, Mother," said Walter, looking sympathetically at Lilith.

"She hates the rain," Miriam said.

"I do not," said Lilith, although of course only Jane heard her. "I'm quite fond of the rain, actually. She just thinks I look cute in this ridiculous getup."

Now ready to brave the elements, the group began to walk through the city. Everyone had been left to their own devices for the early part of the morning, with instructions to meet at their next location precisely at ten o'clock. Jane had not yet told Lucy about her strange experience in the elevator, and it didn't look like she would have time until later. Lucy and Ben were skipping the house tour and instead going to the National Museum of Scotland, where Ben wanted to see the exhibit of the Lewis Chessmen. They would reconvene for dinner at seven at a restaurant selected by Enid.

Miriam, to Jane's dismay, had elected to join the tour, and so it was that at a few minutes before ten Walter, Miriam, and Jane walked up to the front of the Chewgristle Playhouse, where they met the rest of the group—with the exception of Chumsley, who, like Ben and Lucy, had elected to instead visit the museum. His absence had apparently put Enid in a bit of a mood, which at first seemed odd until Jane realized that by not being there Chumsley was depriving Enid of a chance to show off.

"The Chewgristle Playhouse was built in 1867 by my great-great-great-great-grandfather, Laird Birral," Enid said as she posed on the steps of the theater. "At the time it was the most majestic theater in all of Scotland."

"That's all very well, but can we go inside?" Brodie's booming voice carried over Jane's head. "In case you haven't noticed, it's raining cats 'n' dogs out here."

Enid set her mouth in a grim line. "Come on then," she said as she opened the theater doors.

Once inside they stood, dripping, in a lovely marble foyer. As she looked around, Jane had the distinct feeling of having been in the theater before. Then her gaze fell upon a row of framed posters from various productions. One of them was for a production of *He Thinks He'll Keep Her* from 1873. It starred the husband-and-wife acting team of Argyll Peploe and Maisie Longmuir.

I've been here before, Jane realized. *I saw that play.*

It all came back to her. The trip to Scotland. The play. Being introduced to Argyll and Maisie after one of their performances and discovering that they too were vampires. But who had introduced them? She searched her memories for the name.

"The theater's first and most famous director was Wurrick Ogg Runciman," Enid said.

Wurrick Ogg Runciman, Jane thought. *Of course. How could I forget?*

This was a very good question, as Wurrick Ogg Runciman had been rather unforgettable. So short that he was rumored to have been a dwarf, Wurrick made up for his lack of height with his abundance of bluster. Also, he wore specially made high-heeled boots and a very tall top hat. Even thus attired he still was barely five feet tall, and if it hadn't been for his very long black beard and the stream of curses that flowed from his mouth like the Water of Leith, he might easily have been mistaken for a child.

Runciman was not a vampire, but he ran in their circles. Probably because most of the world treated him like a freak, he knew what it meant to be feared, and found in vampires the family he had never had in real life. He in turn provided the undead with gainful employment, hiring them to oversee virtually all aspects of his theater, from costuming and music to scenery and managing the box office. And of course he used many of them as actors.

Jane had been given a letter of introduction by a friend, the actor George Eames. At the time, Jane thought that she might like to write for the stage, and George had suggested she speak to Runciman about perhaps working with him on some small thing.

This had never happened (after reading her first attempt, Runciman had informed her that she had no ear for dialogue), but she had spent a delightful couple of weeks there filling in for a property mistress who had gone and gotten herself staked.

"As we walk up the stairs, please take note of the plaster moldings," Enid said, bringing Jane back to the present.

She followed Walter up the stairs, her fingertips tracing the lines of the brass handrail. How strange, she thought, that she'd forgotten such an unusual period in her life. Of course, if she were human, then not so much time would have gone by since, allowing her to forget. But when your life had no end, there were always new memories piling on top of the old ones and eventually burying them. How much had she forgotten? How many old friends? How many shared moments?

She looked at Walter, walking ahead of her, and suddenly she wanted to grab hold of him and not let go. *What if I forget him?* she wondered. *What if a hundred years after his death I have to see a photograph of him to remember him?*

They had taken almost no photographs on the trip, and none of them together. Jane had to stop herself from grabbing Walter and dragging him outside so that some passerby could take their picture. She needed something besides memories—something tangible that she could hold and look at, so that when her memories faded this part of her life wouldn't just disappear.

When they reached the mezzanine Enid led them through one of the numerous arched doorways and into the interior of the theater. There it opened up, revealing the three horseshoe-shaped galleries rising above the stalls. The seats were upholstered in a deep red velvet that matched the color of the walls and carpets, and the bountiful plasterwork was gilded. An enormous chandelier hung from the ceiling, the thousands of crystals radiating light.

"The theater enjoys protected status," Enid said. "Thanks in no small part, I might add, to my work on the board of Creative Scotland. As such, nothing here may be changed, and any improvements made to things such as lighting and the sound system must be done without interfering with the architecture."

"I have to say, I'm impressed," Walter whispered to Jane. "Do you know how much red tape we would have to untangle to get something like this done in the States?"

"It looks just like it did back then," Jane said, only half listening.

"Have you seen pictures?" Walter asked her.

"What?" said Jane. "Oh. Yes, I have. I forget where. In a magazine, possibly, or a book. I don't know."

"Well, I'll be damned. Take a look at this."

The voice was Brodie Pittman's. He was looking at a series of photographs hung on one of the walls. Several other people were looking as well, among them Genevieve and Sam. Jane and Walter went over to join them.

"Looks just like her, doesn't it?" Brodie said, pointing to one of the pictures.

Genevieve turned and looked at Jane. "A younger, thinner her, perhaps," she said.

"Jane," said Brodie, beckoning her closer. "Look what Suzu here found."

Jane walked to the wall and looked. Brodie indicated a photograph showing the cast and crew of *He Thinks He'll Keep Her*. She saw Argyll and Maisie sitting in chairs on either side of Wurrick, who was standing on a lettuce box so as to appear taller. Around them were other faces, most of which Jane didn't recognize. And then, peering out from between the actor playing the father of Maisie's character and the woman who had designed the hats for the show, she saw her own face. Despite the obvious age of the photograph, she looked exactly as she did now.

"Uncanny," Brodie said. "She could be your twin sister."

Walter put his face up to the photo. "She even has the same dimple you have," he said to Jane. "And if I didn't know better I'd swear I've seen you wearing that same necklace."

He *had* seen her wearing the necklace. It had been a gift to Jane from her sister Cassie, and it was one of Jane's most treasured possessions. She'd almost worn it today, in fact. Now she was glad she'd decided not to. The situation was already more than she wanted to deal with.

"I suppose she does resemble me a bit," she said, trying not to sound too convinced.

"What do you mean a bit?" said Brodie. "If I didn't know any better, I'd swear you just stepped out of that photo there. Look, you're making the same face she is right now."

Jane rearranged her expression before anyone had a chance to verify Brodie's remark. They were all staring at her anyway. Miriam, holding Lilith, looked as if she was holding her breath.

"Jane," Walter said, sounding very serious, "is there something you want to tell me?"

"No!" Jane blurted. "I've never seen that woman before in my life. I have no idea who she is."

"According to the notation on the back of the photo, her name is Beatrice Crump," Genevieve said, peering at a notice posted beside the photo.

"That's not right," said Jane. "Beatrice Crump is the woman on her right. The man on the left is Grandstand Dalrymple." Too late she realized her mistake.

"She's right," Enid said. "That is Dalrymple. He made his name here starring in the Scottish play. But how in the world would you know the name of the costumer?"

"Oh, you know," Jane replied, trying to think. "She's very famous."

"No," said Edith. "She isn't. In fact, Beatrice Crump died not long after this photo was taken, and I'm fairly certain nobody ever thought of her again. The only reason I was able to identify her at all was through a mention in Wurrick Ogg Runciman's journal. Look here."

Enid pointed to another frame. Inside of this one was a page from Runciman's journal. Jane recognized the handwriting.

"This is from an entry about the production of *He Thinks He'll Keep Her*," Enid explained. "Read for yourself."

Jane's eyes scanned the pages. Although the ink had faded, the words were still legible.

Tuesday, 07 October 1873

The play is doing well. Sold out or near every night this week. One foul review in the *Scotsman* but that's to be expected given Pearle's dislike of anything that isn't Marlowe or Skivens. I've half a mind to put an end to the bastard, but A & M say it's not worth the bother as he'd probably come back as something worse and the devil you know, etc., etc.

One bit of trouble. Beatrice Crump has left us. A victim of the needle, I'm afraid. Why any of them listen to Ratcliffe I don't know, as it's clear to me he's a hunter. We've a plan to rid ourselves of him and are waiting for the time.

Beatrice will be sorely missed. She was a lovely girl and made lovely hats.

Tucked into the corner of the frame was a small photograph of Beatrice Crump. She was smiling, and someone had added pink to her cheeks with watercolors. Looking at it, Jane remembered the girl's soft voice and unassuming manner. *She couldn't have been more than seventeen or eighteen*, she thought.

At first she wondered why she couldn't remember the girl's death, but then she realized that the photograph had been taken in September, right before the show's opening. She had left Edinburgh not long after. Beatrice must have died sometime between then and October 7.

"The needle Runciman refers to was of course morphine," Enid said. "Morphine addiction was common at the turn of the century, particularly among theater folk. It was not unusual for certain unsavory elements to prey on those with a taste for the drug. This Ratcliffe was apparently one of them, a hunter of weak and impressionable young women, no doubt, of whom Beatrice Crump was one."

That's not right, Jane thought. *Beatrice was a vampire. Morphine would have no effect on her.*

Suddenly she remembered. She hadn't left Edinburgh, she'd been sent away for her own safety. Someone—a hunter—had been killing vampires, and it was decided that because she was so young she would be most vulnerable. At the time she hadn't really understood, but now she did. The needle wasn't a simple syringe, it was Crispin's Needle. This Ratcliffe was indeed a hunter—a vampire hunter. And apparently he had been convincing vampires that he could save their souls. *But really he was murdering them,* Jane realized.

"You must have seen this letter and photo somewhere," Walter said, bringing her back to the moment. "In a book, maybe?"

"It's possible," said Enid. "It has been reprinted in one book about the theater. But it's rather obscure. I don't know where someone such as yourself would have come across it."

"Jane owns a bookstore," Walter said.

"Yes," Jane said. "I believe I remember now. A customer—the drama teacher at the university—special-ordered a book and it was in there. How odd that the name stuck in my head. I guess because it's such an unusual one." She laughed lightly, hoping her deception would pass muster.

"It isn't really," said Enid. "Crump is actually quite common."

Jane ignored the slight. Something more pressing was on her

mind. "What happened to Argyll and Maisie?" she asked, her voice tight.

"Peploe and Longmuir?" said Enid, her tone suggesting that Jane was being far too familiar with these greats of the theater. "That's a tragic story. Two years after the success of *He Thinks He'll Keep Her* Longmuir too succumbed to morphine addiction. Peploe's end was even more tragic. He died onstage during a performance of *The Black Bird Sings*. Someone substituted a real knife for the prop knife during the climactic fight scene, and he was stabbed through the heart by his best friend, Cecil Baggs-Cowper."

I bet I know who substituted the knife, Jane thought. *Ratcliffe. Bloody vampire hunter.*

She looked over at Miriam, whose smug expression showed Jane that she was thinking the same thing, although with the opposite reaction. Jane wanted very much to bite her at that moment, but there was too much to think about. Also, of course, it would likely alarm Walter. But she would talk to Miriam later. She had questions, and she was fairly certain that Miriam had answers.

"We still don't know who Jane's look-alike is," Brodie said, bringing things back to the matter at hand.

"Probably just some tart," Enid said dismissively. "Shall we move on? There are far more interesting things to see than these old photos."

As the group walked away, Jane took a glance back at the photo of herself, then at Runciman's journal. *Not to me,* she thought, a thousand questions swirling in her head.

Chapter 16

Saturday: Edinburgh

THE STEAM RISING FROM THE HAGGIS BROUGHT WITH IT THE SCENT of oatmeal, onions, and meat. It was not unlike.the smell that came from the can when Jane fed her cat, Tom, his dinner. Ben, who had insisted on ordering the haggis, now looked a wee bit discomfited.

"On second thought, maybe this isn't kosher," he said.

Lucy poked a fork into the haggis and held it to Ben's mouth. "Just try it, you big baby," she said.

Ben shut his eyes and opened his mouth. Lucy fed him the bite of haggis, then watched him chew. His expression changed from one of apprehension to guarded relief and finally to enjoyment. He took the fork from Lucy and attacked the haggis with gusto.

"Isn't he just the cutest thing?" Lucy said. "My little Jewish William Wallace."

"Next year in Edinburgh!" Ben said, raising his glass of whiskey.

"I'm so getting you a kilt tomorrow," said Lucy, kissing him.

Jane laughed. Seeing Lucy and Ben so happy together made *her* happy. She wondered when they would be getting married. It seemed inevitable. They were perfect for each other.

She looked at Walter, seated next to her. He too was laughing at Lucy's remark. Jane reached over and rubbed his neck. "Do you want one too, dear?"

Walter cocked his head. "There is a Fletcher tartan," he said. "My father had a tie made from it. Do you remember that, Mom?"

"No," Miriam said. She stood up. "I need to use the restroom."

Jane, who had been waiting all evening for an opportunity to speak to Miriam, stood as well. "I'll go with you," she said.

Miriam eyed her warily. "I think I can manage this on my own," she said.

"Just walk," Jane said sternly under her breath. She took hold of Miriam's upper arm and steered her away from the table.

"Unhand me!" Miriam snarled.

Jane let go and pushed open the ladies' room door. Miriam went inside and whirled around as Jane entered behind her.

"What do you think you're doing?" she said.

"Tell me about Ratcliffe," said Jane, crossing her arms over her chest and fixing Miriam with a hard stare.

Miriam turned and looked at her face in the mirror over the bathroom's lone sink. She smirked as she fixed her hair. "I wondered when this would come up."

"He was no dope peddler," Jane said. "We both know that."

Miriam turned. "Well, aren't you clever?" she said. "No, he most certainly was not. Peter Ratcliffe was one of the most successful demon hunters of all time. He's a legend."

"Demon hunter," Jane said, rolling her eyes. "He killed vampires."

Miriam shrugged. "That's what they assumed your kind were back then," she said. "And I'm not entirely sure they weren't right."

"I'll have you know that several of the *demons* he killed were my friends," Jane said, baring her teeth.

"Yes," said Miriam. "I gathered by your reaction to seeing the photograph."

"Runciman knew what he was," Jane said. "Why didn't he just kill Ratcliffe?"

Miriam laughed. "That's the best part," she said. "He didn't kill him because he couldn't be killed." She paused for dramatic effect, but Jane guessed what she was going to say and beat her to it.

"Because Ratcliffe was a vampire," she said. "Of course. Now it makes sense. And this needle Runciman wrote about—I assume he means Crispin's Needle."

"Crispin's Needle is a myth," said Miriam. "Ratcliffe invented it to trick vampires into killing themselves. He told them it would free their souls or some such nonsense, but all it did was send them back to hell."

"He could hardly send them *back* when they didn't come from there in the first place," Jane said. "All he did was murder them."

"They murdered themselves," Miriam argued. "He just convinced them to do it."

"That's despicable," said Jane.

"It's *ingenious*," Miriam countered. Then she added, "If it *was* real, would you use it?"

Jane was surprised by the question. Of course, she had been asking herself the same thing ever since Gosebourne had first told her about the Needle, but she never expected to be having this conversation with Walter's mother. And she wasn't sure how to respond. She really didn't want Miriam to know what her thoughts were on the matter. She did, however, want to know what Miriam was thinking.

"Would it make a difference to you if I did?" she said.

Miriam looked at her, saying nothing, and Jane understood that she was having the same reservations about revealing her hand. Now Jane really did wonder whether it would make any difference to Miriam if she could become mortal again. Would her having been a vampire still be a reason for Miriam to hate her? Or would that all be left in the past if Jane could once more be human? She waited for Miriam to say something.

"It's a foolish question," Miriam said when she finally answered. "Crispin's Needle was an invention of Ratcliffe's mind."

Jane thought about arguing. If Ratcliffe had invented the story about Crispin's Needle, how did that explain the windows in the Church of St. Apollonia? Or had Ratcliffe somehow known about the windows and used them as inspiration for his story? It seemed Miriam didn't know about the windows, so probably she didn't know any more about the story than Jane did. Besides, there was no use in arguing with Miriam. Jane understood that in their own way they were declaring a truce, at least as far as discussing their feelings about Jane's soul, or lack thereof.

"What happened to him?" Jane asked, changing course.

Miriam's mouth tightened. "He was killed," she said. "Betrayed. By a woman."

"I like where this is going," said Jane. "Tell me more."

"He was weak," Miriam said. "He fell in love with a fallen woman. He turned her."

Jane gasped, feigning horror. "That's against the rules!" she said.

Miriam frowned. "Don't be disrespectful," she snapped. "The woman seduced him. And when she had what she wanted, she staked him."

"I like this woman," Jane said. "And what became of *her*?"

"The hunters found her and took care of her," Miriam said. "It took a couple of decades, but eventually Eloise Babineaux was sent back to—was sent to hell."

"Eloise Babineaux?" Jane said, trying not to let her excitement betray her. "What an unusual name."

"It's a whore's name," said Miriam. "For a filthy whore."

"Now, now," Jane said. "Let's not go calling people names." She hesitated a moment. "And what became of this needle that Ratcliffe used to kill his victims?"

"I told you, they killed themselves," said Miriam. "Anyway, I don't know what became of it. It was just a piece of iron. I imagine it didn't look much different from any other spike you would use to stake a vampire. Honestly, even a tent peg would do in a pinch."

"Oh, I bet you know all about *that*," Jane said. "Horrible old woman."

"I'm younger than you, missy," said Miriam.

"Yes, but you look *much* older," Jane said, looking at her reflection in the mirror and smiling sweetly.

Having gotten the information she wanted, she turned and started to leave the restroom. She was stopped by Miriam's voice.

"Those vampires Peter Ratcliffe sent to their deaths were vermin," she said.

"Beatrice Crump was a lovely girl," Jane said, her back to Miriam. "She was kind to everyone. She used to feed the stray cats behind the theater. What Peter Ratcliffe did to her was inexcusable."

"What Peter Ratcliffe did was good," said Miriam. "What we as hunters do is good."

Jane whirled around and advanced on her. "The only *good* you've ever done is give birth to Walter," she said. "And believe me, the only reason I haven't drained you dry already is because he loves you."

Miriam flinched, but quickly regained her composure. "The same goes for you," she said tersely. "The difference is that he'll always love his mother."

Jane was about to tell Miriam that she shouldn't be so sure about that. But she knew it was true. Walter *would* always love his mother. That's the kind of man he was. *But will he always love me? When he finds out what I am?*

She turned and left the washroom before Miriam could see the tears forming in her eyes. And they weren't there just because of Walter. They were there because of Beatrice, and Argyll, and Maisie. They were there because of Peter Ratcliffe and all of the vampires he had lied to and murdered.

And he *had* murdered them. Jane didn't care what Miriam called it. They hadn't wanted to die; they'd wanted to live. She imagined Beatrice driving the spike into her own heart, and she felt she might collapse. She could see in her mind the look on the girl's face as she realized that her soul wasn't returning to her body, that in fact she was dying without salvation. Had Peter Ratcliffe watched, enjoying this moment of betrayal? Jane's heart raged with anger. Her fangs clicked into place, and the muscles of her neck tightened. She wanted revenge.

She forced herself to calm down. There was nothing she could do about Ratcliffe now. But she *could* keep looking for Crispin's Needle. Miriam had said it was a myth, but Jane didn't believe it. *Or maybe you just want to believe in it so much that you're refusing to see the truth,* she told herself. *Maybe it was just a trick of the hunters.*

"Are you okay?"

Jane turned around and saw Walter standing beside her, looking confused.

"I'm fine," Jane said, forcing a smile. "I just felt a little dizzy. I think the smell of the haggis got to me."

"I thought maybe you and my mother got into a rumble in the loo," said Walter.

Jane was amused by his use of the British word for the bathroom. He had been picking up little pieces of her culture here and there throughout the trip, like one of those crabs that decorated its shell with snips of seaweed and tiny rocks. It was endearing, although the accent that crept into his voice from time to time was going to have to be dealt with. It was bad enough when Madonna did it; Jane couldn't have her husband doing it as well.

Except that he's not your husband, she reminded herself.

The bathroom door opened and Miriam came out. Seeing Walter and Jane in the hallway, she smiled awkwardly and passed by without comment.

"What did you do to her?" Walter asked Jane.

"I asked her if she was looking forward to being a grandma," Jane answered.

They returned to the table, where Ben was looking at the half-eaten haggis with a look of grim determination.

"You don't have to eat the whole thing," Lucy told him.

"It's taunting me," said Ben.

"Don't listen to it, man," said Brodie, who had wandered over from where he'd been drinking at the bar. "A haggis is like a mermaid. If you follow its song, you're doomed."

Ben lifted his fork. Before he could take another bite, Brodie grabbed the plate of haggis and ran off shouting, "You'll thank me later!"

Ben stared at where the haggis had been a moment before. "I just wanted a little more," he said sadly.

"Finish your whiskey," Lucy ordered. "You'll feel better."

Jane, sitting beside her, whispered in her ear, "I think Eloise Babineaux may have taken the Needle."

Lucy's eyes widened. "How do you know?"

Jane cut her eyes at Miriam. "The fearless hunter told me," she said. "But she thinks the whole thing is made up anyway. Still, I don't want her to know that we're going to Babineaux's house."

"How will we get away from the group?" Lucy asked.

"We'll think of something," said Jane. "In the meantime, we'd better get our boys out of here before Ben decides to wrestle Brodie for the rest of that haggis."

Back at the hotel, Jane packed for the morning's flight to Paris. Walter, remembering the ordeal of the flight to Edinburgh, was watching the weather report on BBC Scotland.

He lay back on the bed and sighed. "This trip has been crazy," he said. "And I thought it was going to be relaxing."

Jane folded a sweater and tucked it into the suitcase. "Oh, it hasn't been that crazy," she said. "Unless you count my ex-husband interrupting our wedding, Ryan falling off the keep, and the fact that pretty much everyone on the trip is completely mad. Other than that it's been a perfectly delightful six days."

"Is that all it's been?" Walter said. "Six days?"

Jane nodded. "Does it seem longer?"

"Much," said Walter.

Jane closed the suitcase and sat beside him. "You're not having a good time?"

Walter took her hand. "I'm having a good time being with you," he said. "I'd be having a better time if we were married, but I can't have everything."

"You're taking the whole business with Joshua rather well," said Jane. "I don't know that I would be as calm about the whole thing if the shoe were on the other foot."

"I'm probably not as calm about it as I look," Walter admitted. "But I figure I've waited this long to be married to you, so I can wait a little while longer."

Jane stretched out beside him on her side. Walter turned and put his arm around her.

"I haven't made it very easy for you," Jane said.

"No," Walter agreed. "You haven't."

Jane took his hand and held it to her chest. "Why *do* you put up with me?" she asked. "There are dozens of women who would want to be with you and wouldn't be nearly as much trouble."

"Only dozens?" Walter said.

"At least two," Jane joked.

Walter kissed the back of her head. "Maybe," he said. "But none of them is you."

"I just hope I don't disappoint you," said Jane.

"I don't see how you could," Walter told her. "I already know everything about you and I'm still madly in love with you."

"You didn't know about Joshua," Jane reminded him.

"True," Walter said. "But I do now, and I'm still not disappointed. There aren't any other husbands floating around, though, are there? One I can handle. Maybe even two. But any more than that and all bets are off."

"There's just the one," Jane said. "And I told you, he doesn't really count. Only *you* do."

"Then I think we're okay," said Walter.

I hope you're right, Jane thought.

She'd begun to wonder if she might be able to get away with never telling Walter that she was a vampire. If Crispin's Needle *was* real, and if she *could* find it, perhaps she could make herself mortal again and he would never have to know what she'd been. Of course, Miriam could always tell him, but her story would sound incredible. Jane didn't think Miriam would risk it.

Tomorrow they would be in Paris. With some luck she and Lucy would get to Eloise Babineaux's house and see if the Needle was there. Again Jane remembered the voice in the elevator. Someone was on her side, even if she didn't know who it was. And she had the key—whatever the key was for. Everything seemed to be falling into place.

Almost too easily, she thought. But she pushed the thought away. Everything was happening for a reason. That was all there was to it. She was meant to find Crispin's Needle. It was her destiny. Everything in her life had brought her to this point, and she was poised on the brink of a life-changing moment.

Or you're just making an ass of yourself, a voice in her head said. *That's a distinct possibility.*

"Oh, shut up," Jane said.

"What?" Walter mumbled. He had drifted off to sleep. Now he rolled onto his back and started to snore.

Jane turned off the light. Outside the window the moon was visible, a half circle that glowed with silver light. Jane realized that the clouds that had covered the sky for the past few days were gone.

The storm is over, she thought. *Tomorrow is going to be a beautiful day.*

Chapter 17

Sunday: Paris

IT'S SAID THAT THE ONLY PEOPLE WHO DON'T FALL IN LOVE WITH Paris at first sight are those who have no souls. Jane, who very much did love Paris, wondered if the opposite was true. Although the city was not yet bursting with the warmth and colors of springtime, it was on its way. March had brought with it sunshine and hope, and this was reflected in the buds on the trees and in the faces of the people on the streets, who walked here and there with a renewed sense of purpose after the long, cold days of winter.

The flight from Edinburgh had been, thankfully, completely uneventful. Having left very early, they'd arrived in Paris in time for lunch and were now about to visit the first of their two destinations in the city. Chumsley, whose selection it was, had kept them completely in the dark as to the location, herding them all onto a bus and saying nothing as they wound their way through the narrow streets of the city.

Eventually they had passed into the Fourth Arrondissement, which everyone on the bus discovered when Genevieve Prideaux told them as much. She was very excited about being back in her own city and was pointing out all of the things she thought they should notice as the bus passed by them.

"There is the Hôtel de Ville," she said loudly. "And of course you don't want to miss Notre-Dame de Paris." She made similar remarks regarding the Place des Vosges, the Pompidou Centre, and both Île de la Cité and Île Saint-Louis. When no one responded to her attempts, she settled into a gloomy sulk, occasionally muttering to herself in French.

"And here we are!" Chumsley announced as the bus came to a stop. "Follow me, ducklings."

They tumbled out into a narrow street lined on both sides by shops with a decidedly unmodern appearance. Jane felt as if she'd stepped back in time at least a century. It was a pleasant feeling.

"We are now standing in the middle of what is known locally as the Pletzl, or the Jewish Quarter," Chumsley told them. "The beginnings of this community date back more than six hundred years, and it's one of the most interesting parts of the city."

"*Oui, oui, oui,*" Genevieve said. "The Jewish Quarter is *très intéressant.* But there is nothing of architectural importance *ici.*"

"Why is she going in and out of French?" Walter whispered to Jane. "It's like switching back and forth between two radio stations."

Jane covered her mouth to hide a giggle, but a bit of it escaped nonetheless. Genevieve turned and glared at Jane.

"I am delighted to tell you that you are mistaken," Chumsley said to Genevieve. "There is a great deal here to see—if only you know where to look. Now if you'll just follow me."

He led them down the street and turned right, into an even narrower lane with even less impressive buildings than those they'd just passed by. Jane, looking around, found herself wondering if perhaps Genevieve wasn't right in her assessment of the neighborhood. *It certainly seems very ordinary,* she thought.

Chumsley came to a stop in front of a *boucherie.* The window was filled with various meats, and there was a postcard-worthy quaintness to it, but there was nothing to set it apart from the hundreds of other *boucheries* in the city. Even the black-and-white cat sitting on the step and licking its paw seemed familiar, as if it were a prop placed there by a set decorator instructed to create a "typical Paris street" for a film shoot.

The door to the shop opened and an elderly man emerged. Short and stout, he wore a white apron over a long-sleeved blue shirt and tan pants. His white hair was full and thick, and his dark eyes were bright. He smiled broadly and hugged Chumsley tightly, kissing him on both cheeks.

"My old friend," he said in heavily accented English. "It is good to see you again."

Chumsley turned to the group. "Ladies and gentlemen, I would like to introduce you to my friend Daniel Halphen."

Daniel nodded. "Welcome to my little shop," he said.

"Daniel is being uncharacteristically modest," said Chumsley, earning himself a chuckle from the old man. "His shop is actually one of the most fascinating places in all of Paris."

"What about it is so fascinating?" Bergen asked, saying what was on all of their minds. "It looks to be a perfectly ordinary butcher's shop."

"And that is what it's supposed to look like," Daniel said. "Come. I will show you."

He went inside and beckoned for them to follow. As they filed into the small store, Chumsley said to Ben, "I think you will find this of particular interest, rabbi."

The inside of the *boucherie* did little to change the impression of it being nothing more than a place to purchase a brisket or a piece of tongue. But Daniel led them past the cases of meat and into a small room, made of stones joined neatly together in the old fashioned manner, in which rows of salamis hung from wood beams. The room could barely contain the baker's dozen people now inside it.

"As you may know," Daniel said, "the Jews have had a home in Paris for centuries. But life has not always been easy for us. Several times we have been expelled, and often we have been the target of persecution."

As Daniel spoke he knelt down and picked up one of the smooth, flat rocks that formed the floor. Jane was surprised to see that underneath it was a piece of wood into which was set a metal ring.

"In 1940 the Germans invaded France," Daniel said. "I was seven years old at the time. My father, who like myself was a butcher, knew that the worst was yet to come. He gathered together the men of the community and told them that we needed to be prepared."

He took hold of the metal ring and lifted. A section of the floor came up, and Jane saw that it was a kind of trap door. The square of wood was perhaps three feet by three feet, and pieces of stone had been affixed to it so that when it lay flat it was indistinguishable from the rest of the floor. Beneath it was a set of steps.

"It took nearly two years to complete what you are about to see," Daniel told them. "By then we knew what was happening to our people. We knew as well that eventually the Nazis would come for us. They did so in July of 1942, in what we refer to as the Rafle du Vel' d'Hiv. This roundup conducted by French police resulted in the arrest of more than thirteen thousand Jews, almost all of whom were sent to Auschwitz to be exterminated."

He indicated the steps. "Please," he said to Sam Wax, who was standing closest to him.

Sam descended into the hole. She was followed by Suzu, then Orsino and the rest. Jane followed Lucy and Walter; Chumsley and Daniel brought up the rear. The steps went down about twelve feet and ended in a room only a bit larger than the one above it. The walls there were of stone, and the air was decidedly cooler.

"I'm sure you are all familiar with the story of Anne Frank and her hiding place," Daniel said. "There were such hiding places all across Europe. This is one of them. But it is more than that, as you will see in a moment."

He passed through a narrow archway, and once again the group followed him. This time Jane found herself in a narrow corridor that went on for a short way before once more opening into a room. Unlike the earlier stone-walled room, this one had walls covered in white plaster. The vaulted ceiling was made of bricks cleverly fitted together and similarly whitewashed. In the center of the dome was painted a red Star of David amidst a sea of smaller six-pointed stars.

"It's a synagogue," Ben said, his voice a whisper.

Daniel nodded. "Yes," he said. "A place for us to worship in safety."

Something was written on one of the walls in Hebrew. Jane, pointing to is, asked Ben what it said.

"Da lifnei mi attah ome," he said. "'Know before whom you stand.' It reminds us that we are always in the presence of God."

Jane understood now why Chumsley had brought them to the unassuming *boucherie.* No, it wasn't an example of exquisite architecture, but it was even more beautiful for its simplicity and meaning. The grandest cathedral could not best it, because it had been built purely out of love. Jane imagined people gathered there, asking God for mercy in the face of what must have seemed like certain death. She couldn't imagine having that kind of faith.

She remembered 1942 all too well, if not fondly. She'd spent it in various cities across Europe, doing what she could to help the war effort. When Daniel had mentioned Auschwitz her mind had flashed back to a time spent liberating the victims of the camps. Not just the Jews, but all those who were being murdered by Hitler's army: Gypsies, dissidents, the men with the pink triangles, the old and the sick and the feebleminded. The undead had been particularly suited to rescue work, although most of Jane's kind preferred to stay out of what they considered a human conflict. Those who did choose to get involved, like Jane, were generally those who remembered their own mortality.

Long-buried memories came back to her. She closed her eyes, afraid of being overwhelmed. She felt Walter's arms go around her and heard his voice in her ear. "It's hard to imagine what they went through, isn't it?"

Jane nodded. She wished she could tell him that she *did* know. She wished she could tell him that even in the midst of all that darkness there had been beacons of light, and that hope never really died as long as there was one person who believed that things would get better. But she couldn't tell him any of that, because he didn't know who she really was.

She opened her eyes. The others were walking around the room as much as they could, examining the walls and the symbols painted on them, talking in hushed voices. Daniel stood in the midst of them, watching her. There was a look of sadness on his face, and Jane wondered what he was thinking about. *His family,* she thought. *Of course, he's thinking about his family.*

Miriam came and drew Walter away to show him something. Even she seemed to be awed by the hidden synagogue and its story. She hadn't so much as glared at Jane since they'd entered the room. Jane couldn't help but wonder if Miriam would have become a hunter if she'd known about the vampires' role in rescuing so many people during the war. *Of course, there were just as many of us on the other side,* she reminded herself. *And Miriam probably wouldn't believe it anyway.*

Daniel walked toward Jane. He stopped in front of her and looked into her eyes. "It is you," he said. "I thought at first you merely looked like her, but no."

Jane didn't know what to say. Who did Daniel think she was? Before she could ask his hands went to the left cuff of his shirt. He unbuttoned it and rolled it back, revealing his forearm. The ink was faded now, but the numbers tattooed there were still visible.

"You don't remember me," Daniel said. "I should not be surprised. It was many years ago, and I was a boy. But you have not changed."

He must have been one of the ones we saved, Jane thought. But she couldn't acknowledge that, not here and not now.

"It's all right," said Daniel, taking her hand. "I understand. Well, not everything, but enough. There were stories."

Jane didn't know what to say. Did Daniel know what she was? What stories had been told about her and the others? She wanted to know, but she couldn't ask.

Chumsley came over to them. "Do you know Jane?" he asked his friend.

Daniel laughed. "Why would an ugly old man like me know such a beautiful young woman?" he said. "No, I was just telling her that she reminds me of someone who was a good friend to my family many years ago."

"Ah," Chumsley said. To Jane he added, "I've seen him use this trick before. Never trust a Frenchman!"

Jane laughed along with Daniel. "I'll keep that in mind," she said as Chumsley went to speak to Enid, who was standing with her arms crossed, a look of irritation on her face.

Daniel was still holding Jane's hands. She felt his hands shake a little as he pressed hers tightly. "The Lord bless you and keep you," he whispered. "The Lord make his face shine upon you and be gracious to you; the Lord turn his face toward you and give you peace."

He looked into her eyes. "My father said that prayer to me every night," he told her. "After he was gone I said it to myself. And now I say it to you."

"Thank you," Jane said. She hesitated a moment before asking, "You're not afraid of me?"

Daniel smiled. "Why would I be afraid of one of God's angels?" he replied.

"I'm not an angel," Jane said sadly. "Far from it. And God doesn't have anything to do with it."

"You saved a little boy from death," said Daniel. "To me you are an angel, whatever else you may be. As for God, well, he has something to do with everything. He's very busy that way."

He kissed Jane on both cheeks, then announced, "If you will follow me back upstairs, I will show you why my grandmother's chopped liver was the talk of the Pletzl."

The group filed back into the passageway. Jane lingered, wanting to spend a moment in the synagogue when it wasn't so crowded. Finally it was just her and Walter in there.

"It's pretty amazing, isn't it?" Walter said.

"It is," Jane agreed. "I think it's the most beautiful place we've seen yet."

She looked up at the Star of David hanging above her head. Was Daniel right? Did God have anything to do with what she was? She was searching for Crispin's Needle because she'd been told it might restore her soul to her, but what if she'd never had a soul to begin with? What if she really was just a body kept alive by an accident of biology? She didn't even know if she believed in God, and if she couldn't believe that much, then how could she believe that a relic might make her human again?

She thought about Daniel as a boy, surrounded by death and evil. Yet still he'd believed that God would send someone to save him. *And whom did he send?* Jane thought. *Me. Not an angel. Me.* And she *had* saved him, as well as many others. Maybe God had something to do with it, maybe not. She had her doubts.

But if you are *up there, and you can hear me,* she thought, *I could use a little help.*

Chapter 18

Monday: Paris

"YOU'D THINK THAT WE'D BE SAFE FROM ST. PATRICK'S DAY CELE-brations in Paris," Lucy said as she and Jane exited the Métro and made their way through a crowd of revelers wearing green.

"When it comes to needing an excuse to drink beer, everyone is Irish," Jane joked.

She looked at the piece of paper in her hand, glanced at the plaque on the nearest house, and headed north, away from the raucous celebration.

"That's better," Lucy said as the noise died down and they found themselves in a quiet street of old homes that, while still beautiful, had their grandest days behind them.

Extricating themselves from the rest of the group had been relatively easy, although it had required some lying on Jane's part. The others were taking a day trip outside of the city to see what Enid assured them was the most exquisite little winery in the Champagne region, with a visit to the cathedral at Reims on the return. Jane had invented a weekend literary festival to which she and Lucy were to go in order to connect with some French publishers. She'd made it sound very boring (which in all likelihood it would have been, had it been real), and although both

Walter and Ben were disappointed that the ladies wouldn't be joining them, the promise of a dinner out that evening lessened the blow.

Another check of the map the front desk clerk at the hotel had given to her caused Jane to make a left turn onto Rue des Roses Cent-Feuilles. Halfway down, another street intersected this one. Inscribed on a tablet and affixed to the wall of the first house whose front faced the new street was Rue des Violettes.

"This is it," Jane said. "We need to find number thirty-seven."

Not two minutes later Jane and Lucy were looking up at the windows of what had once been the home of Eloise Babineaux. Constructed in the Second Empire style, the house was lovely, a four-story brick lady of a certain age who, like many of her kind, had managed to retain an air of sophistication despite the inevitable effects of time. The glass in her windows was clear and bright, her lines elegant, and her mansard roof charmingly patinaed. Here and there the faces of stonework ladies looked down upon those coming to visit.

According to Clare Marlowe, the current owner of the house was one Ninon Grosvenor. That's all Jane knew about the woman as she rang the bell and waited for someone to answer.

The woman who opened the door was tall, thin, and absolutely stunning. Her skin was deep brown, her eyes golden brown, and her hair fell in thick dreadlocks halfway down her back. She was dressed in a simple red shift, and the nails of her bare feet were painted the same color. She was young, and when she spoke her voice was rich and smooth.

"Do you have an appointment?"

"Appointment?" Jane said. "No, we don't. We were hoping to speak to Ninon Grosvenor. Clare Marlowe sent us. Well, she didn't *send* us so much as she just gave us the address."

The young woman cocked her head. "And what business do you have with Ninon?" she asked.

Jane suddenly found herself at a loss for words. She hadn't

really thought this far ahead. She'd assumed that she would just tell Ninon Grosvenor why she was there when she met her, but now it all sounded so strange that she wondered how she could ever have thought she could do that. But the young woman was waiting for an answer.

"It's about the stained-glass window in the chapel," she said, deciding that it was best to be direct. "The one with the heart being pierced by a needle."

She expected the young woman to say something, but all she did was raise one eyebrow.

"I—we think we understand what the window represents," Jane continued "And we think we might have some information about it."

The young woman looked at Jane for some time, then at Lucy. "Information?" she said. "What kind of information?"

Jane hesitated. "That's a little difficult to explain," she said. "It's a bit complicated, and I'm afraid it all sounds slightly silly, but we think that—perhaps—the window is a clue to solving a great mystery."

"A mystery?" said the young woman. "What kind of mystery?"

Jane looked at Lucy, unsure if what to say next.

"Vampires," Lucy said. "It's about vampires. We think the window is a clue to finding something that might be able to help a vampire get her—or his—soul back."

Jane held her breath. She couldn't believe Lucy had just blurted out everything. Now, surely, the young woman would think them completely mad and tell them to go away. Then they might never discover if the secret to finding Crispin's Needle was in Eloise Babineaux's house.

"You should have said so in the first place," the young woman said, holding the door open. "Come in."

Jane entered quickly before the woman could change her mind. Lucy followed. When they were inside, the woman said, "I am Ninon Grosvenor. Welcome to my house. I'm sorry I didn't introduce myself earlier, but you cannot be too careful."

"That's true," Lucy said. "One of my mother's neighbors was robbed by men pretending to be with the electric company."

Ninon laughed. "Oh, I'm not worried about burglars," she said. "It's reporters I am always on the lookout for."

"Reporters?" Jane said. "Why would reporters be bothering you?"

Ninon looked at her. "You don't know who I am?" she asked.

Jane, embarrassed, said, "Oh, I'm so sorry. I probably should, shouldn't I? You *do* look familiar. Are you a singer?"

Ninon laughed again. "No," she said. "I thought perhaps Clare would have told you. I am a courtesan."

"Courtesan?" Lucy said. "Didn't they go out of fashion, like, a hundred years ago?"

Ninon shook her head. "They just started calling us hookers," she said. "But of course that's not what we were then and not what I am now. Come with me."

She led them up a sweeping staircase to the next floor, where they entered a beautifully appointed sitting room. It was decorated in modern furnishings that somehow blended perfectly with the age of the house. Ninon indicated a Charlotte Perriand sofa upholstered in pink leather.

"Please," she said. "Sit."

Ninon herself sat down in an unusual armchair that looked very much like a hollowed-out football floating in the air. It too was upholstered in leather, although it was red.

"Is that a Fasanello?" Lucy asked, admiring it.

Ninon nodded. "My aunt was a collector of modern furniture," she said, running her fingers over the chair's curved arm. "I inherited it along with this house."

"Eloise Babineaux was your aunt?" Jane asked.

Ninon shook her head. "My aunt's name was Isobel Marchand," she said. "Eloise Babineaux was our relative going back many generations. Although this house did belong to Eloise at one time."

"Clare said that Eloise was a courtesan," Lucy said.

"That's right," said Ninon. "The women in our family have been for centuries. Of course, things have changed a great deal since Eloise's time. Now there is great interest in my gentlemen friends on the part of the press. I have to be very discreet."

"Understandable," Jane said. "It must be very . . . interesting."

"It is," said Ninon. "People assume that men come to me for sex. Some do, of course. It would be ridiculous for me to deny that. But mostly they just want me to listen. This seems to be something that many wives and girlfriends don't wish to do. I, however, am a very good listener."

As she spoke she picked up a cigarette case from a table beside the chair. Opening it, she removed a cigarette and lit it using a small gold lighter shaped like a skull embedded with crystals. The flame emerged from the skull's mouth. Ninon inhaled and blew out three perfect smoke rings.

"So," she said. "You have come to talk to me about the vampire needle."

"Is that what you call it?" Jane asked.

Ninon nodded. "I remember my aunt calling it something else, but I've forgotten what it was," she said.

"Crispin's Needle," said Jane. "What else did your aunt tell you about it?"

More smoke rings emerged from Ninon's mouth and floated toward the ceiling. "She said that Eloise Babineaux believed that it was a tool for the killing of vampires."

Jane didn't contradict her. Then Ninon looked at Lucy. "But you said that it does the opposite," she said.

Lucy glanced at Jane, clearly not sure how to respond.

"That's right," Jane said as Ninon's gaze returned to her. "From what we understand, it was believed that Crispin's Needle could restore a vampire's human soul."

Ninon tapped her cigarette on the edge of an ashtray. The end glowed brightly as she took another drag. "I had not heard that," she said.

Jane couldn't read the woman at all. Did she think Jane and Lucy were mad? Did she know more than she was telling them? It was impossible to say.

"I understand that there's a chapel in the house. That's where the stained-glass window is, correct?"

"I don't know that I would call it a chapel," said Ninon. "A sanctuary, perhaps."

Jane was confused. "I don't understand," she said.

"Eloise Babineaux was a very superstitious woman," Ninon said. "She believed in all kinds of things—ghosts, werewolves, vampires. She thought that one of her suitors was a vampire. His name was Edward St. John. He was English, a secretary to the ambassador, the Earl Granville."

"Granville Leveson-Gower," Jane said. "Of course. I knew hi—"

Lucy coughed.

"I remember him from history class," Jane concluded.

Not only had she known the Earl Granville, she had known Edward St. John as well. He *had* been a vampire, and a rather nasty one at that. If Eloise Babineaux had been mixed up with him, she probably did have reason to be afraid.

"Eloise heard about this needle," said Ninon. "I don't know where. She had the window made and placed in a room at the top of the house, thinking it would protect her. She slept in there every night."

"Apparently it worked," said Lucy. "I mean, she was never turned into a vampire, right?"

"She died of consumption," Ninon replied. "Everybody did back then. It was very romantic, apart from the spitting up of blood."

It was, Jane felt, time to get to the point. "Do you know if Eloise ever actually found the Needle?" she asked.

Ninon looked at her quizzically. "You think it exists?" she said.

"I don't know," Jane answered. "We think perhaps it might."

"Would it be very valuable?" asked Ninon.

"That's difficult to say," Jane said. "Some people believe it was made from the nails used to crucify Christ."

Ninon snorted. "Another fairy tale," she said.

"Yes," said Jane. "Well, to answer your question, Crispin's Needle might indeed be very valuable."

"If it exists," Lucy added.

"If it exists," Jane agreed.

"And what makes you think it might be here in the house?" Ninon asked.

Jane hesitated. "Just the window," she said, knowing that any other explanation would sound insane. "As you know, it's the same as the one in the Church of St. Apollonia."

"Well, you're certainly welcome to look for yourself," Ninon said. "But understand that if you do find anything, it belongs to me."

This thought had not occurred to Jane. Now that it had, she saw that there might be a problem. If Crispin's Needle indeed was in the house, Jane wanted it for her own use. But of course Ninon would have a claim on it.

I might have to bite her, she thought. *That would be most inconvenient.*

Ninon rose from the chair. "Follow me," she said.

They walked up two more flights of stairs, until they came to the top floor. Here the house was far less elegant, with plain wood floors and faded wallpaper patterned with shepherdesses. Ninon walked to the end of the hall and opened a door.

The room behind it was small, perhaps nine feet on any side. It was painted white, and there were no rugs on the floor. A narrow iron-framed bed was pushed against one wall. The only other furniture was an old wooden traveling trunk at the foot of the bed. It was banded in brass and secured with leather straps. The room's lone window had been replaced by a stained-glass panel. Like the one in the church at Cripple Minton, it depicted a red heart being pierced by a long needle.

"Have you looked inside that?" Jane asked Ninon, indicating the trunk.

"Of course," Ninon replied. "It was filled only with old night-gowns. Now it is empty."

"There could be a false bottom," Lucy suggested.

"Look for yourself," said Ninon.

Lucy knelt and undid the buckles on the straps. She lifted the lid and peered inside. Then she put her hand in and tapped on the trunk's bottom. She shook her head at Jane. "That's it," she said.

"And you didn't need the key to open it," Jane said.

"Key?" said Ninon. "You have a key?"

I might as well show her, Jane thought. She pulled the key out of her pocket and held it up.

Ninon took the key from Jane and examined it. "Come with me," she said.

They left the room and retraced their steps, going back down the stairs and then down yet another flight. They passed through a kitchen and down a final set of stone steps into a very damp basement. It was filled with broken things: an old wringer washer, dolls with no heads, mirrors spotted with age. Everything was covered with cobwebs and dust.

Ninon went to a corner where several large cardboard boxes sat, their bottom edges fuzzed with mold. She opened one and pawed through the contents, then shut it and tried another box.

"Here it is," she said, lifting out what looked like a small body.

She brought it over to where Jane and Lucy stood and set it on a table.

"It's a clown doll," Lucy said.

"A Pierrot, actually," said Ninon.

The doll was quite large, about two feet in length from the top of its white conical hat to its black-shoed feet. It was dressed in the traditional costume of white pants and a long white coat with three large black pom-poms down the front. Around its neck was a wide white ruffle edged in black, and its ceramic face was painted white with black around the eyes and a single black teardrop sliding down the right cheek. Its lips were painted a faded red. There was a crack running from its left ear down its neck.

"This used to sit in my bedroom when I was a girl," Ninon said. "It frightened me quite badly, though, and eventually I hid it down here and told my mother that it had been destroyed by our dog. She was angry because it had been in the family for many years."

She lifted the doll's coat. "The hands and head are ceramic," she said. "But the main body is a cylinder of wood. And under here"—she pulled the clown's pants down, exposing what would have been its backside if it had had one—"is the keyhole."

Jane looked more closely. Sure enough, there was a small key-hole in the clown's posterior.

"I always assumed it was some kind of wind-up mechanism," Ninon said. "Perhaps for a music box of some kind. But there was never a key."

"What made you think *this* key might work?" Jane asked her.

Ninon looked at her. "I don't know," she said. "I hadn't thought about this Pierrot in years. But when you showed me the key, somehow I knew what it was for."

"Well, let's see if you're right," said Lucy.

Ninon took the key and inserted it in the hole. It slipped in easily. When she turned it there was a slight clicking sound. Then the doll's body opened up. Inside it was lined with red velvet, and down the center was an impression that was designed to hold something long and needle-shaped. The impression was filled with what looked like iron filings. The velvet had several rust-colored stains on it.

Lucy looked at the empty doll. "There was something here," she said. "It was real."

Jane picked up some of the filings and rubbed them between her fingers. The remnants of what she was certain had been Crispin's Needle fell like dirty snow.

"But now it's gone," she said.

Chapter 19

Monday: Paris

"IT WAS NICE OF NINON TO GIVE YOU THE DOLL," LUCY SAID. SHE and Jane were walking back to the hotel. Jane had the Pierrot cradled in her arms.

"I suppose," Jane said glumly. "Clowns are creepy, though. I don't think I can be in the same room with it."

"You're just upset that the Needle wasn't in it," said Lucy.

"Well, it *was* in there," Jane said. "Just not in any usable form."

Lucy shrugged. "Maybe it just wasn't meant to happen. The universe doesn't always work the way we want it to."

"Oh, shut up," said Jane. Under her breath she muttered, "Stupid universe."

"I'm serious," Lucy said. "Don't you think things happen for a reason?"

"Maybe," said Jane. "But if that's true, then why has everything on this trip pointed me toward finding Crispin's Needle? You have to admit, there have been a *lot* of coincidences since we got here."

"True," Lucy admitted. "It does seem a little odd that you'd keep getting pointed in one direction, only to have it be a dead end."

"Maybe it's God's idea of a joke," said Jane. She looked up at the sky. "Well, it's not funny!" she said.

"At least you've gotten to meet a lot of interesting characters," Lucy said. "And look at it this way—if it really all was a story made up by Ratcliffe, you've actually done yourself a huge favor."

"What are you," said Jane, "the author of *Chicken Soup for the Vampire's Soul?*"

"I'm just trying to make you feel better," Lucy said. "Geez."

"I know," Jane said. "I'm sorry. It just all feels off somehow, like I picked the wrong door in a choose-your-own-adventure story. I can't help thinking that the Needle is still out there somewhere and I just need to retrace my steps and go in a different direction."

They reached the hotel and went inside. The tour group hadn't come back yet, and wouldn't for several hours. Jane and Lucy made plans to reconnect for dinner, then went to their respective rooms.

Jane set the Pierrot doll on the dresser, then lay down on the bed and closed her eyes. She was exhausted, and not just because she and Lucy had walked a great deal. Her entire body felt heavy and drained of energy. Her head was pounding and her thoughts felt dull and insubstantial. The only thing she could focus on was her disappointment, and even that was vague and insubstantial.

What am I really upset about? she wondered.

She considered the question. Was she disappointed that she hadn't found the Needle intact? Yes. *But a week ago you hadn't even heard of it,* she reminded herself. This was true. But once she *had* learned of its possible existence, it had become the most important thing in the world to her.

Maybe that's the problem, she thought. *Maybe you should have been happy with what you had.*

That was it. She should have been happy. And she *had* been. She had Walter, and Lucy and Ben, and all of her other friends. She had the bookstore and her career. There was also Miriam, of course, and she *was* a problem, but not an insurmountable one.

Her only real problem was the fact that she was a vampire. And *that* wasn't even really the problem. No, the real problem was that she hadn't told Walter what she was, and that she didn't want to. In short, she'd looked upon Crispin's Needle as the thing that would save her from having to tell Walter anything at all. She could have just (assuming the legend about the Needle was true) restored her human soul, married Walter, and lived out the rest of whatever her natural life would have been.

If that's how it would have worked, she reminded herself. *For all you know, the instant you pierced your heart with the Needle you might have dropped dead. You really ought to ask these kinds of questions before you get excited.*

She thought about this. All she knew was that supposedly Crispin's Needle made a vampire human again. But maybe it did so only for a moment, so that when death came seconds later (after all, there was a needle stuck through the heart, and that couldn't be entirely good news) the restored soul flew up to heaven. Or wherever.

If this was the case, Walter would then be grieving her death. She herself wouldn't be particularly thrilled about the matter either. But was that worse than letting Walter marry her not knowing that she would in all likelihood outlive him by centuries, that she would never age physically while he would suffer the inevitable ravages of time? Looking at things this way, there seemed to be no option that didn't end in unhappiness.

But you were *going to let him marry you without knowing what he was in for,* her conscience argued.

"I was going to figure it out later," she said aloud.

When? she asked herself. *When you got pregnant? When*

Miriam spilled the beans? When Suzu or someone else caught you feeding and told him?

"Leave me alone," she said, turning onto her stomach and putting a pillow over her head.

That's what I thought.

The bottom line was, she had been looking for an easy way out. Now that the way had been blocked, she was back where she had started and still no closer to knowing what to do than she had been when she'd accepted Walter's proposal in the first place.

Remarkably, she fell asleep. The next thing she heard was the sound of the door to the room opening and Walter's voice saying, "Honey! I'm home!"

She rolled over and discovered that her cheek was wet. She'd been drooling. She wiped it away with the pillowcase and sat up.

"What time is it?" she asked, yawning.

"Almost nine," said Walter. "We just got back."

He came over and gave her a kiss. "How was the festival?"

"The what?" Jane asked, momentarily forgetting the lie she'd told. "Oh, it was boring. You didn't miss anything. How was the winery?"

"Beautiful," Walter answered. "I wish you'd come with us."

"So do I," said Jane. She glanced at the dresser, thinking, *Then I never would have seen this stupid clown.*

Only the clown wasn't there.

"Did you move the Pierrot?" she asked Walter.

"The what?" Walter said as he took off his shoes.

"The Pierrot," said Jane. "A clown. It was sitting on the dresser."

Walter shook his head. "I didn't see any clown," he said.

"But it was right there," said Jane. "I put it there when I came in."

"You bought a clown?" Walter shuddered. "Clowns give me the creeps."

Jane got up and went to the dresser. She stared at the place where the clown had been, as if perhaps she just couldn't see it. She looked on the floor around the dresser, then behind it. It wasn't there. She then checked the closet, under the bed, her suitcase, and even the shower. There was no Pierrot anywhere to be found.

"Where could it possibly have gone?" she wondered aloud.

"Maybe it came to life," Walter suggested. "Like the clown in *Poltergeist.* Maybe it's hiding and just waiting for us to go to sleep so it can come out and murder us."

Jane ignored him. "It has to be here somewhere," she said.

"Forget about the clown," Walter said. "Are you ready to have an amazing dinner with your almost-husband?"

"I can't wait," said Jane, opening the minibar and peering inside.

"Good, because we're meeting everyone in ten minutes," Walter informed her.

"Everyone?" Jane said. "In ten minutes? What happened to our quiet dinner with Ben and Lucy?"

Walter looked sheepish. "Well, it's just that everyone got along really well today, and on the way back Suzu suggested we all have dinner at this restaurant she knows of."

"Suzu?" said Jane. "She actually spoke? She hasn't said more than a dozen words the entire trip."

"She talked to me quite a bit today," Walter said.

Jane felt her stomach tighten. "Really?" she said. "About what?"

"I don't know," said Walter. "Lots of things. She's really very interesting."

"I bet she is," Jane said as she checked the wastepaper basket beside the desk.

"For example," Walter said, "did you know Genevieve hated Ryan because he won the Pecker-Deadbird?"

Jane turned around. "Excuse me?"

"The Pecker-Deadbird," Walter repeated. "It's an award given to an architect whose work reflects the aesthetics of John Pecker-Deadbird."

"Who was . . . ?" Jane said.

"The father of post-minimalist modernism in institutional design."

"Oh," said Jane. "*That* John Pecker-Deadbird."

"Apparently Genevieve thought *she* should have won the award that year for some juvenile detention facility she built in Manchester, but according to Suzu, Ryan was very *close* to at least two of the judges on the committee, if you know what I mean."

Jane was surprised to hear Walter talk like this. He was never one to gossip, and here he was wagging his tongue like a fishwife. She wondered what else Suzu had told him.

"Even if he wasn't involved with the judges, I don't know why Genevieve would think she had a chance at the Pecker-Deadbird," Walter continued. "Her work is clearly post-modernist minimalism."

Astonishing, Jane thought. *It's as if he's been possessed by the spirit of a fifteen-year-old girl.*

"Oh," said Walter as he changed his shirt, "I also found out that Ryan was the reason Sam didn't get the teaching position at Columbia. She asked him to write her a letter of recommendation—you know, because they worked together on that project in Charleston—and he did. Only it wasn't at all flattering. He totally threw her under the bus."

"Suzu told you this too?" Jane asked.

Walter shook his head. "No. Sam did. She had a couple of glasses of champagne and started talking."

Aha, Jane thought. *He's rambling because he had a little too much to drink. That explains it.*

She was still searching for the clown doll. It had to be there somewhere. *Clown dolls don't just get up and walk away,* she thought as she checked behind one of the room's two chairs.

"You should have heard Bergen at lunch," said Walter. "He was telling the filthiest jokes. There was one about three plumbers, a goat, and a bottle of—"

"Bergen?" Jane said. "Bergen Faust?"

"Bergen *Faust,*" Walter said, as if there were two of them. "The guy is hysterical. Hang on. Let me remember how it goes. Okay, so these three carpenters are hired to build a barn. And one of them has a rash, so he has to put liniment on it three times a day." He stopped and looked at Jane with a bewildered expression. "Or maybe it's the goat that has the rash. Anyway, they all end up—"

"Yes, yes, yes," Jane said, holding up her hand. "I've heard it before."

She had not heard it before, and didn't want to hear it now, but thankfully this shut Walter up. At least momentarily. He very quickly moved on.

"Another thing about Bergen—he had a beef with McGuinness too."

"Really?" Jane said. She was much more interested in this line of conversation. "What kind of beef?"

"McGuinness stole a commission from him," said Walter. "I forget what. A shoe museum or something."

"Shoe museum?" Jane said. "Who would want to build a shoe museum?"

"They have one for chewing gum," said Walter. "In Minsk, I think. Why not shoes?"

"Why not, indeed," Jane replied. "It sounds as though Ryan McGuinness was quite the topic of conversation today."

"Not really," Walter said. "His name just came up a couple of times. By the way, what are you looking for?"

Jane put the cover back on the ice bucket. "The Pierrot," she said. "The clown doll," she added when Walter looked at her blankly. "Remember?"

"No," Walter said. "I don't think you mentioned it."

Jane started to ask him how he could possibly have forgotten, when something occurred to her. *He's been glamored*, she thought. *That explains the chattering and the forgetfulness. But who glamored him?*

"Walter," she said, "did you happen to run into anyone on your way up here?"

"Not that I recall," Walter said. "Why? Are you expecting someone?"

"What's the last thing you remember doing?" asked Jane.

Walter thought for a moment. "I remember getting in the elevator," he said. "And then I came into the room."

"Good," Jane said. "Now, was there anybody in the elevator with you?"

Walter thought for a moment. "Now that you mention it, there was. But I can't remember who. Probably just some other guests. Why?"

"No reason," Jane answered. "I was just curious. By the way, how do your teeth feel?"

Walter ran his tongue over his teeth. "Now that you mention it, they feel a little tingly. Must be that toothpaste the hotel puts in the bathrooms. Who knows what's in French toothpaste, right?" He laughed, sounding slightly mad.

There was no new toothpaste. The tube Walter had been using was the one Jane had packed from their own bathroom back home. The tingling sensation was one of the symptoms of having been glamored. There was no doubt in Jane's mind—there was another vampire in the hotel, and he had gotten to Walter.

Joshua, she thought. *I'd bet my fangs he's the one who stole the Pierrot.*

It all made sense. After pretending to return to London, Joshua had been following them the whole time, letting Jane do all the work looking for Crispin's Needle. He'd waited until Jane found it—or until he *thought* Jane had found it—and then moved in to steal it. Only there were two things he hadn't counted on: first, that the Needle had either rusted away to nothing or been stolen, and second, that he would run into Walter as he fled the room. That's when he must have glamored him.

"You always were too clever by half," she said, as if Joshua could hear her.

By now he would have discovered that the Pierrot was empty. But would he know that it was because the Needle was gone, or would he assume that Jane still had it and had hidden it somewhere for safekeeping? Jane suspected the latter. And if Joshua thought that Jane still had the Needle, he was still a danger.

"Wow," Walter said. "My teeth are really buzzing now. It's like my mouth is full of bees."

Jane sighed. The glamor was wearing off. Next would come the pounding headache.

"We'll get you some aspirin on the way to dinner," Jane said as she picked up her purse. "And whatever you have for dinner, make sure it has lots of garlic in it."

Chapter 20

Tuesday: Venice

HALF AN HOUR INTO IT, JANE WAS REGRETTING THE GONDOLA RIDE. For one thing, the singing was annoying. For another, it looked like it might rain. But mostly she was irritated that Miriam had managed to sit between her and Walter, making what might otherwise have been a romantic affair merely a study in tedium. Lilith was sitting on Miriam's lap, and she was enjoying the experience only slightly more than Jane was.

"I hate Venice," Lilith said, although of course only Jane could hear her. "What moron thought it was a good idea to build a city in a lagoon?"

"They're Italian," Jane said. "They're all mad as a basket of rats."

"Who are you talking to?" asked Lucy, who was sitting behind Jane.

Jane had forgotten that she didn't need to speak aloud when communicating with Lilith. In fact, it was best if she didn't, as having a seemingly one-sided conversation with oneself was likely to bewilder anyone who—like Lucy—happened to overhear what was being said.

"She's lost her mind," Miriam said under her breath. "Someone should check *her* basket for rats."

"Don't make me pitch you into the canal, old woman," said Jane in a tone that only Miriam could hear. "Remember what happened to Katharine Hepburn when she fell in while filming *Summertime*." Jane bugged out one eye and twitched it, mimicking the results of the infection that supposedly plagued Hepburn for the rest of her life following her dunking.

Miriam turned her face away and pretended to look at something on the other side of the canal. Jane, pleased with herself, turned around. "Just having a chat with my dear mother-in-law," she said to Lucy, enjoying the way Miriam stiffened at the reference.

"Coming up you will see Ponte dei Sospiri," said the gondolier, who despite being named Napoleon was actually quite tall and very good-looking. "You will know it as the Bridge of Sighs, a name that was given to it by the famous poet Byron."

Jane rolled her eyes. *Enough with him already,* she thought. It was bad enough that they were staying at the Byron Hotel. She'd forgotten how much the Venetians considered him an adopted son of the city. *It's a good thing he's not here,* she told herself. *He'd be impossible to live with.*

"It's said that if lovers kiss beneath the Bridge of Sighs just at sunset, their love will be eternal," Napoleon informed them. He then glanced up at the sky. "If we wait a few minutes, we can put this to the test."

"That's all right," Miriam said loudly. "We don't need any of that."

"Just because nobody wants to kiss *you*," Jane murmured in her ear. She made kissing sounds just to be irritating. Miriam swatted her away as if fending off a mosquito.

"Listen to this," said Ben.

At a bookshop in a narrow street just off Piazza San Marco he had picked up a battered copy of Mark Twain's classic piece of travel writing, *The Innocents Abroad*. He had been reading them bits and pieces of it throughout the day, focusing, naturally, on the chapter devoted to Venice. It had become bothersome, but he was so enthusiastic about it that no one wanted to tell him to stop. Also, because he was a rabbi, there was a feeling that it would be too much like poking God with a stick.

"'The gondolier is a picturesque rascal for all he wears no satin harness, no plumed bonnet, no silken tights,'" Ben read. "'His attitude is stately; he is lithe and supple; all his movements are full of grace. When his long canoe, and his fine figure, towering from its high perch on the stern, are cut against the evening sky, they make a picture that is very novel and striking to a foreign eye.'"

Napoleon beamed as if Twain had written the words after having taken a ride in that very gondola. "Apart from calling such a fine craft a canoe, I can find no fault with that," he said.

"I love Twain," Walter said, surprising Jane. "He had such a wit."

"He did indeed," said Miriam. "Do you know what he said about Jane Austen?" She didn't wait for anyone to answer before continuing. "'Every time I read *Pride and Prejudice* I want to dig her up and beat her over the skull with her own shinbone.'"

Miriam laughed loudly, and Jane was horrified to hear Walter laugh along with her, although he didn't laugh nearly as loudly. Lucy, ever the true friend, remained silent, and Jane chose to believe that Ben did not join in the mockery because he found Twain's assessment rude and not because he was too busy reading Twain himself.

"How interesting that he said 'every time I read *Pride and Prejudice*,'" Jane remarked, keeping her temper in check. "If he really detested the book, I wouldn't think he'd want to read it ever again."

She saw Miriam open her mouth to rebut, and cut her off. "And of course *Pride and Prejudice* has outsold, well, all of

Twain's books combined, I would think." She smiled. "I imagine that would take a bit of the sting out of such a remark. If Austen was alive to hear it, of course."

"Do you know why Byron called this the Bridge of Sighs?" Napoleon asked, bringing the exchange to an end.

Jane spent the remainder of the ride rubbing her right foot against her left shinbone and wondering just how much damage it might do if applied to a head with the proper amount of force. She regretted not having heard of Twain's remark while he was still alive, so that she could have provided him with the opportunity to find out. She made a mental note to remove all of his books from her store when she got back, or at least to hide them in the stockroom so that people would be forced to ask for them. Customers seldom asked for anything; they either left when they didn't find what they were looking for or, more often, selected something else. Jane knew this because until Lucy had found out and made her stop, she'd kept any book by a Brontë in the back room as well, and generally suggested one of her own to anyone foolish enough to inquire about *Wuthering Heights* or *Jane Eyre*. (She made an exception for *The Tenant of Wildfell Hall*, keeping a single copy on the shelf out of curiosity to see what kind of person might buy it. So far, no one had.)

When the gondola ride ended, Jane clambered out and onto the dock, happy to be out of the narrow boat and away from Miriam. She was even more relieved to get back to the hotel and into the shower, where she spent a good long time washing away the feelings of irritation aroused by the afternoon's activities. By the time she got out she was looking forward to the rest of the night.

First to come was dinner, which promised to be excellent. She and Walter had been invited—along with Lucy, Ben, and the rest of Team Chumsley—to join Orsino at a restaurant he knew from having lived in Venice for several years. Miriam too had been invited, but to Jane's relief she had declined. Jane hadn't cared enough to ask her what other plans she might have, and Miriam had not offered any explanation.

Following dinner they were to attend a performance of *La Traviata*. But rather than sitting in the stuffy, albeit lovely, La Fenice they would be in the Palazzo Barbarigo Minotto, a fifteenth-century home in which operas were performed in the actual rooms of the palace, moving from room to room with each act. The idea thrilled Jane no end.

Fitting the occasion, Jane wore a strapless blue crushed velvet dress, with a beautiful vintage diamond and sapphire necklace. The jewels were paste, but no less wonderful for that, and when Jane looked at herself in the mirror she felt very elegant indeed. Her hair was up, and she had applied some blush to give her naturally pale skin a soft, pinkish glow.

"You're stunning," Walter said, coming up behind her and putting his hands round her waist. "I'm not sure I want anyone else seeing you tonight. They might fall in love."

"You're quite dashing yourself," said Jane.

"Aren't you going to be cold in that?" Walter asked. "It's freezing out there."

"I bought a cloak," Jane told him. "While you were taking a nap after lunch, Lucy and I did some shopping. Look."

She went to the closet and took out the cloak. Made from lightweight black wool, it fell all the way to her feet and had a hood that could be pulled up for protection from the elements or (Jane theorized) to create an aura of menace. It likely wouldn't keep one terribly warm in the event of truly inclement weather, but she didn't require it for that and so it was perfect.

"You look positively Venetian," Walter told her as she modeled her purchase.

"I thought it was nicer than my Paddington raincoat," Jane said.

They went downstairs, where they met up with Ben, Lucy, Chumsley, Sam, Brodie, and Orsino and proceeded to the restaurant. La Caverna Nascosta was, as its name implied, impossible to find if one wasn't accompanied by someone who knew the way. It was not on any lists of restaurants recommended for vacationers, and no amount of Googling or Binging would reveal its whereabouts. It had no sign.

Nor did it have menus. Having found it, diners were seated at a single large, round table in the middle of a beautiful dining room that was lit by dozens, if not hundreds, of candles. The windows of the room overlooked a canal, and the walls were frescoed with faded scenes from Roman mythology, not all of them appropriate for the prudish. Jane found them delightful.

Once seated, guests were brought dish after dish of delights, the menu created by the whims of the chef. *Sarde in saor* came out, the grilled sardines atop a bed of onions, pine nuts, and currants. This was accompanied by *polenta e schie* and *baccalà mantecato* spread on crostini. A creamy *risotto nero alle seppie*, rich with squid ink, was followed by *fegato alla veneziana, galletto alla brace, branzino del doge,* and *stinco di agnello brasato.*

As each dish arrived it was sent around the table to a chorus of delighted oohs and aahs. Forks and knives clinked against china, and much prosecco and amarone was drunk as glasses were quickly refilled by the attentive waitstaff. The conversation was lively, and all in all, Jane couldn't imagine a more delightful evening.

She was seated with Walter to one side and Sam to the other. She hadn't really had a chance to talk to Sam very much, and despite her initial wariness of the woman due to her connection to Walter, she found herself chatting easily with her.

"How are you getting along with Miriam?" Sam asked during the short period between the last dinner dish being swept away and the arrival of small dishes of *zabaglione* and plates of *baicoli, zaletti,* and *galani.*

Jane laughed. "How well do you know her?"

"Well enough to know what a bully she can be," Sam replied. "Did you know she tried to get Walter to marry me?"

"No!" Jane said. "Really?"

Sam nodded. "Oh, she really put the screws to him. Mind you, I'd only met her once, at a party for the opening of a building Walter and I worked on together. But apparently she decided I was going to be the new Mrs. Fletcher. She wouldn't stop nagging him about it."

Jane felt the fingers of jealousy tickling her. "Had you and Walter been dating long at that point?" she asked cautiously.

Sam smiled. "I don't think my girlfriend would have been too happy if anything like that had been going on," she said. "Well, she was my girlfriend then."

"I'm sorry," Jane said, enormously relieved. "I assume Miriam's behavior had nothing to do with the breakup?"

"Breakup?" Sam said, accepting a cup of espresso from a waiter.

"Your girlfriend," Jane said. "You said she was your girlfriend *then*."

"Oh," said Sam. "I meant that then she was my girlfriend. Now she's my wife. We got married in Massachusetts—gosh, almost eight years ago."

"Congratulations," Jane said, marveling at how the world had changed for the better since her time.

"Thank you," said Sam. "I can't believe it's been that long. Of course, I can't believe we have two boys either."

"Two?" Jane said.

Sam nodded. "Gus and Max," she said. "They're five. Twins. I have to remember to get them something before we leave tomorrow. Do you know where Miriam got that clown doll?"

Jane choked on a *galani*, spraying powdered sugar down the front of her dress. "Clown doll?" she said.

"She had one when I ran into her in the elevator as I was coming down to meet everyone tonight. It looked really old, but she said she had just bought it. Max and Gus love clowns, and I thought a doll like that would make a great present. I was going to ask her where she got it, but she seemed to be in a hurry to get wherever she was going."

Jane was seized by a sudden panic. "Was it black and white?" she asked.

"That's the one," said Sam. "Do you know where she got it?"

"I'm afraid not," Jane said. "But I'll be sure to ask her. Will you excuse me a moment?"

She turned to Walter. "Sweetie, I'm having a bit of heartburn. I'm going to run back to the hotel and take something. You go ahead to the opera and I'll meet you there."

"I'll come with you," Walter said, just as Jane knew he would.

"Aren't you sweet?" she said, kissing his cheek. "But I'll be fine. You finish your espresso."

She left before he could object again. Fortunately, the hotel wasn't that far away, and she made it there in under ten minutes. She took the elevator to the third floor and strode briskly to Miriam's door.

As she raised her hand to knock she heard a commotion from inside. Then Lilith's voice was in her head.

"Let me out of here!"

Jane tried the knob and found the door unlocked. Pushing it open she saw Miriam on the bed. Straddling her was Bergen. His mouth was on her neck. The sound of Lilith's barking came from the bathroom, where apparently she had been locked in. Bergen turned his head and looked at Jane. His eyes were wild, and he hissed at her.

Bergen's the vampire? Jane thought vaguely as she tried to figure out what to do. *That's unexpected.*

Bergen leapt off the bed and ran at her. Jane, acting on instinct, hauled off and punched him as hard as she could in the face. Her fist connected with Bergen's nose, there was a disturbing yet satisfying crunch, and the little man fell backward. He stared at Jane for a moment, blood just starting to drip from his nose, then collapsed.

"Quick!" Jane said to Miriam. "Get me a stake!"

Miriam, who was getting up from the bed, said. "Don't be stupid. He's not a vampire."

"But he was biting you!" Jane said.

Miriam patted her hair. "Actually, he was kissing me," she said.

"That's even worse!" said Jane.

"I was trying to find out who he's working for," Miriam said.

"Working for?" Jane said. "What are you talking about?"

Miriam poked Bergen with her toe. He remained still. She looked at Jane. "You really are the worst vampire I've ever met. Can't you recognize a familiar when you see one?"

Jane looked at Bergen. She remembered what Walter had said about the odd man reminding him of Renfield, Dracula's bug-eating assistant.

"Whose familiar is he?"

Miriam sat on the end of the bed and sighed. "That's what I was trying to find out," she said, "before you barged in here. What are you doing here, anyway?"

Jane, remembering why she'd come, stood up. "That's right," she said. "Before we talk about what to do with Mr. Faust here, you've got some explaining to do."

The sound of wild scratching distracted her. It was coming from the bathroom. "Oh, right," Jane said. "But first you should probably let Lilith out."

Chapter 21

Tuesday: Venice

> *Libiam libiamo, ne' lieti calici,*
> *che la bellezza infiora;*
> *e la fuggevol fuggevol'ora*
> *s'inebrii a voluttà.*
> *Libiam ne' dolci fremiti*
> *che suscita l'amore,*
> *poiché quell'occhio al core*
> *onnipotente va.*
> *Libiamo, amore; amor fra i calici*
> *più caldi baci avrà.*

ALFREDO LIFTED HIS GLASS AS HIS VOICE FILLED THE *PORTEGO* OF the Palazzo Barbarigo Minotto with the opening lines of his famous drinking song. The small group of listeners, now understanding their role in the night's performance, lifted their own glasses in return.

"Very clever," Jane whispered to Walter, who stood beside her. "We're not only the audience, we're the guests at Violetta's party."

Walter sipped his glass of champagne. "It's too bad my mother has a stomachache," he said. "She would love this."

Jane said nothing. She felt terrible about the lie she'd told Walter. But Miriam had insisted on interrogating Bergen herself. She'd ordered Jane to go to the opera and make an excuse for her absence. A stomachache had seemed the easiest explanation, and so Jane had invented a bad oyster and the resulting digestive distress to explain her mother-in-law's failure to appear.

She was still unclear on several points regarding the night's events, and as the performers continued to toast the joys of friendship and love, Jane went over again what she knew and did not know. She had gone to Miriam's room assuming that Miriam was the one who had stolen the Pierrot from her room in Paris. Miriam, however, had not taken it. She had found it, she said, sitting on the floor of the elevator at the hotel just moments before Sam had gotten on and seen her holding it. Assuming this was true—and Jane had no reason to think that it wasn't—the identity of the real thief remained a mystery.

Then there was the matter of Bergen. Miriam continued to insist that she had lured Bergen to her room with the promise of a tryst. The very notion filled Jane with a horror beyond imagining. She tried very hard not to remember seeing Bergen kissing Miriam's neck, but of course, having thought about it, it was all she *could* think about. She shuddered and drank some more champagne, hoping its intoxicating effects would dim the disturbing image.

What she didn't fully understand was why Miriam had suspected Bergen of having nefarious intentions in the first place. That he was a vampire's familiar was, frankly, not surprising. From a casting point of view he was perfect for the role in every possible way. Which was probably why it had never occurred to Jane to seriously entertain the thought that that's exactly what he was.

Miriam, though, had suspected something. *Of course, she suspects* everyone *of something,* Jane reminded herself. Still, she couldn't help but be reluctantly impressed. It had been a brave move to invite Bergen to her room, and it could have ended very badly for her. Jane hated to think, for several reasons, what might have transpired had she not arrived when she did. Miriam had promised to explain her suspicions later, and Jane was looking forward to that conversation.

The primary question, though, was who Bergen's master or mistress was. Naturally, being a vampire's familiar required having a vampire, otherwise the role was nothing more than a pretentious affectation. And where Bergen was concerned there were a number of possibilities. Jane's immediate assumption was that he was working with Joshua. That made the most sense, as it allowed him to gather information without having to expose himself to possible discovery. But the more she thought about it the more she realized that she couldn't rule out the Tedious Three, Charlotte, or really any other vampire in existence. If Gosebourne knew about the Needle, there was every reason to suspect that a lot of other vampires did as well, and while many of them would write it off as a legend, many would not. And the easiest way to get it would be to keep an eye on Jane, wait for her to find Crispin's Needle, and then take it.

Returning to the matter of the stolen doll, she again considered various explanations. Certainly Bergen could have broken into her room and taken the clown. Really, that made the most sense. But Jane was troubled by the fact that Walter had clearly been glamored. Her assumption was that he had interrupted the thief in the act and had been glamored to make him forget what he'd seen. But Bergen was human and would have no glamoring ability. A vampire had to be involved. And *that* meant that whoever Bergen was working for, she or he was nearby, or at least had been as recently as their time in Paris.

She hoped that Miriam was getting to the bottom of these matters at that very moment and that there would be news when they returned. In the meantime, she tried to enjoy the opera. When the first act ended the entire party moved into the Sala

Tiepolo, so named because it featured glorious frescoes done by the artist of that name. It was the perfect setting for Violetta to be miserable in, and the soprano worked both her voice and the gilded furnishings with great success. By the time it came to move into the *camera da letto* for Act Three and Violetta's inevitable tragic end, Jane had almost forgotten about Bergen and Miriam. Despite being very familiar with the libretto, she found herself hoping that this time Violetta would rally, marry Alfredo, and live happily for the rest of her life.

But of course she didn't. People in operas seldom do. And so they watched, tears in their eyes, as Violetta rose from her bed for one last duet with Alfredo and then expired. To preserve the mood of the evening, the audience was escorted out while Alfredo remained weeping over the corpse of his beloved. It was all very tragic and wonderful, and Jane exited into the Venetian night with a strong impulse to throw herself off a tower, or perhaps drink some poison.

The rest of the party, however, was more inclined to drink espresso, and so off they went to a coffee bar. Not wanting to call undue attention to herself by once more claiming heartburn or fatigue, Jane went along. Miriam would be fine for another hour or so, she figured, and as it was their last night in Venice, she wanted to enjoy it as much as possible.

Seated next to Lucy at the table, she told her friend as much as she could about the night's events. Lucy listened, her eyes getting wider with every new detail. Thankfully, Walter and Ben were engaged in a conversation with Brodie about the architectural details of the Palazzo Barbarigo Minotto, and Brodie's booming voice drowned out the sounds of Jane and Lucy's conversation.

"So you don't think Our Gloomy Friend is behind it?" Lucy said.

"I really don't," said Jane. "For one thing, I think she likes being undead. I don't know why she would want the Needle."

Lucy thought for a moment. "Maybe she doesn't," she said. "Maybe the Needle has nothing to do with it."

"How so?" Jane asked.

"Think about it," said Lucy. "Ever since we got here, one thing after another has gotten in the way of your wedding. First your husband shows up."

"*Technically* he's my husband," Jane reminded her.

"Then Ryan McGuinness is killed and all fingers point at you," Lucy continued.

"I'd forgotten that bit," said Jane.

"And we're fairly certain a vampire is behind that," Lucy continued.

"Oh, and there's Walter's glamoring," said Jane. "But honestly, apart from Joshua showing up and Ryan getting thrown off the keep, nothing else has happened."

"What else *could* happen?" Lucy said. "And it's only been five days since Ryan was killed."

"Is that all?" said Jane, surprised. "It seems like ages ago."

"My guess is that there's something big coming," Lucy said.

"But why would Our Gloomy Friend care if Walter and I get married?" Jane asked. "It doesn't affect her one bit."

"Why does she have to have a reason?" said Lucy. "Maybe she just wants to see you be as miserable as she is."

Jane sniffed. "That would be just like her," she said. "That whole family was obsessed with being unhappy. No wonder it rains so much in their books."

"Who else would want to put a stop to your wedding?" Lucy asked.

"Miriam," Jane said instantly. "But she wouldn't do anything as extreme as killing someone. At least I don't think she would. It seems a bit much, even for her."

"I agree," said Lucy. "Which brings us back to Our Gloomy Friend."

"I still don't know about that," Jane said. "Whoever it is, he or she has been hanging around during the entire trip. Frankly, I don't believe Charlotte is clever enough to keep herself hidden for that long."

"Even if Bergen was doing all the dirty work?" Lucy asked.

"She's too vain," Jane said. "I just can't see her being content to hide in the shadows."

Lucy sighed. "You vampires and your need to be the center of attention," she said. "For creatures of the night, you certainly do like the spotlight."

Jane looked at her watch. "It's almost midnight," she said. "We should be getting back. Maybe Miriam has gotten some more information out of Bergen."

She waited until there was a break in the conversation the others were having, then suggested to Walter that they return to the hotel. He was only too happy to oblige, and half an hour later they were back in their room. Jane had removed her evening wear and slipped into a decidedly unglamorous pair of sweatpants and a sweatshirt. Walter was in bed, reading.

"I'm just going to pop in and check on your mother," Jane said. "See if she needs anything."

Walter raised one eyebrow. "Really?" he said.

"You sound skeptical," Jane said.

Walter laughed. "I *am* skeptical," he replied.

"For heaven's sake," said Jane. "You make it sound as if I slipped her that oyster myself."

Walter grunted and returned to his book.

"What's that supposed to mean?" Jane asked.

"Absolutely nothing," said Walter, still reading. "Tell Mother I said I hope she sleeps well."

"I will," Jane said, opening the door and going out into the hall. As she walked to Miriam's room she congratulated herself on having played things just so. *I really do make a convincing concerned daughter-in-law,* she thought. *Well, a semi-convincing one, at any rate.*

When she reached Miriam's room she rapped three times on the door. When there was no answer she knocked again. And when there was still no answer, she tried the handle. She experienced a moment of déjà vu as, for the second time that night, the door opened easily. Only this time there was no one on the bed. The room was empty.

She went inside.

"Miriam?" she called softly.

When there was no answer she looked in all of the usual places—the closet, the bathroom, under the bed—that a body, dead or alive, might be concealed. She found nothing. Nor was there any sign of a struggle. In fact, the room was as neat as if it had just received maid service.

That's when Jane realized that not only was Miriam gone, so was her luggage. There were no suitcases, no toiletry bags, no clothes thrown over the back of the chair or tossed carelessly on the floor. No Lilith or her carrying case. It was as if Miriam had never been there at all.

Where on earth could she have gone? Jane wondered. *And why?*

Clearly, something had happened. The most obvious answer was that Bergen had overpowered Miriam and done her a mischief. Really, it was the *only* answer. Miriam would never have just allowed Bergen to go free. And Jane doubted very much that she would have taken off without so much as a note for Walter.

But what was Jane to do? She could hardly tell Walter that his mother had been kidnapped by a vampire's familiar. Nor did she have any idea where to start looking for Miriam and her captor. For all she knew, Miriam was dead. She was surprised, and a little relieved, to find that this idea saddened her.

She picked up the phone and dialed Lucy and Ben's room. When Lucy answered Jane said, "We have a problem. Miriam is gone. Can you come down here?"

"Of course I have that book you wanted," Lucy said. "I'll bring it right down."

"Good girl," said Jane, knowing Lucy had just given herself an alibi that Ben would not question.

She hung up. Not two minutes later Lucy knocked on the door. Jane opened it.

"Wow," Lucy said when she'd looked around the room. "She's not just gone, she's *gone.*"

"We have to figure out what we're going to tell Walter," Jane said.

"Well, obviously we can't tell him the truth," said Lucy. "So we'll have to stall. Tell him she's still not feeling well and wants to be left alone."

"But we're leaving for Switzerland in"—Jane looked at her watch—"less than fourteen hours."

"At least it gives us some time to think," said Lucy. "He won't expect to see her until breakfast, and with a little luck we can put him off even longer while we look for Miriam."

"I should never have left her alone with Bergen," Jane said. "But she insisted."

"She's a vampire hunter," Lucy reminded her. "She's dealt with things a lot worse than Bergen."

"Good point," said Jane. "I really shouldn't blame myself. None of this is my fault."

"Well, that's not exactly true," Lucy said. "It's a little bit your fault."

"Some friend you are," Jane said.

"You know it's true," said Lucy.

Jane sighed. "Yes, I suppose I do," she said. "Still, you needn't remind me."

"You'd better get back to Walter. He's going to wonder why you've been gone so long. Make sure you tell him Miriam is feeling worse. But don't overdo it. We don't want him coming down here to check on her. Do you think you can do that?"

Jane nodded.

"Good," Lucy said. "Oh, should we check Bergen's room?"

Jane shook her head. "That would be too obvious," she said. "Wherever they are, I'd bet anything they aren't in the hotel."

"Then I guess there's nothing else we can do tonight," said Lucy. "At least not without causing more trouble. So try to get some rest. Maybe we'll think of something during the night."

"And if we don't?" Jane asked.

Lucy looked at her. "If we don't, you'll be explaining to Walter how his vampire hunter mother disappeared while interrogating a familiar."

Jane turned out the lights and followed Lucy into the hall.

"You're really quite horrid. You know that, don't you?" Jane said.

Lucy turned and smiled at her. "I love you too," she said. "Now get back to your little Indian."

"My what?"

"Your little Indian," Lucy repeated. "Remember, the Agatha Christie novel?"

"I'd forgotten all about that," said Jane. "Yes, I'll get back to my little Indian. Good night."

While Lucy took the stairs to the next floor, Jane walked back to her room. As she did she found herself humming the rhyme about the ten little Indians. She couldn't remember all of it, but one verse came to her.

"'Four little Indian boys going out to sea,'" she sang. "'A red herring swallowed one and then there were three.'"

She stopped just as she reached the door to her room. An idea was forming in her head. She stood very still, allowing it room to grow. Then she laughed lightly. *Oh, Agatha,* she thought. *You are a clever old bird.*

Suddenly she couldn't wait for the morning.

Chapter 22

Wednesday: Venice

"GOOD MORNING," JANE SAID PLEASANTLY AS SHE WALKED INTO the hotel dining room.

"Good morning," Chumsley called out. "Come and sit by me, my dear girl."

"Thank you, but no," Jane replied. "I have something to say, and I would prefer to do it standing."

Walter, who had come down a few minutes before Jane (she had purposely arranged it that way), set down the glass of orange juice in his hand and looked at her. Jane avoided his gaze.

They were all of them staring at her now, some with expressions of curiosity, some with expressions of annoyance, and some with no expressions whatsoever. Jane stood for a moment in silence, letting the tension build, then announced, "I know the identity of the murderer of Ryan McGuinness."

Genevieve, who was eating a croissant, set it down. "Are you confessing?" she asked.

"No, I am not confessing," Jane snapped. "I am identifying."

"And what makes you think you know who the murderer is?" said Enid. She was holding an egg cup and, with a spoon, was poking with great determination at the soft-boiled egg inside it.

"We'll get to that," Jane replied. "In the meantime, Lucy and Ben, would you please shut and guard the doors leading out of this room?"

This too had been prearranged, just in case the guilty party tried to make a run for it. Lucy and Ben walked quickly to the doors on either side of the room and closed them. They then took up positions in front of them, their arms crossed and frightful scowls on their faces. Lucy had suggested they wear sunglasses so as to look more like Secret Service agents, but Jane had dismissed the idea as too gimmicky.

"You're locking us in?" said Chumsley. He looked at Walter, who shrugged.

"If you look around you," Jane said, "you will notice that one member of our party is not here."

Everyone looked about, taking inventory.

"Miriam isn't here," Sam said.

"She's not feeling well," Walter told her. "A bad oyster."

"There was no bad oyster," Jane informed him. "And I wasn't referring to Miriam, as she isn't technically a member of the party."

"What do you mean there was no bad oyster?" Walter asked. "I thought you said—"

"It's Bergen," said Genevieve, interrupting. "Bergen isn't here." The tone in her voice suggested that she expected some kind of reward for having guessed correctly, like perhaps a gold star or a piece of candy.

"Is Bergen the murderer?" Orsino said.

"I knew it!" Brodie declared, banging his hand on the table so that the coffee cups rattled. "It's always a German!"

"Strong words coming from an Australian," Enid said. "Your country was founded by criminals, as I recall."

"Like the Scots are any better," said Chumsley, snorting. "Woad-faced skirt-wearers."

"Just because Ryan was a better lover than you ever were—" Enid began.

Chumsley stood up. "Let me tell you something about how good a lover he was—"

"Shut up!" Jane yelled. "You're ruining everything!"

All eyes turned to her.

"Sit *down*!" she ordered. "Now!" she added when Chumsley didn't move quickly enough.

When everyone was seated she took a breath. "Now then, let's start over, shall we? And please, no more interruptions until I'm finished."

Walter raised his hand.

"Yes, darling?" Jane said.

"I was wondering if, before you begin, you could tell me what's happened to my mother?"

"Of course," Jane replied. "I'm fairly certain that she's been kidnapped by Bergen."

A chorus of voices erupted as everyone began to speak at once. Jane picked up a teaspoon and banged it against the side of a chafing dish filled with sausages. The cacophony ceased.

"I'm afraid that's all I know at present," Jane told Walter. "But I have every reason to believe that she's safe. At least for the moment."

"Then Bergen *is* the murderer?" Sam asked.

Jane shook her head. "No," she said. "Bergen is the murderer's assistant."

"Then who *is* the murderer?" said Genevieve.

"A very good question," Jane answered. "As everyone is aware, initially I was considered by some to be the most likely suspect."

"And you're not now?" Enid said.

"Perhaps in the minds of some," said Jane. "But that will soon be cleared up, as I intend to unmask the murderer in a few moments."

She looked around, waiting for someone to leap up. She half hoped someone would, as it would confirm her suspicion. But she was also rather pleased that no one did, as she was enjoying herself.

"Almost everyone in this room had a reason to despise Ryan McGuinness," she began. "Except you, Walter. Of course you're not the murderer."

"But I didn't like him," Walter said. "I thought he was a jerk."

"That's not generally a strong enough reason for wanting to fling someone from the top of a tower," Jane said. "However, there are people here who do have very good reasons for wishing ill will on Ryan McGuinness."

She turned to Enid.

"Let's begin with you," she said. "We all know that you and Ryan were lovers."

Enid nodded. "Which makes it highly unlikely that I would want him dead," she said, rolling her eyes. "Any child should be able to see that."

"Except that you had reason to believe he might be seeing someone else," Jane said. "Isn't that right?"

Enid shrugged. "I might have heard some things," she admitted.

"But what you didn't know was that the other object of Ryan's affections was"—she swung around and pointed at Chumsley—"your ex-husband."

A collective gasp went up from the table. Chumsley threw down his napkin. "Who told you that?" he said.

"I saw you coming out of Ryan's compartment on the train to Pembroke," Jane said. "At first I thought you were telling him to stay away from Enid." She glanced at Enid. "But the notion that you were still in love with her made no sense. Then Orsino mentioned having had an affair with Ryan before Ryan took up with Enid."

Orsino looked deeply into his coffee cup as everyone turned their attention in his direction.

"That's when it made sense," Jane continued. "You weren't warning him away from Enid because you wanted her, you were telling him to stay away from her because you wanted him all to yourself. Isn't that right?"

Chumsley reddened. "I didn't kill him!" he said.

"No," Jane said, nodding. "You didn't. And neither did Enid."

"So it was Orsino, the jilted lover!" Genevieve cried. She was sitting next to Orsino, and now she leaned away from him, her eyes wide.

"It was *not*!" said Orsino.

"Was it?" Brodie asked Jane.

Jane didn't answer. Instead she moved on, standing behind Sam.

"Love is only one avenue to murder," she said. "There are many others. Revenge, for instance. Sam, it must have made you very angry to learn that Ryan was the reason you didn't get that teaching job."

Before Sam could respond, Jane continued. "And Genevieve, you think he unfairly won a prize that you deserved to have."

Genevieve tore a croissant in half but said nothing.

"Brodie, he stole your design idea when you were in school," Jane said. "And then there's the small matter of his having stolen Bergen's commission for the shoe museum."

"And now we're back to Bergen," said Enid. "I think it's clear to everyone here that of all of us he's the most likely suspect, particularly if, as you claim, he's absconded with Walter's mother."

"I agree that that would be the most likely explanation," Jane said. "But then I asked myself, what would Agatha Christie do?"

"Agatha Christie?" said Orsino. "What has she got to do with this?"

"Oh, nothing directly," Jane answered. "But I assume you've all read her at some point, yes?"

All around the table heads nodded.

"And what's the most maddening thing about an Agatha Christie novel?" she asked.

There was a long silence. Finally Enid said, "She always withholds key bits of information."

"Exactly!" Jane said. "In every Agatha Christie novel there's always a scene in which the murderer is revealed, and it always involves the person who has solved the murder informing everyone that Mrs. So-and-so is really the daughter of the maid whom the victim treated unkindly thirty years before, resulting in her family's descent into poverty, or that the young man who spends every day reading by the pool isn't a nice young man at all but an alcoholic gambler with designs on the victim's diamond brooch."

"That always annoyed me," said Sam. "You could never figure out who the murderer was because it could be any of them, and Christie never gave you all the clues you needed to figure out which one it was."

Murmurs of agreement rippled around the table.

Jane cleared her throat. "I'm not done yet," she said. "There's something else about Christie's novels that is a bit predictable, and that is the character who is largely invisible throughout the book but who then becomes enormously important at the end. In fact, you can often identify the murderer simply by looking at who gets the least amount of time in the story."

"In our case that would be Genevieve," Orsino said.

"I beg your pardon?" said Genevieve.

"I'm sorry, but it's true," said Orsino. "I've barely seen you at all this trip."

"You're just trying to get back at me because you think I called you a murderer!" Genevieve said.

She started speaking in rapid-fire French. Orsino responded in equally rapid and equally loud Italian. Jane put her fingers in her mouth and gave an ear-piercing whistle. This stopped their bickering.

"Although Genevieve has indeed contributed little in the way of conversation during our excursions, it is not she to whom I am referring."

As she spoke she moved quietly around the table, until she was standing just behind the chair of her prime suspect. She smiled triumphantly. "Ladies and gentlemen, I give you our murderess."

"Suzu?" Sam said as they all stared at the diminutive professor.

"I'd forgotten all about her," said Brodie.

"Well, the poor thing almost never speaks," added Genevieve.

"What makes you think it's her?" Enid asked. "What motive does she have?"

"None that I know of," said Jane. "Which according to the rules of every Agatha Christie novel I've ever read means that she *must* be the guilty party."

Suzu remained motionless as they discussed her. She said nothing, sitting with her hands folded in her lap.

"We really don't know anything about her," Orsino said.

"Now that you mention it, Bergen was the one who suggested I invite her," said Enid. "I'd never heard of her before."

"Exactly," Jane said. "She masterminded this from the beginning."

"Wait a minute," Genevieve said. "Suzu was standing with us at the bottom of the tower when Ryan fell. How do you explain that?"

"Oh, that," said Jane. "Well, she's a vam . . . "

Unfortunately, she hadn't quite gotten this far when imagining how the big reveal would go. Now that she was there, she realized that there was one big question she wasn't going to be able to answer.

"Yes, Jane," Suzu said in a calm, even voice. "How do you explain that?"

Jane looked down. Suzu was looking up at her, not smiling.

Her dark eyes flashed anger, and Jane could sense that more than anything Suzu wanted to destroy her.

At least I know I'm right, she thought as she searched frantically for words—any words at all.

"And she's hardly big enough to fling a cat," said Brodie. "How could she hurl a great big thing like McGuinness over a four-foot-high wall?"

Then Jane heard a sound that made her heart shrink to the size of a pea. It was laughter. It started at one end of the table, where Enid was grinning and pointing at Jane, and then it seemed to roll like a great, sweeping wave toward the chair in which Suzu sat with Jane behind her.

"Stop it!" Jane shouted.

But they didn't. They only laughed harder and louder. All except Walter, who sat looking at Jane with a perplexed look on his face.

Jane wanted to die. She couldn't even muster the energy to try again. Then, beneath the laughter, she heard Suzu speaking to her. Only it was more like the way Lilith spoke to her, the words forming in her mind instead of reaching her ears.

"It took you long enough to figure me out," Suzu said. "But of course, as you now realize, you can't make them believe you. They think you're insane."

"Where has Bergen taken Miriam?" Jane asked.

"Don't worry," Suzu said. "She's not dead. Yet. I'll return her when you give me the Needle."

"I don't have the Needle," Jane said. "I don't think it even exists."

"Nice try," said Suzu. "I've seen the doll. Just give the Needle to me."

"I just told you, I don't have it," Jane said. "There was nothing inside the doll."

"Then you'd better find it," Suzu told her.

The laughter had died down now, and the people around the

table were looking at Jane, waiting for her to say something. Before she could speak there was a knocking at the door. Lucy looked at Jane, who shrugged. There was no reason to keep it locked now.

Lucy opened the door and a girl wearing the shirt of a hotel employee came in. She walked over to Walter and handed him an envelope.

"Your mother asked us to deliver this to you at nine-thirty this morning," she said.

Walter took the envelope. "When did she leave it at the desk?"

"Last night, I believe," the girl said.

"Thank you," Walter said as he opened the envelope and removed a single piece of paper. He scanned it, then cleared his throat and began reading.

> Dear Walter:
>
> Since your father and I divorced I've been looking for a man who understands me and loves me for who I am. I've found that man in Bergen Faust. I know this will come as a surprise, but I want you to know that we are very much in love.
>
> Bergen and I are going away to spend some time together alone. We don't even know where we're going. We're just getting a car and driving where our hearts take us. But don't worry, we won't do anything foolish. I'll let you know in a few days where we are.
>
> Love,
> Mom

"Well, that explains that," Enid said.

"It does not!" said Jane. "It's obviously a forgery!"

Walter held the letter up. "It's her handwriting," he said.

"They made her write it," Jane insisted.

"Jane, you know as well as I do that nobody makes my mother do anything she doesn't want to do," Walter said.

"I think you should apologize to Suzu," said Genevieve.

Suzu stood up. "There's no need," she said. "Jane meant no offense, I'm sure."

"She accused you of being a murderer," said Enid.

"Jane is a writer," Suzu said, her voice still soft and light. "Perhaps her imagination simply ran away with her."

Everyone looked at Jane. She felt the weight of their stares. Suzu was lying. She *was* a murderer. But there was no way anybody was going to believe her. No one except Lucy, anyway, and that wasn't enough.

She was beaten.

"Yes," she said. "Perhaps it did. I'm very sorry."

Suzu touched her arm gently. "We won't speak of it again."

She left the room. Jane, not knowing what else to do, went and sat down beside Walter. "I feel like such a fool," she said.

"Can hardly blame you for that," said Brodie, who was seated across from her. "But it was very entertaining."

"And you weren't wrong about all of us having reasons for wanting Ryan dead," Sam added kindly.

"Especially you, eh, Chumsley?" Brodie called out. He chuckled. "Who knew you had it in you, you old dog?"

"Yes," Chumsley said. "Well." He glanced at Enid, who glared at him and stomped out of the room.

"At least we know where my mother is," said Walter. "Well, sort of."

"But *Bergen*?" Sam said. "No offense, but ick."

"I'm just happy she's found someone," said Walter.

Jane wanted to shake him and ask him if he really thought Miriam would run off with someone like Bergen. But she didn't. She'd caused enough trouble for one morning. She was surprised any of them were speaking to her at all, especially after she'd aired their dirty laundry. Walter looked at his watch. "We're supposed to meet in front of the hotel in fifteen minutes to go to today's house," he said.

"I don't think anyone wants me to come," Jane said.

Walter smiled. "I do," he said. "But you don't have to if you don't want to."

Jane didn't want to. In fact, it was the last thing she wanted to do. Not only would she have to be around all of the people in front of whom she'd embarrassed herself, she would have to be around Suzu. Now that her suspicions about the woman were confirmed, she was determined to find out who she was and why she was so anxious to get her hands on Crispin's Needle. She couldn't do that if Suzu was watching her.

On the other hand, she can't do anything while you're watching her, she thought.

She smiled at Walter. "I can't imagine anything better than spending the day with you," she said. "I'll go get my coat."

Chapter 23

Thursday: Geneva

THE PEUGEOT HUGGED THE CURVE OF THE ROAD AS WALTER AC-
celerated, causing the car to shoot forward when it came to the
straightaway. Jane, looking out the window, watched as the moun-
tains opened up and the car descended into the Val d'Aosta. The
late afternoon sun had burned away most of the fog, and the
glacier-fed waters of the Dora Baltea turned it into a silvery rib-
bon that wound back and forth across the landscape.

A bus had been arranged to take the group from Venice to
Geneva, but Walter had suggested to Jane that they rent a car
and drive on their own. That way they would be able to stop if
they wanted to. Also, it would give them some time alone.

It was the time alone that worried Jane. Following the debacle
of her unmasking of Ryan McGuinness's murderer, she might be
expected to relish being away from those she had offended,
amused, or both. But being alone with Walter was also problem-
atic, as it meant she couldn't avoid discussing either her seemingly erratic behavior or his mother's disappearance.

They had discussed the latter subject during the first two
hours of the trip. Walter accepted the explanation—provided by

the letter allegedly written by Miriam and left for him at the desk of the Byron Hotel—that his mother had run off with Bergen Faust, and Jane chose not to disabuse him of this notion. Things were actually made easier for her by Walter's belief that his mother was simply off on a romantic adventure, as it gave Jane more time to figure out her next move.

The second two hours of the journey had been spent talking about the scenery, the various buildings they'd seen, and the charms of European cities in general. Now, as the final third of the trip began, Jane felt it was time to address the topic they had both been avoiding.

"You're probably wondering what got into me this morning," she began.

"I haven't the faintest idea what you're talking about," Walter said.

"Oh, good," said Jane. "Then just forget I said anything."

Walter laughed. "Somehow I don't think you'll let me off that easy."

"Excuse me," Jane said. "But *I'm* the one who has to provide an explanation."

"And I'm the one who has to listen to it," said Walter.

Jane wasn't sure if she should be relieved or offended by his tone, but she chose to believe that Walter was joking with her. This made her want to be open and honest with him, and so she decided to be as truthful as she could be.

"It's all Lucy's fault," she said, her resolve crumbling before the first word had left her mouth. "She had me thinking all kinds of crazy things. You know how she is."

"Uh-huh," Walter said.

"What?" said Jane.

"Lucy had *you* thinking all kinds of crazy things?" Walter said. "Pardon me for suggesting such a thing, but is it possible that it's actually the other way around?"

"What are you implying?" Jane asked.

"I'm implying that you're the one whose imagination occasionally gets the better of her," said Walter.

"It does not!" Jane objected. A moment later she said, "Well, perhaps once or twice."

"Yes, once or twice," Walter agreed.

Jane sighed. "I don't know how you can put up with me."

"Because I love you," Walter said. "If I got upset every time you did something odd, I would have given up years ago. But I've gotten used to it."

"You get *used* to ugly carpeting," Jane said huffily. "And Jennifer Aniston's new haircut. You make it sound as though I need to be *endured*."

"Are you saying that you *want* me to be disturbed by your behavior?" asked Walter.

"Of course not," Jane replied, wondering how the conversation had gone so horribly wrong.

"Look," said Walter. "I don't always know what goes on in that head of yours. And yes, on occasion you do things that are, well, unusual. But that's what makes you who you are, and I wouldn't want you to be any other way."

"All right then," Jane said. "And thank you."

"You're welcome," Walter said.

"I'm probably going to get odder, you know," Jane told him.

"I'll be surprised if you don't," said Walter.

Jane looked at him. "What's that supposed to mean?"

"And here we go," Walter said.

Half an hour later they passed Courmayeur, entered the Mont Blanc Tunnel, and emerged in France. Another hour brought them to Geneva, and then they were driving up a long, narrow road. Jane, who had been napping, awoke when she felt the car stop. She opened her eyes and promptly uttered a very unladylike word.

"Is something wrong?" asked Walter, who had gotten out of the car and was stretching the stiffness from his limbs.

"No," Jane said quickly. "I'm just surprised is all. I didn't know we were coming here. I mean, I knew we were coming to Geneva. I didn't know we were coming to this particular house."

Villa Diodati had changed little since her last visit nearly two hundred years before. As Jane got out of the car and looked at the house, she remembered quite clearly walking up the drive and seeing Byron standing on the pillared porch. Only a few roses had still been in bloom, and the lavender had been cut back for the year. The cool touch of autumn had brought out the color in the leaves, and the days were growing shorter. But in her heart it had been summer.

"You know who lived here, don't you?" Walter asked.

Jane nodded. She was staring at the green-shuttered windows, imagining a face looking back at her. Then she realized there *was* a face looking back at her. It was Lucy, and she was waving. Jane raised her hand and waved back.

"I do," Jane said, answering Walter's question.

"We're really lucky that we get to stay here," said Walter as he opened the trunk and removed their suitcases. "It's not open to the public. But Chumsley knows the—"

"We're *staying* here?" Jane said, whirling around.

"Yes," said Walter. "Chumsley is friends with the owner. He's not here, so we have the run of the place."

"Couldn't we stay in a hotel?" Jane asked.

"I thought you would be thrilled to stay here," said Walter. "How many people can say they slept in the same house where Mary Shelley dreamed up *Frankenstein*?"

Jane didn't know how to respond. After all, Walter was right—anyone with any literary inclinations at all would jump at the chance to spend a night in such a fabled place as Villa Diodati. It was the center of much fascination, all of which Jane understood all too well. That same fascination had brought her there when she was still mortal.

She took a deep breath and walked with Walter to the front door, where they were met by Lucy. As Walter carried the bags inside, Lucy hugged Jane.

"Are you all right?" she whispered in her ear.

Jane nodded. "I think so," she said.

She looked around. Although the outside of the villa was mostly unchanged, the inside had been greatly renovated. This brought some measure of relief, although Jane could still envision exactly where a chaise longue had been and where a painting of cows in a field had once hung. It was as if two houses existed, one inside the other, and wherever she turned she caught glimpses of the older house peeking through.

"Where is everyone?" she heard Walter ask Lucy.

"All over," Lucy told him. "There's really nothing planned. Everyone is just kind of hanging out. Chumsley, Brodie, Sam, and Orsino are playing cards and smoking cigars in the living room. Enid and Genevieve are looking at the gardens. And Ben's taking a nap."

"What about Suzu?" Jane asked hesitantly.

"Gone," said Lucy.

"Gone?" Jane said. "As in gone to town?"

"As in gone," said Lucy. "She had us drop her at the airport. She said something about needing to get back to Tokyo tonight."

"Well, I guess you don't have to worry about seeing her again," Walter said to Jane.

"I suppose not," Jane said. She looked at Lucy. "Any other interesting developments?"

Lucy shook her head.

"Are we in any particular room?" Walter asked.

"We saved you the one next to ours," Lucy said. "It's just up those stairs, on the right."

"I'll take these up then," said Walter.

When he was gone Lucy said, "Did you know we were coming here?"

"No," said Jane. "It's a bit of a shock."

"I know you're wondering, so I'll just tell you—they think you were off your meds this morning."

"My meds?" Jane said. "What meds?"

"The ones for your bipolar disorder," said Lucy.

"But I don't have—" Jane began.

"You do now," said Lucy. "And when you don't take your meds you start to imagine things."

Jane opened her mouth to protest, then shut it. She opened it again, and again shut it. Finally she said, "That's not a bad explanation."

"Thank you," Lucy said. "I thought it worked rather well."

"Am I on my meds now?" Jane asked.

Lucy nodded. "Walter made sure you took them," she said.

"Good," said Jane. "Do they still think I pitched Ryan over the wall?"

"That's unclear," Lucy answered. "I think they kind of like the idea that you might have, though, so I wouldn't worry about it."

"This morning went rather badly," said Jane. "And now what am I supposed to do about Suzu? She demanded that I give her Crispin's Needle in exchange for Miriam. But if she's run off, how can I possibly give it to her? Never mind that it either has disintegrated or was a myth to begin with."

"Somehow I suspect she'll turn up again," Lucy said. "There's no way she's just disappeared. I think she was just trying to make everyone believe she was gone."

"You're probably right," said Jane. "I'd just feel better knowing where she is."

"Jane!" Walter called from upstairs. "You have to see this room."

"Should I tell him I already have?" Jane murmured to Lucy.

She went upstairs and pretended to be appropriately awed by

the room. She was relieved that it wasn't Byron's room, which was down the hall and was being occupied by Orsino. She then endured a tour of the house narrated by Chumsley, who not surprisingly focused on the summer of 1816 and the visit paid to Byron by Percy Shelley, Mary Godwin, and Claire Claremont.

"It was the eruption of Mount Tambora the year previous that caused what was later referred to as the 'year without a summer,'" Chumsley told them. "It was perpetually gloomy and rained nearly every day."

This was true. Jane remembered it well. At the time, the notion that the eruption of a volcano in Indonesia could affect the weather in Europe had seemed fantastical. Some of the more superstitious among the population even suggested that black magic played a role in the events, inventing covens of black-robed witches summoning forth the demons of hell. For what reason they might do this no one ever fully explained, but it was a thrilling idea and the subject of more than one penny dreadful.

Chumsley continued with his story. "Because there was little that could be done outside, the party amused themselves by telling ghost stories," he said. "Several of them—most notably Mary Godwin and Byron's personal physician, John Polidori—committed their stories to paper and gave us *Frankenstein* and *The Vampyre.*"

"We should do that," Sam said.

"Do what?" Genevieve asked.

"Tell ghost stories," said Sam. "Tonight. After dinner."

"What a wonderful idea," Chumsley said.

And so they did. Following a light supper of salad, grilled trout, and *apfelküchlein* prepared by a girl from the village, they gathered in the salon, where Chumsley surprised them by producing a bottle of absinthe. He poured it into eleven delicate reservoir glasses, then for each one repeated the process of pouring water over a sugar cube balanced on a cunning slotted spoon. The air was soon filled with a woody, herbal smell.

"You've counted wrong," Enid said as Chumsley handed round the glasses. "There's only ten of us."

"The eleventh glass is for our friend Lord Byron," Chumsley said. "I'm hoping he will be kind enough to join us for the evening's storytelling."

Oh, good gods, you have no idea what you're asking, Jane thought. But part of her did wonder what Byron would make of their little party. She would have to tell him about it when they got home.

There was a fire in the fireplace, and for the occasion the lights had been turned off and candles placed throughout the room. The flickering flames cast shadows on the walls and lit up the faces of the assembled group. All in all, Jane thought, it was very atmospheric, even if it did make her feel wistful. She leaned against Walter, who sat beside her on the sofa, and he put his arm around her shoulders.

"Who will start us off?" Chumsley asked.

"Jane likes to tell stories," Genevieve said. "I think she should begin."

Jane bristled at the implication but decided to take the high road. "All right," she said. "Just give me a moment to think."

She considered various tales she had heard throughout the years. In the end, though, she decided to make up one of her own. It was about a girl who had no heart. The girl tried to make a heart out of many things—the innards of a clock, a rose, a bell. But nothing made her feel alive. Then one night she awoke to the sound of a thunderstorm. Going to the window, she watched as lightning lit up the sky. She ran outside with a jar and waited until the lightning flashed again. She caught it in the jar along with some wind and rain, then screwed the top on tightly. She placed the jar where her heart should have been, and she felt the storm raging inside her. Then she felt truly alive.

It wasn't really a ghost story, but Jane was pleased with it nonetheless. When she finished, there was polite applause.

"I do believe *la fée verte* is working its magic," Chumsley said, saluting Jane with his glass of absinthe. "That was a most macabre tale. Now who's next?"

Jane sipped some absinthe and snuggled closer to Walter. She only half listened as Sam began to tell a story about a church haunted by a headless vicar. Closing her eyes, she let the sound of the voices around her become a gentle murmur, the tone changing as each story finished and a new one began. She was very tired, and when Walter shook her gently to wake her she wondered if she'd slept all night. But it was only a little past midnight.

She went upstairs with Walter and got ready for bed. Walter fell asleep almost immediately, but Jane's nap had revived her, and she found herself awake. Her thoughts turned to Crispin's Needle, then to Suzu and Miriam. *What am I going to do?* she wondered.

It had begun to rain, and the pattering on the window distracted her. When lightning flashed, followed by the boom of a thunderclap, she decided to get up. The storm was reminiscent of the one that had shaken the valley the night of her transformation into a vampire so long ago. She wondered how Walter could sleep through it, but he dozed peacefully as another crackle of lightning lit up his face.

Jane got out of bed and went into the hallway. The house was quiet. *I'm the only one awake,* she thought as she crept downstairs. She was drawn to the front door of the house, which she opened, then stepped out onto the porch. She stood there as the rain fell, not caring that she was getting wet.

"It's just like the night he turned me," she said.

"Isn't it?" said a voice. "Although I believe you were wearing a different nightgown. One a bit sexier."

Jane jumped. When she turned she saw Byron standing on the steps. Despite the shorter hair and modern clothes, he looked just as he had the first time she saw him. For a moment she thought she might be dreaming. Then she saw the suitcase at his feet.

"What are you doing here?" she asked.

"I thought you might be in need of my assistance," he said.

"But how did you—"

"Second sight, vampire powers, cosmic woo-hoo," Byron replied, waving his hands in the air. "Something like that."

Another figure emerged from the storm, coming to stand beside Byron.

"Oh," Byron said. "And I brought a friend."

Chapter 24

Friday: Geneva

"YOU LOOK AWFULLY FAMILIAR," CHUMSLEY SAID AS HE SPREAD marmalade on a scone. "I could swear I've seen you somewhere before."

"I hear that a lot," said Byron. "I have one of those faces."

Indeed you do, Jane thought. *And if anyone looks at the portrait of you hanging in the sitting room, they'll know why that is.*

"How did you say you know Rosemary and Guy?" asked Chumsley, referring to their absent hosts.

"I didn't," Byron replied. "But since you asked, I'm the godfather to their baby. I saw them at the Berlin Film Festival last week—Rosemary won a Silberner Bär, by the way—and mentioned that I would be passing through Geneva. They suggested I overnight here. I know they wish they could be here with all of us, but you know how it is when you have a film to promote."

"Of course," said Chumsley. "Well, it's certainly a happy coincidence that you've come at the same time your friends are here."

"Isn't it?" said Byron as he poured himself another cup of tea.

Jane was still getting over the shock of Byron's midnight arrival. She was also still wondering exactly who his friend was. The man was very good-looking, with thick blond hair, dark eyes, and a rugged physique. He appeared to be in his early forties. His name, as Byron had introduced him, was William. Byron had yet to explain why they were there. He and William had retired for the night shortly after Jane had encountered them. The only information she'd gotten out of Byron was that Sarah was being looked after by Shelby, a bit of news that greatly relieved Ben when he walked into breakfast to see the man supposedly taking care of his daughter seated there leisurely drinking a cup of coffee.

This left Jane with numerous unasked, and therefore unanswered, questions. Nor could she ask them now, as the room was filled with people getting their breakfasts. Byron and William were proving to be quite popular with both the ladies (apart from Sam) and the gentlemen (particularly Orsino and Chumsley) of the party. Jane was used to this kind of response to Byron's brooding good looks and flirtatious charm, but William was proving to be nearly his equal in the reactions he elicited from those around him.

Jane had to remind herself repeatedly to call Byron Brian. This was always difficult for her, and was made even more so by the current setting. She couldn't see him in the villa without thinking of him as the great Lord Byron. But at least in front of those who didn't know his true identity (meaning everyone save Jane and Lucy) he was Brian George, writer of romance novels.

"I'm sorry you all have to leave today," Byron said to the assembled table. "If I'd known this was to be your last day, I might have come sooner."

In fact, the breakfast they were eating was to be their last meal together. A bus was coming at ten o'clock to take them all to the airport, where they would board planes and return to their respective homes. Jane, Walter, Lucy, and Ben were scheduled to return to London for a few more days, but Jane had a feeling those plans were about to change.

She waited impatiently for a chance to speak to Byron alone.

She finally got it when, half an hour before the bus was to arrive, everyone scattered to their rooms to finish packing. Jane sent Lucy on a mission of distraction, telling her to request a tour of the villa's smaller guest house from Walter, who she knew would be only too happy to talk about the various architectural features of the building.

Now, alone with Byron and William, Jane got down to business.

"Why are you here, and who is he really?" she asked.

"*He* has a name," said Byron.

"I'm sorry," Jane apologized, smiling at William.

William nodded. "Not at all," he said. "Byron always has been a bit maddening."

"I told you, you have to call me Brian," Byron said, putting his hand on William's knee. He looked at Jane and winked, "Unless we're in the bedroom. Then he calls me Daddy."

"I believe it's the other way around," said William, raising an eyebrow. This gave him a rakish look that Jane found rather appealing.

"I'm guessing you're a vampire," she said.

"Very good," Byron said. "I'm impressed." He turned to William. "I told you she's not terribly good at the whole being-undead thing."

"It took me some time too," William said kindly.

"Thank you," said Jane. To Byron she said, "Now I'll ask you again. Why are you here?"

Byron sighed. "Fine, fine, fine," he said. "I heard a rumor that you might be having a little trouble with Our Gloomy Friend."

Jane was surprised. "Charlotte?" she said. "You mean it isn't Joshua?"

"Joshua?" said Byron. "Why ever would you think it was Joshua? The man's an imbecile. Very sweet, and an excellent kisser, but really rather stupid."

"Charlotte?" Jane said again. "And who told you that?" she asked.

"Do you remember our trip to New York?" Byron said.

"Of course," said Jane. She immediately pictured Solomon Grundy, remembered what day it was (Friday), and felt a pang of sadness that he would be dead on the morrow. "Why?"

Byron indicated William. "William's sister happens to be Alice, Solomon's wife."

"But you said she's not a vampire," Jane reminded him.

"Darling, just because people are siblings it doesn't mean they have to be the same type of creature," said Byron. "Remember, most of us are made, not born. Anyway, Alice happened to mention to William that we had come in."

"She's an inveterate gossip," William said.

"Which in this case is a good thing," said Byron. "Because as it happens, William is friends with your husband."

"Walter?" Jane said.

"No," Byron said. "The other one."

"Oh, him again," Jane said. "How do you know—Never mind. Go on," she told Byron.

"William happened to mention to Joshua that he'd had news of you," Byron continued.

"Which explains how he knew I was in London," Jane said, ticking that particular mystery off her list.

"And Joshua told William that he'd recently seen Our Gloomy Friend and your name had come up," said Byron. "So when William told *me* all of this I got suspicious."

"You think Joshua told Charlotte I was coming?" Jane said.

"I didn't know it was a secret," said William. "I'm very sorry."

Jane waved a hand. "Oh, it's not your fault," she said. "You had no way of knowing."

"So that's why I'm here," said Byron. "And from what I've heard, it's a good thing I came."

"What have you heard?" Jane asked, wondering whom he could possibly have spoken to.

"Well, about Miriam," Byron answered. "I understand she's gone missing."

Jane nodded. "Suzu's behind that," she said. "She and Bergen—"

"Who?" said Byron.

"Suzu," Jane said. "She's a vampire. From Japan."

"I've never heard of her," Byron said. He looked at William. "Have you?"

William shook his head. "Not that I can recall."

"And there are so few of us from that part of the world," Byron said. He looked a Jane. "Are you sure she's a vampire?"

"I'm not a complete imbecile," Jane said. "Yes, she's a vampire. She arranged for Miriam to be kidnapped. And she told me that if I don't give her Crispin's Needle she'll kill her."

"Crispin's Needle?" said Byron. "Really? That old story?"

"I haven't heard anyone speak of that in over a century," William said.

"Well, I'd never heard of it at all," said Jane. "It's one of the many things you've never told me about," she added, giving Byron a look of disappointment.

"Because it's hardly worth mentioning," Byron replied. "It doesn't exist." He paused. "You haven't been looking for it, have you?" he asked Jane.

Jane shrugged. "Here and there," she admitted. "I didn't set out to, but once Gosebourne told me about it I thought it might help with my situation with Walter. And then I kept finding little clues here and there, so even though it seemed like a wild goose chase I let myself hope it might be true."

"Gosebourne," Byron said. "Now it all makes sense. You know that he and Our Gloomy Friend were lovers."

Jane gasped. "No, I didn't know that either. Apparently I don't know anything."

"She probably set the whole thing up," William said. "She hoped you would find the Needle and save her the trouble."

"That sounds like her," Jane agreed. "But then what does Suzu have to do with any of this?"

"That I don't know," said Byron. "But we'll find out. And we'll find Miriam."

"How?" Jane asked.

"You're going to find Crispin's Needle, of course," Byron said.

"But you said it doesn't—Oh, I see," said Jane. "We're going to lie. But I still don't know how to contact Suzu."

"Trust me, she'll be in touch," Byron said. "We just need to be ready for her when she comes."

"How are we going to fake the Needle?" Jane asked.

"Questions, questions, questions," Byron teased. "Why is the sky blue? Where do babies come from? Why is a raven like a writing desk?"

Jane glared at him.

"There's a blacksmith shop in town," said Byron. "We'll have him make something more or less needlelike. After all, nobody knows what this thing looks like anyway."

Jane could find no fault with this plan other than the fact that it all hinged on a million variables over which they had no control. She just had to hope it worked.

"I can't believe Joshua knows Our Gloomy Friend," she said.

"She knows a lot of people," said Byron. "You've hidden yourself away in the colonies for so long that you've lost touch with the community here."

"I was never in touch with it," Jane reminded him. "At least not very much. But I suppose it's still my fault. It generally is."

"I told you she was like this," Byron remarked to William.

"Like what?" said Jane.

"Like you are," said Byron. "Now let's get into town and get this needle made. We want to be ready when what's-her-name calls."

"Suzu," Jane said.

"When Suzu calls," said Byron. "William, can you handle this?"

"I think I can manage," William answered, standing up and pulling on a coat. "I'll see you two later."

"What are we going to do?" Jane asked Byron.

"We're going to say goodbye to all your new friends," said Byron.

This was a much more emotional experience than Jane expected it to be. Although she was not at all sad to be saying goodbye to Enid and Genevieve, she found herself clinging tightly to Orsino as she wished him *buon viaggio*, and telling Sam not to be a stranger. Brodie kissed her for slightly longer than was probably polite, but she didn't mind, and when she hugged Chumsley it was with genuine affection that she told him to keep his pecker up. As the bus drove away, she stood next to Walter and waved until the bus turned the corner and no one could see her anymore.

"That was some trip," Ben said as they went back into the villa.

"I know I'll never forget it," Walter added. "One interrupted wedding, a death, and my mother running off with a German architect. I'd say that's pretty memorable."

"That reminds me," said Byron, reaching into the pocket of his jacket. "This came for you. I've been picking up your mail. This looked important, so I thought I should bring it."

He handed Jane an envelope.

"It's from the General Register Office," Jane said as she opened it. She took out a piece of paper and ran her eyes over it. "It says that the marriage between Joshua Mobley and Elizabeth Jane Fairfax has been declared null and void due to the presiding vicar having improperly acquired credentials."

She looked at Byron, who suddenly seemed to have something in his eye, as he looked away and rubbed it vigorously.

"Joshua said he would look into this," she said. "I must say, I didn't expect him to actually do it." She turned to Walter. "I suppose I'm free to marry you now. If you'll still have me."

"You're sure there are no other husbands floating around?" Walter asked.

"Very sure," Jane said.

"Then I'm game if you are," said Walter. "But I would like to wait until my mother decides to come back, if that's all right."

Jane's happiness flooded away. "Of course," she said, forcing herself to sound happy. "We wouldn't want her to miss it."

"That reminds me," said Walter. "I want to call home and see if she's left a message there. I'll be right back."

"Don't be long," Jane said. "And if you talk to Miriam, tell her that if she wants to be my matron of honor, she'd best get herself back to us."

When Walter was out of earshot she turned to Byron. "How did you arrange this?" she asked, holding up the letter.

"I know a guy," Byron said, in a perfect imitation of a Brooklyn accent. "Don' worry 'bout it."

"Well, thank you," said Jane. She sighed. "You do take awfully good care of me."

"You forget what I did to you the last time we were here," Byron said. "After that, looking out for you is the least I can do."

"It is strange being here, isn't it?" said Jane.

Byron looked around. "That was all so long ago," he said. "I like to think I'm a different man now. You weren't the only woman I was cruel to that summer, you know."

Jane took his hand and they started to walk back to the house. "I don't know that we ever really change," she said. "I think we just learn which parts of ourselves to lock away and which ones to bring out more often."

"Perhaps you're right," said Byron.

"I generally am," said Jane. "I wish I didn't have to keep reminding you. By the way, something is puzzling me. If the Needle doesn't exist, why have the Tedious Three been looking for it for so long?"

"The Tedious Three?" Byron said. "Have you run into them as well?"

"No," Jane said. "I've only been told about them. Why? Do you know them?"

"Thankfully, no," said Byron. "I know *of* them, of course, but I've never encountered them. As I understand it, they tend to keep to themselves, in all probability because no one can stand having them around. Hence the name, you see."

"Yes, well they seem very interested in the Needle," Jane said.

Byron snorted. "They're *librarians,*" he said. "All they're interested in is obscure, impossible things. Just forget about them."

Jane did just that. An hour later William returned from town. Finding Jane and Byron in the kitchen, eating gherkins out of a jar and arguing over the proper way to make a croque-madame, he asked, "Is it safe?"

"Walter is taking a shower," Jane told him. "Ben and Lucy are upstairs. Did you get the needle?"

William placed a bundle on the table. Untying the twine that held it closed, he unrolled a piece of thick canvas and revealed an iron spike. About nine inches long, it was completely unremarkable in appearance. One end was pointed and the other had a wide, flat head.

"It's a bit plain," Jane remarked.

"What would you have it look like?" asked Byron.

Jane shrugged. "I don't know," she said. "I just thought it would be more . . . mystical."

"You mean like covered in runes?" Byron said. "Or perhaps a bit of elvish verse? This isn't a Tolkien story."

Jane rolled her eyes. "I'm just saying, it's supposed to be capable of restoring a soul. This looks like something you would use to keep the corner of a tent from blowing away."

"I had him age it a bit," William said, ignoring their bickering.

"It's perfect," said Byron. "This Suzu woman has no idea what it's supposed to look like anyway."

A thought occurred to Jane. "What if she insists on seeing if it works before handing over Miriam?"

"We'll worry about that when the time comes," Byron told her. "Right now we just have to wait for her to contact you."

As the afternoon dragged on, Jane became more and more concerned that she wouldn't hear from Suzu. She tried to be cheerful for Walter's sake, but as the hours passed her anxiety grew. They had plans to return to London in the morning, and Jane worried that once they left Villa Diodati Suzu wouldn't know where to find them.

Then, shortly before seven o'clock, the telephone in the hall rang. Jane, hearing it, went and picked it up. "Hello?" she said.

"Waiting for my call, I see." Suzu's voice was unmistakable. "Do you have the Needle?"

"Yes," Jane said. "Is Miriam safe?"

"She's alive," said Suzu. "But not safe. She won't be until you've handed over the Needle to me."

"Where are you?" Jane asked her.

"London," said Suzu. "You're coming here tomorrow, I believe."

"That's right," Jane said. "How did you know?"

Suzu laughed. "I know everything about you, Jane. Now listen carefully."

Jane listened, memorizing Suzu's instructions. Before she could ask anything more, Suzu hung up.

"Who was that?" Walter asked, coming out of the kitchen and handing Jane a glass of wine.

"The hotel," Jane said. "I called them earlier to confirm our reservation."

"Oh," said Walter. "Is everything okay?"

"Fine," Jane said. "Everything's fine."

Walter sighed. "I kind of hoped it was my mother," he said. "I changed the message on the machine at home and told her where we are. I knew I should have brought my cell phone with me."

"I'm sure she's all right," Jane said. "She's probably living it up on the beach in St. Tropez or somewhere."

"It's March," Walter said. "She'd need to wear a sweater on the beach in St. Tropez."

"I'm sure she's fine," said Jane. "This is your mother we're talking about. She's traveled all over the world on her own. She can handle herself."

"You're right," Walter said. "And who knows, maybe when we get to London tomorrow she'll be waiting for us."

"Maybe she will," Jane said, hoping she sounded convincing. "Maybe she will."

Chapter 25

Saturday: London

Iron Lilly had been standing in Carting Lane, just around the corner from the Savoy, for well over a century. Day and night she was there, whatever the weather, enduring the people who wanted their photos taken with her (usually while holding their noses and making rude faces) and pretending not to hear the childish name they used to describe her street. Year after year she had done her duty, inhaling the gases sent up by the local sewer and burning them off in her cleverly-engineered pneumatic hood.

To the unaware she seemed to be an ordinary street light, albeit of a charming old-fashioned type, but in fact she was a Webb Patent Sewer Gas Lamp. Once her kind had been plentiful, but now she was the only one left in London. In her time she had blazed without ceasing, thanks to the prodigious digestive activities of the customers of the nearby hotel and theater. Improvements in the city's sanitation systems had lessened her workload, but she was still sometimes called into service and was more than just a curiosity.

It was beneath Iron Lilly's watchful gaze that Jane waited for Suzu to appear. She carried in her arms, much as Mary surely must have held the newborn baby Jesus, the impostor Needle nestled safely in its canvas swaddle. She rocked it gently as she paced in a circle, hoping that things would go smoothly.

Suzu's instructions were for Jane to be standing beneath Iron Lilly at precisely three-thirty in the afternoon. Ensuring that this happened had not been easy. A seven o'clock train from Geneva had gotten them to the Gare de Lyon station in Paris an hour before noon. Their train to London left Gare du Nord at one. Normally this would have given them ample time to get from one station to another, but Byron had insisted on making a detour to his favorite pastry shop for what he assured them were the most exquisite *tartelettes au citron meringuée* in all of creation. They may very well have been, but Jane and the others never found out, as apparently the shop in question had closed in 1937. This resulted in hard feelings all around, especially when they arrived at Gare du Nord with only five minutes to spare and were forced to run in an undignified manner to catch the train.

In the end, though, they had arrived in London as scheduled and checked back into the Savoy with just enough time for Jane to pee, splash some water on her face, and go over the plan with Byron one final time before leaving for her rendezvous with Suzu (a phrase, Jane couldn't help but notice, that would make an excellent title for a film). Now she had nothing to do but wait.

She was slightly concerned about the plan, which hinged on Suzu being unaware of Byron and William's presence. Not knowing the extent of her abilities, it was entirely possible that they had underestimated her. Jane hoped this was not the case, but as things had not gone smoothly up to this point, she was prepared to once again be met with difficulty. Compounding her anxiety was the fact that Walter knew nothing about what was going on and that his mother's safety hung in the balance. He thought that Jane had run out to the chemist in search of dental floss, a flimsy last-second alibi she now regretted employing.

"Stop fidgeting," said a voice in her ear, startling her.

"Must you do that?" she asked.

Byron, who was invisible, replied, "William has gone to make some inquiries. I'll be right over there. When Suzu arrives, give her the Needle. I'll then follow her and see where she goes. With any luck she'll lead us right to Miriam."

"And if she doesn't?" Jane asked.

"Your optimistic outlook is just one of the many things I'm sure Walter finds delightful about you," said Byron, and left before she could respond.

She resumed waiting. Twice she had to stand aside as tourists posed beside Iron Lilly, and once she was asked by a man wearing a Paris Disneyland T-shirt if she could point the way to "Farting Lane"; she was offended by his vulgarity and sent him seventeen blocks in the wrong direction. By this point whatever novelty had surrounded the plan had worn off and she just wanted it to be over with.

It was then that she completed what felt like her millionth trip around Iron Lilly's base and saw Bergen standing not half a dozen feet away. He regarded her dully and scratched his nose. At his feet was a small bag of the sort used to hold gym clothes.

"What are you doing here?" Jane asked. "Where's Suzu?"

"I don't know," Bergen replied.

"What do you mean you don't know?" said Jane.

Bergen shrugged. "She told me to come here and get something from you," he said. "When I have it I'm supposed to call her on this." He fished a cellphone from his pocket and held it up.

Jane groaned. "Wonderful," she said. "Just wonderful."

"Do you have the item?" Bergen asked.

"Of course I have it," Jane snapped. "What do you think I'm holding?"

Bergen held out his hands. "Give it to me," he said. "Then I'll call and find out what the next step is."

Jane didn't know what to do. She'd been expecting Suzu herself to appear. That she might send Bergen to fetch the Needle had never occurred to her. And apparently Suzu was keeping him in the dark as well.

"Where's Miriam?" she said.

Again Bergen shrugged, a gesture Jane was beginning to find aggravating. "I don't know," he said. "My mistress moves her from place to place. I know where she was this morning, but not where she is now. However, I have been authorized to give you this as a goodwill gesture."

He reached down, unzipped the bag, and removed Lilith. The little dog turned her head and bit him on the hand, causing him to let out a shrill scream. To his credit, however, he did not drop her.

"Put me down!" Lilith barked.

"He can't understand you," Jane reminded the Chihuahua. She addressed Bergen. "Put her down."

He did, and Lilith ran to Jane. She then turned and bared her teeth at Bergen, growling loudly.

Jane wished Byron would appear, or at least tell her what to do. Since Bergen had given her Lilith, she felt obligated to hand over the Needle. But then what would they do?

"Jane?" said a voice.

For a moment she thought Byron was speaking to her. Then she saw Walter jogging toward her. Walter looked down at Lilith, then over at Bergen. For a moment his face brightened.

"Bergen!" he said. "Where's my mother?"

Bergen, looking distinctly nervous, started to speak. Then he stopped, looked at his feet, and said, "I'm not sure."

Jane hid the bundle containing the Needle behind her back. "What he means is that Miriam wanted to do a little shopping before meeting us," she said.

"Oh," Walter said. "Well, where are we meeting?"

Jane looked at Bergen, who was looking more and more uncomfortable. A bead of sweat formed at his brow and rolled down his nose as his fingertips scratched anxiously at his thighs.

"Why don't you call her and ask her?" Jane suggested.

Bergen looked at her.

"On your phone," Jane prodded. "Why don't you call and ask her where she wants to meet?"

Bergen nodded. "A fine idea," he said. "Just a moment." He took the phone from his pocket and walked off a few feet, turning his back so that they couldn't hear his conversation.

"Did you know they were here?" Walter asked Jane.

Jane shook her head. "I just happened to run into him," she said. "Why are you out here, anyway?"

"After you left I remembered that I needed shampoo," said Walter. "I went looking for you but couldn't find you. I was on my way back to the hotel when I saw you standing here."

"And I'm so glad you did," Jane remarked.

Walter bent down and picked up Lilith. "Hey, little girl," he said. "Did you have fun with your mother and her new boy-friend?"

"Seriously?" Lilith said to Jane. "Is he really this stupid?"

"Look how happy she is to see you!" Jane said brightly.

Bergen turned back to them and walked forward. "Miriam says we're to meet her at Boswell's grave. She said Brian will know where it is."

"Brian?" said Walter. "But where is *he*?"

"Did someone say my name?"

Smiling as if he'd just been strolling along and happened to stumble upon his friends, Byron walked up. He nodded at Bergen. "Good to see you again. I trust Ms. Ellenberg is well?"

"The last I saw her she was," Bergen replied.

"Do you know where Boswell's grave is?" Walter asked. "I have no idea why my mother would want to meet us there, but it seems she does."

"Boswell was buried in Scotland, wasn't he?" Jane said.

Byron shook his head. "I believe this is a different Boswell."

They walked to a busier street, where Byron hailed a black cab and gave the driver instructions to take them to Hyde Park.

Once there, he directed him to Victoria Gate, where they all piled out as Byron paid the fare.

"This way," he said, walking through the gate and past the lodge. "It's just round here."

They passed through a garden gate that, although it seemingly was locked, Byron opened with ease, and found themselves in a spacious clearing filled with hundreds of tiny tombstones. Jane peered at one of the nearest ones and read aloud the words engraved upon it. "'Dear Pupsey, September twelfth, 1894.' Pupsey? What an odd name."

"Not for a dog," said Byron.

"A dog?" Walter said.

"Mmm," said Byron, looking around. "This is a pet cemetery. Begun by the lodge keeper, a Mr. Winbridge, back in, oh, the 1880s, I think. One of London's hidden treasures. Not many know of it."

"Why would my mother want to meet us here?" Walter wondered.

"I'm afraid it's not your mother," said Byron.

"Then who—" Walter began.

"It would be she," Byron said, pointing.

Suzu stood among the graves. She was dressed in black, as if she were preparing to attend a funeral. She walked toward them slowly, wending her way through the tightly packed stones.

"I'm really confused here," Walter said.

"Wait a few moments, my friend," said Byron, clapping Walter on the shoulder. "You're going to be even more confused."

Walter looked at Jane, bewilderment furrowing his brow. She took his hand and held it tightly, terrified of what was coming. But she trusted that Byron knew what he was doing. At least, she hoped he did, because she certainly didn't.

"I knew you would figure it out," Suzu said to Byron.

Byron smiled. "How could anyone forget Boswell?"

"Indeed," Suzu said. She knelt and ran her finger lightly over a gravestone. "My dear Boswell," she said with a sigh. "Taken too soon."

Byron turned to Jane and Walter. "A cat," he said. "Gray, as I recall. Excellent mouser."

"Boswell is a cat?" Walter said.

"Not just a cat," said Suzu. "The most wonderful cat in all the world. I miss him terribly."

Walter, looking at the dates on the surrounding stones, said, "When did he die?"

"You don't really want to know that," Byron warned him.

Suzu turned her gaze to Walter and smiled tightly. "Eighteen ninety-two," she said. "August the second. He fell from a tree while trying to catch a robin."

"You mean nineteen ninety-two," Walter said.

"No, she doesn't," said Byron.

"But that's impossible," Walter argued. "That would mean she was over a hundred years old."

"I told you that you were going to be even more confused," said Byron. To Suzu he said, "Where's Miriam?"

"All in good time," Suzu answered. "Where is the Needle?"

Jane held up the bundle she'd been carrying. "Right here."

"Take it," Suzu ordered Bergen. "Bring it to me."

Jane looked at Byron.

"Give it to him," he said.

Walter watched as Bergen took the parcel from Jane.

"What's going on here?" he asked.

"I'll explain later," Jane said. "If I can."

Bergen carried the Needle to Suzu and presented it as if it were an offering. She took it and unrolled the canvas. Holding up the Needle, she ran her fingers lightly along its length.

"If you don't mind my asking, how did you know who Boswell was?" Jane asked Byron as they waited for Suzu to say something.

"Sorry," Byron said. "I forgot to mention that. See, she isn't

Suzu. I mean, she *is* the person you've known as Suzu. But she's not who she says she is."

"Then who is she?" Jane asked.

"Charlotte?" Byron called.

Suzu looked up. "What?"

"There you go," Byron said to Jane.

Jane looked at Suzu. "You've got to be kidding me."

Suzu smiled tightly. "How *did* you know, dear heart?" she asked Byron.

"Well, I confess that it wasn't I who figured it out. It was William." He looked around. "William? Are you here?"

William materialized behind them.

"Where did he come from?" Walter said. "And how did he do that?"

"It wasn't that difficult, really," William said. "First I checked with the university. No one there had ever heard of someone called Suzu. Then I asked around among our people and no one had ever heard of you."

"His people?" said Walter. "What people? Is he with the Secret Service or something?"

"Shh," Jane said. "I want to hear this."

"Of course, that still didn't tell me who you were," William continued. "But then a friend I asked about you—a fellow who works in the Asian antiquities department of the British Museum—remarked upon your name. Suzu, as you undoubtedly know, means 'little bell' in Japanese. What better alias for the author once known to the world as Currer Bell?"

"Currer Bell?" Walter said. "Isn't that the name Charlotte Bro—"

"Try not to say her name," Jane interrupted. "It's bad luck."

Suzu clapped her hands together. "I'm impressed," she said. "You figured out in a handful of hours what some people"—she glanced triumphantly at Jane—"didn't even suspect."

"But the hair," Jane said. "And the . . . eyes," she finished, wondering if drawing attention to them was racially insensitive.

"Makeup and a wig, you idiot," Suzu said. "And before you ask, yes, I was the one who threw Ryan McGuinness from the tower."

"See?" Jane said to Walter. "I was right all along."

Walter was staring at Suzu. "She's Charlotte Bro—"

"Our Gloomy Friend!" Jane said.

"And that thing she's holding?" he asked.

"It's called Crispin's Needle," Jane answered. "It's a kind of relic."

"If you don't mind telling us, why *do* you want the Needle?" Byron asked Charlotte.

"For the simplest reason of all," Charlotte told him. "So that no one else can have it." She sneered at Jane. "Especially you."

"Now it makes sense," said Byron. "You think that by denying Jane her mortality that you'll ruin her life because then she either won't marry Walter or will have to turn him."

"Something like that," Charlotte said.

"Turn me into what?" asked Walter.

"Well, now you have the Needle," Byron said. "Give us Miriam."

"I really should kill her," said Charlotte. "Do you know what she is?"

Byron nodded. "I do," he said.

"She's my mother!" Walter cried.

"Oh, she's far more than that," said Charlotte. "You have no idea the treachery the women around you have wrought."

"Just hand her over," Byron said firmly.

Charlotte huffed. "Fine," she said. "She's tied up behind that tree over there."

Walter handed Lilith to Jane and ran in the direction of Charlotte's pointing finger. A minute later he returned leading a very annoyed Miriam. She was cursing and gesturing with her hands.

"I should never have taken my eyes off that little bastard!" she shouted, pointing at Bergen.

She rushed at him, her hands clawing the air, and knocked him down. Immediately Byron and Walter leapt forward and tried to pull her off.

"I'm going to stake him!" Miriam shouted. "I don't care if he isn't a bloodsucker. He deserves it!"

"She's much stronger than she looks," Byron remarked as Miriam and Bergen rolled around on the ground, wrestling madly. Finally they managed to pull Miriam off the architect, who lay on the ground, whimpering softly.

"Where's the other one?" Miriam asked. "That one I *will* stake."

Jane looked around for Charlotte, but she was nowhere to be found. In all of the commotion, she had disappeared.

Miriam, searching the cemetery, stopped short when she saw William. Jane was surprised to see her start to tremble. She shook her head back and forth.

"What are you doing here?" she asked, her voice barely a whisper.

"Hello, Miriam," William said. "It's lovely to see you again."

Walter looked at his mother. "You know him?"

Miriam nodded but said nothing.

"Mom?" Walter said. "Are you all right?"

Miriam took a deep breath. "No," she said. "I'm not all right."

Walter pointed at William. "Is it him? Is he what's upsetting you?"

When Miriam didn't reply, Walter turned to William. "What's going on here?" he said, his voice heavy with confusion and anger. "How do you know my mother?"

William looked at Miriam, who nodded. "Tell him," she said. "It's time he knew."

Chapter 26

Saturday: London

JANE DRAINED THE REST OF THE PINT OF CIDER AND SET IT DOWN. Byron, seated across from her at a table in the Tipsy Shrew, bit a pickled egg in half and offered Jane the smaller of the two pieces. She took it and popped it into her mouth.

"I haven't had a pickled egg in ages," she said. "I'd forgotten how dreadful they are."

"Every twenty years or so I have one to remind myself," said Byron.

Jane took a sip of his ale to wash away the bitter taste of the egg. "How do you suppose he's handling it?"

Byron shrugged. "How would any man handle being told his father isn't really his father and that, by the way, his real dad is a vampire?"

"And that's just the beginning," said Jane. "Then I have to tell him about myself. His entire world is being turned upside down."

"Yes, well, perhaps if he'd been told sooner . . . " Byron said.

Jane wagged a finger at him. "Don't you even start with that," she said. "I still can't believe that it never occurred to you that William might be Walter's father."

"Why would it?" Byron asked. "Fletcher is a very common name."

"Still, it never crossed your mind? Not even in a 'wouldn't it be funny if' kind of way?"

"No," Byron said. "It really didn't."

"I'll never understand men," Jane said. "William Fletcher was your almost constant companion from the time you were sixteen. And apparently you've kept in touch ever since. Are you saying that not once did he mention to you that he seduced a vampire hunter who shared his last name?"

Byron looked uncomfortable. "He might have mentioned the seducing a vampire hunter part," he admitted. "But that must have been at least forty years ago. I can hardly be expected to have remembered it."

"I'm assuming you turned him," Jane said.

"Surprisingly, no," said Byron. "That was just a happy accident."

"How did Miriam find him anyway?" Jane asked, signaling the waitress that she would like another pint.

Byron leaned forward. "Apparently after she married George Fletcher she became interested in researching the family tree. Our William was George's sixteenth uncle thrice removed or some such thing. When Miriam couldn't find a death certificate for him, or really any information on him at all, she became suspicious and did some more digging. This brought her to London, where she managed to track William down. Her plan was to stake him, but as you know he's a man of considerable charms."

"So I've heard," Jane said.

"William managed to seduce her," Byron continued. "And apparently it took, if you catch my meaning."

The waitress arrived with Jane's drink and took away the empty glass. Jane held the glass in her hand, feeling the coolness of the sides and thinking.

"I assume George never knew," she said.

"I would think not," said Byron. "That would certainly be awkward. Can you see Miriam sitting him down and saying, 'Dear, the bad news is that I've had an affair. The good news is that he's an ancestor. Oh, and by the way, the bairn has a good chance of being a vampire.'"

Jane almost choked on her cider.

"What?" Byron asked.

"The bairn," Jane said. "I mean Walter. He's *not* a vampire."

"More's the pity," said Byron.

"You're missing the point," Jane said. "This proves that vampires and humans can . . . well, you know."

"Make bairns?" Byron suggested.

"Precisely," Jane said. "What's more, it apparently doesn't mean the child will turn out like us. And Miriam knew all along and didn't say a word. That horrible old woman!"

"Now, now," said Byron. "Can you blame her for being suspicious of our kind after what William did?"

Jane started to reply, but stopped. "I suppose not," she said after a few moments. "Poor Walter," she added. "What must he think?"

"You've told people about yourself before," Byron said.

"Just Lucy," Jane said. "And she'll believe anything. I mean, she's *willing* to believe anything. Walter's different."

"Is he?" asked Byron. "Maybe you just need to give him a chance."

Jane shook her head. "It may be too late," she said. "I've been lying to the poor man for years. His *mother* has been lying to him for years. He'll probably never trust a woman for as long as he lives."

"That will take him far," Byron remarked. "And speaking of the devils, here are William and Miriam now."

Walter's parents came to the table and sat down, Miriam next to Jane and William next to Byron. Both of them looked exhausted.

"Well?" Byron said.

Miriam looked up. "It went fairly well until we got to the vampire part," she said.

"We considered not telling him about that, but it would have been rather difficult to explain why his father is the same age he is," William added. "Also, he was a wee bit curious about the fact that his mum was kidnapped by Charlotte Brontë."

"He must think we're all mad," Jane said.

"I don't think he knows what to think," said Miriam. "He's probably hoping it's all a dream."

"Where is the boy now?" Byron asked.

"Taking a walk," said Miriam. "With Lilith. She seems to soothe him for some reason."

"That's because he can't hear her talk," Jane said. She hesitated before asking, "Does he know about me?"

William shook his head. "We thought it best to leave that to you," he said.

"*He* thought it best," Miriam said, cocking her head at William. "I was all for getting everything out in the open."

"I guess I should go find him," Jane said. "Do you have any idea where he went?"

"Kensington Gardens," William answered. "He said he wanted to see the statue of Peter Pan."

"It was his favorite book when he was a boy," said Miriam.

Jane stood up. "Wish me luck," she said.

It wasn't difficult to find Walter. For one thing, he was letting Lilith walk on her own three legs, which meant they couldn't walk terribly quickly. For another, he was exactly where William had said he would be, near the statue of Peter Pan. As Lilith sniffed around Walter stood looking at the figure of the little boy who never grew up.

"If you're looking for Neverland, I believe it's second star to the right and straight on to morning," Jane said.

Walter turned around. "You know they added the word 'star' for the Disney film," he said. "It's not in the book."

"I know," Jane said. "I tried to get him to put it in, but he wouldn't have it."

Walter, apparently either not hearing her or not registering the meaning of her words, went back to looking at the statue.

"I used to pretend I was Peter," he said. "My mother bought me a cap like his and I found a cardinal feather in the yard and stuck it in the band. I even had a little bell I carried around and rang whenever Tinker Bell was part of the game I was playing."

"You had quite an imagination even then," Jane remarked.

Walter looked over at her. "My mother told me a pretty unbelievable story today," he said.

"Did she?" Jane said.

"She claims she's a vampire hunter," said Walter. "And William, he's supposedly a vampire. Also, he's my father."

Jane tread carefully, unsure of how solid the ground on which she now walked was. "You do resemble him," she said.

To her surprise, Walter laughed. "Oh, and Suzu was really Charlotte Brontë. I forgot that part."

Jane waited for him to question her about her role in the drama that had unfolded in the pet cemetery, but he didn't. She wondered if perhaps he'd forgotten. He seemed transfixed by the statue of Peter Pan.

"What would you say if your mother sat you down and told you that story?" he asked, breaking the silence.

Jane thought for a while before speaking.

"Did you read the Narnia books when you were small?" she asked Walter.

"Yes," he answered. "I loved them. Why?"

"Do you remember in the first book when Lucy has told the others that she's found Narnia inside the wardrobe? They don't believe her, so they go to the old Professor and ask him what he thinks. He tells them that there are only three possible explanations for what she's said—she's telling lies, she's mad, or she's telling the truth."

"I remember that," Walter said. "And they decide that since they've never known her to tell lies, and she isn't crazy, then she must be telling the truth."

"Right," said Jane. "Well, suppose we apply those same rules to what your mother told you today. Have you ever known your mother to lie?"

"Not until today. She never even tried to get me to believe in the tooth fairy or the Easter bunny or Santa Claus. She never *let* me believe in them. She always told me that I should know the difference between what was real and what was imaginary."

"All right," said Jane. "And although it pains me to say this, I don't think she's mad. Which leaves the possibility that she's telling the truth."

Walter shook his head. "That's ridiculous. Jane, she wants me to believe that vampires are *real*."

"How do you know they aren't?"

"*Everybody* knows they aren't," said Walter.

"Who's to say what's real and what isn't?" she asked him. "Some of the most unbelievable things are real. Did you know there's a type of sea slug that eats anemones and then uses their stinging cells for its own defense? If you ask me, that's far weirder than the notion of vampires. And what about the platypus? It's the Frankenstein's monster of the animal world, as if somebody sewed together parts of a beaver, a crocodile, and a duck and then added some poison sacs for good measure."

"If I didn't know better, I might think you *want* me to believe in vampires."

"I'm just saying it's an option," Jane replied.

"Let me ask you this," Walter said. "What would you think if *your* mother told you that vampires were real?"

"I wish she had," Jane said, snorting. "Then I wouldn't be

here right now. Not that I don't want to be here," she added. "I mean I wouldn't be here the way I am, although even if she *had* told me about vampires I wouldn't have known Byron was one, so it probably all would have turned out like this anyway."

"Are you going to start making sense anytime soon?" Walter asked.

"Walter," Jane said, looking him in the eyes, "your mother isn't lying to you. She *is* a vampire hunter, and William *is* a vampire. I know this because *I'm* a vampire. So are a couple of other people you know, but I'll let them tell you themselves. We're really not supposed to out one another."

Having said it, Jane now wondered why she had worried so much about it. The words had come out fairly easily, and despite her fears she already felt immensely better.

"I'm sorry I didn't tell you before," she said. "I know I should have. But now you know why I said no all those times you asked me out."

Walter looked at her for long enough that some of her relief began to turn to worry. "I can't believe you," he said. "Here I am freaking out about the fact that my mother might very well be a raving lunatic, and you're making fun of me."

"I'm not making fun of you," Jane protested. "I'm telling you the truth."

Walter laughed. "You're a vampire?" he said.

Jane nodded. "Yes."

"You drink blood?"

She cringed. "Only when I have to. And never from you. I want you to know that."

"Well, that's a relief," said Walter. "Anything else I should know? Is Lucy a werewolf? Maybe old Sherman at the paper is really Satan in disguise?"

"Now you're being ridiculous," Jane said.

"*I'm* being ridiculous? Are you listening to yourself? Have you heard *anything* you've said in the last five minutes?"

"This really isn't going well."

Jane looked down and saw Lilith looking up at her.

"Don't you start," she told the Chihuahua.

"Who are you talking to?" Walter asked. "The dog? Wait. Let me guess. She's really an alien. From Mars or from Jupiter?"

"I told you it wasn't going well," Lilith said. "You should have quit while you were ahead."

"I was never ahead," said Jane.

"Would you please stop it?" Walter said. "You know, as odd as you can be sometimes, you've always been there for me. Now, when I need you the most, this is how you behave? I can't believe you, Jane."

He turned and started to walk away. Lilith trotted beside him, using her strange hop-skip-hop technique.

"Walter," Jane called.

"Leave me alone," he said.

Jane started to cry. "Walter," she said. "Please come back."

Walter whirled around. "You want me to believe that you're a vampire?" he said. "Then bite me."

Jane stared at him, unable to speak.

"Go on," Walter said. He tilted his head, exposing his neck. "Go on, Jane. Bite me."

Jane closed her eyes. *No, no, no, no, no,* she thought. *This isn't how it's supposed to happen.*

"Did you hear me, Jane?" Walter yelled. "I told you to bite me!"

Jane opened her eyes.

"I heard you," she said, and her fangs clicked into place.

Chapter 27

Saturday: London

WALTER OPENED HIS EYES, SAT UP, AND GROANED.

"What happened?" he asked.

Jane, who was sitting on the side of the bed, handed him a glass of water and two aspirin. "Take these," she said.

Walter swallowed the pills and handed back the glass. "I feel as if someone hit me in the head with a line drive," he said, rubbing his temples.

"It's the aftereffects from being bitten," said Jane. "They'll wear off in a couple of hours."

"What bit me?" Walter asked. "It wasn't Lilith, was it? I know she can be a little snippy, but—"

"It wasn't Lilith," said Jane. "It was me."

"You?" Walter said. "Why would you bite me?"

"You'll remember soon enough," said Jane. "I didn't glamor you, so eventually it will all come back. Probably in bits and pieces."

Walter shut his eyes and groaned. His fingers went to his neck, where the two small puncture wounds caused by Jane's bite had already healed. "It hurts," he said.

"I'm sorry about that," said Jane. "But you wanted proof."

"Proof of what?" Walter asked, leaning back against the pillows.

"Try to remember," Jane told him. "Just relax your thoughts."

Walter took a deep breath, then another. He kept his eyes closed, but Jane could see that he was concentrating. Beneath the lids his eyes moved back and forth. After a minute or two his eyes flew open and he stared at Jane.

"You're a vampire!" he said.

"I'm afraid so," Jane said.

"Everything my mother told me is true," Walter said, looking confused and hurt and angry all at the same time. "My father—"

"Is a vampire too," said Jane. "And your mother is a hunter. Not the best pairing imaginable, but these things happen."

Walter tried to get up but wobbled and lay back down. Jane moved closer, but Walter recoiled from her. She felt her heart break a little bit as she saw him move away.

"I'm sorry," she said. "This isn't the way I wanted you to find out."

Walter laughed bitterly. "As if there's a *good* way to find out?" he said.

"No," said Jane. "I suppose there isn't."

"Who else knows?" Walter asked her.

"Lucy," Jane said. "Ned and Ted at the shop. Brian."

"So I'm the last one to find out," said Walter.

"Not the *last* one," Jane said. "Ben doesn't know."

"Ben has known you less than a year," said Walter. "I've known you for ten. And Ben hasn't been living with you for the past nine months and isn't your fiancé. So excuse me if that doesn't make me feel any better."

Jane set the glass on the nightstand. "I really don't know what to say," she told Walter.

"Am I one of you now?" he asked.

Jane shook her head. "No. I didn't take very much. Just enough to make you believe."

Walter grunted. "I suppose I should be thankful for that," he said.

"This probably isn't the best time to mention this," Jane said. "But you *are* half vampire."

"I can't believe I'm having this conversation," Walter said. "Do you know how ridiculous this all sounds?"

"It's a lot to take in," said Jane. "I know it took me a long time to accept it after I was changed."

"And when did that happen?" Walter asked.

Jane wondered if she should lie, then decided against it. *There's been too much lying already,* she thought. *He might as well know everything.*

"Eighteen sixteen," she said. "And there's something else you might as well know. My real name isn't Jane Fairfax, it's Jane Austen."

Walter stared at her.

"I know it isn't terribly original," Jane said. "At first I considered Sophronia Kindleysides, but it seemed a bit much. Besides, I was already used to Jane, so changing just the surname was easiest."

"I suppose you're *the* Jane Austen," Walter said.

Jane nodded. "I'm afraid I am."

"No wonder my mother doesn't like you," said Walter. "She hates your books."

"Yes," Jane said. "She's made that clear on several occasions."

"She thinks your characters are boring," Walter continued.

"I believe I've heard her say as much," Jane said, keeping an even tone.

"She also says there are far too many coincidences in your plots and—"

"I *know,*" Jane said. "And she's one to talk. Too many coincidences! What about *her* plot? A vampire hunter marries a man who just happens to have a vampire in the family? She gets pregnant by that vampire and forty years later her child falls in love with another vampire? Oh, and the father of that child just happens to be the best friend of another vampire who lives in the same town? There are far more coincidences in that story than in any of mine."

"William's best friend is Brian," Walter said, catching up with her. "Are you saying Brian is a—"

"Oh, for heaven's sake, yes, he's a vampire. And he happens to be Lord Byron. I know I said we aren't supposed to out one another, but I think as far as this is concerned he owes me. After all, he's the one who turned—"

"Brian?" Walter interrupted. "*Brian* turned you. But I thought he was—"

"He is," said Jane. "Well, he mostly is. Back then he was a little less discriminating."

"And my father?" Walter asked. "Who is he really?"

"Oh, he's just William," said Jane. "Well, not *just* William. He's pretty extraordinary in his own right. Did you know Byron selected him to be his companion after seeing him working in the fields? He was extraordinarily good-looking. It's no wonder Byron fell in love with—"

"La la la la la," Walter wailed, putting his hands over his ears.

"Sorry," Jane said. "I suppose thinking about that would be a trifle unsettling."

"What?" said Walter. "You mean the fact that apparently both my fiancée *and* my father slept with the same man? Yes, I think 'unsettling' is a good way to describe it."

"To be fair, he *is* Lord Byron," Jane said. "I don't know many people who *haven't* slept with him at one time or another."

Walter held up his hands and Jane stopped. She wasn't doing a very good job of making things better. They sat in silence for a time as Jane waited for Walter to say something. But he didn't. He just looked out the window. Finally, he cleared his throat.

"So how does this work?" he said. "Do I have to become a vampire?"

"No," Jane answered. "You don't."

"But I'm guessing that you don't get any older," said Walter. "I mean, your body doesn't. You stay the same, right?"

Jane nodded. "That's right."

"I see," Walter said.

Jane knew that he was thinking about what it would mean for her to stay the same while he grew old and eventually died. "I thought there was a chance that I might be able to become mortal again," she said. "I was going to try it."

Walter looked over at her. "But you decided not to?"

"It turned out to be a legend," Jane said. "An unfortunate bit of irony there, I suppose."

"Is that what Suzu was talking about in the cemetery?" Walter asked. "That iron spike?"

"It's called Crispin's Needle," Jane said. She didn't correct him regarding Suzu's identity, hoping that perhaps he hadn't heard or didn't remember. "But it's a fake. We made it to fool her."

"To save my mother," said Walter.

"Yes," Jane said. "To save Miriam."

"Thank you for that," Walter said.

"Well, she *is* my mother-in-law," Jane reminded him. Then she remembered that they were yet to be married. "Will be my mother-in-law," she said. "Might be my mother-in-law."

Walter said nothing. Jane, unable to stand the uncertainty, finally asked, "Where does this leave us?"

Walter didn't look at her. "I don't know," he said.

"Do you still love me?" asked Jane.

"Yes," Walter answered. "I do."

"It's the vampire thing, isn't it?" said Jane.

"Strangely enough, no," Walter replied. "It's that you didn't think you could tell me the truth. And you were going to marry me without telling me."

"I was hoping I could find a solution," Jane said. "That way you would never have had to know."

Walter took her hand. "But don't you see how that's even worse?" he said. "We should know everything about each other—the good *and* the bad. If there's something about yourself you feel you have to hide away from me, that's always going to be between us. There's always going to be that one hidden room you won't let me into. And you'll be so worried that someday I might accidentally open the door to that room that you'll never be able to fully be yourself. You'll always be on guard. And the worst part is that the person you'll be afraid of is the one who loves you the most."

Jane felt tears forming in her eyes. "But you know now," she said. "I don't have to keep that door closed anymore."

Walter squeezed her hand. "But you didn't open the door on your own," he said. "It was forced open."

Jane sniffed as a tear rolled down her cheek. "Ben can still marry us," she said. "Tomorrow. We can start fresh. No more secrets."

Walter looked into her eyes. "I don't know if I can," he said.

Jane began to cry. "Please, Walter," she said. "Don't say no. I don't think I can bear it."

Walter took her in his arms and held her tightly. "I love you more than anything in the world," he whispered. "But I don't know."

They stayed that way for a long time, Walter just holding Jane while she wept. Eventually he let go and she wiped her eyes.

"I'm going to go now," Jane said. "I'm going to go away and give you time to think. Tomorrow morning at nine o'clock I'll be standing in the White Tower, waiting for you. If you still want to marry me, you meet me there."

"And if I don't come?" asked Walter.

Jane forced a smile. "La la la la la," she said, putting her hands over her ears. She took them away again and kissed Walter lightly on the lips. Then she stood up and without another word left the room.

Byron found her a few hours later, sitting in the American Bar listening to the piano player and drinking gin and tonics. She'd had three, and was working on her fourth.

"Lucy has been looking all over for you," Byron said as he sat down at her table. "She's worried."

"You told her what happened?" Jane asked.

"An abbreviated version of the story," Byron said. "Dare I ask how things went with our dear Walter?"

Jane took a long sip from her glass. "I told him that I'll be waiting for him in the Tower tomorrow morning at nine," she said.

"How typically passive-aggressive of you," said Byron.

Jane glared at him. "I'm not in the mood for you," she warned.

"Don't worry," Byron said. "I haven't come to torment you. I came to give you a wedding present."

He laid a long, thin black velvet box on the table. Jane looked at it. "Is it a necklace?" she asked hopefully.

"Open it," Byron said.

Jane picked up the box, which was surprisingly heavy, and opened it. Inside, nestled in a narrow trench pressed into the velvet, was a piece of metal about nine inches long. One end came to a very fine point, while the other was rounded.

"It's Crispin's Needle," Byron informed her before she could ask.

Jane, confused, set the box down. "The Needle is a myth," she said. "You told me as much yourself."

"Yes, well, I lied," said Byron. "It very much exists, and there it is. Happy returns of the day and all that."

"I don't understand," Jane said. "Where did you get it?"

"Do you remember when I told you about Ambrose?" Byron asked.

"The vampire who turned you," Jane said. "Of course."

"He gave it to me," said Byron. "It was given to him by Crispin himself. He wanted me to use it. Even though he turned me, he thought the greatest gift he could give me was to restore my humanity. He begged me to do it. But I didn't want to be human."

Jane reached out her hand and held it over the Needle.

"You can touch it," Byron said. "It won't harm you. It only works if you drive it into your heart."

Jane touched her finger to the nail. It was cool to the touch.

"Is it really made from the nails used to crucify Christ?" she asked.

"Who knows?" said Byron. "You know what happens with these things—someone makes up a story and then someone else adds something to it, and before long you've got a hammer that was forged from the tongue of a frost dragon."

Jane ran her finger down the length of the Needle. She let her fingertip rest against the point, pressing down until she could feel the Needle just begin to pierce her flesh. She pulled her hand away.

"You've had this all along," she said. "And you've never told me about it. Why?"

Byron looked at her, and Jane was surprised to see sadness in his eyes. "Can't you guess?" he asked. "I was afraid you would want to use it."

Jane couldn't speak. She understood exactly what Byron meant. Hadn't she been doing the same thing by hiding from Walter the fact that, should he choose it, she could grant him eternal life? Wasn't this the same reason why she hadn't offered to turn her sister Cassie, or anyone else from her family? *I was afraid they would say yes,* she told herself.

"Are you going to use it?" Byron asked her.

Jane still couldn't speak. She simply shook her head and shrugged.

"Tell you what," said Byron. "I'll be at the Tower tomorrow at nine as well. We'll see then." He bent down and kissed Jane on the cheek. "Either way, I'll always love you," he said.

He started to walk away, then returned. "I almost forgot," he said. "I got something for Sarah." He reached into his pocket and placed on the table a small toy replica of one of the Daleks from the *Doctor Who* television show.

"I've been introducing her to the Doctor," he said. He then adopted the peculiar high-pitched voice of the Daleks. "Exterminate!" he said, using their famous line.

Jane laughed. "She's going to love it," she said.

Byron left. Jane sat very still, looking at the Needle and thinking. When she could think no more she closed the box and picked up the Dalek. This one was aluminum in color, with a single eye that lit up with a blue bulb. When she pressed a button on the bottom, the toy spoke just as Byron had. "Exterminate!" it said.

She pressed the button again. This time she heard a noise resembling radio static. Then a voice came from the Dalek.

"I told you the Needle was real."

It was the voice from the elevator.

"Yes, but you might have been a bit more helpful as to where it was," Jane said.

"Sorry about that," said the voice. "I can't be expected to know everything. But you've got it now, that's the important thing. So, are you going to use it?"

Jane, feeling very self-conscious about holding a conversation with a toy Dalek, looked around before replying. "I don't know," she said.

The voice sighed. "It's what you wanted," it said.

"I thought I did," Jane said. "Now I don't know. And by the way, who are you?"

"Haven't you guessed?" asked the voice. "I'm Apollonia."

"The saint?" Jane said. "So you do exist."

"Of course I do. Didn't you see the windows?"

"Yes," Jane said. "But you know how it is. Tongue from a frost dragon and all that. If you don't mind my asking, are you in heaven?"

"There's no more time for questions," Apollonia said. "I just wanted to know if you'd decided to use the Needle. If you don't want it, you really ought to give it to someone who does, you know."

"That's very saintlike of you," Jane remarked.

"I do try," said Apollonia. "Look, I have to go now. Do try to make up your mind soon, will you?"

"I will," Jane told her. "And you take care of yourself. Give my regards to God. Or whomever."

The Dalek was silent. Jane held it in her hand for another few minutes, in case Apollonia had anything else to say. When it seemed she didn't, Jane slipped the Dalek into her pocket and picked up the case containing the Needle. Then she left the bar and went in search of Lucy.

It never hurts to get a second opinion, she told herself.

Chapter 28

Sunday: London

"OH, YOU'RE BACK."

Prince Edward the Fifth of England materialized in front of Jane. He was joined a moment later by Richard of Shrewsbury, First Duke of York. They were wearing the same outfits Jane had seen them in before.

"Do ghosts never get to change their clothes?" Jane asked.

Richard shook his head. "No. You get just the one set."

"We're just thankful that we didn't get stuck with our night-clothes," Edward said.

"You mean you don't get whatever you had on when you were mur—when you died?" Jane asked.

"Some do, some don't," Edward answered. "I think they go with what's the most dramatic."

"That makes sense," Jane said.

"Are you really getting married this time?" Richard asked.

Jane sighed. "I don't know," she said. "I hope so."

"And did you find Crispin's Needle?" said Edward.

"Yes and no," Jane told him. "I didn't find it, but it eventually found me."

"And did you use it?" asked Richard.

Before Jane could answer they were interrupted by the arrival of Lucy and Ben. Jane was surprised to also see Miriam and William. She hoped their presence was a sign that Walter was coming as well.

"Is he with you?" Jane asked Lucy, her heart beating madly.

Lucy shook her head. "He wasn't in his room when we left. We don't know where he is."

It was ten minutes before nine.

Jane wrung her hands as she paced back and forth. The two ghosts watched her, which only made her more anxious. Lucy stood by looking as if she didn't know what to do.

"Did you talk to him?" Jane asked Miriam.

"I tried," she said. "*We* tried." She cocked her head at William.

"The boy didn't want to hear anything we had to say," said William. "I'm afraid he's still quite angry with all of us."

"He must get his stubbornness from you," Miriam said.

"Quiet," Lucy said. "Remember, Ben still doesn't know everything."

"You ought to tell him," said William. "Nothing good can come out of keeping it a secret. Just ask Jane."

Jane glared at him, and William suddenly became very interested in his fingernails.

"It's not going to matter if they don't get married," Miriam said.

Jane thought she detected a note of disappointment in Miriam's voice. This surprised her, and she said, "I thought you'd be happy about that."

Miriam shrugged. "I did too," she said.

"But?" said Jane.

"Don't make me say it," Miriam said.

"Go on," said William. "Out with it, woman."

"Fine," said Miriam. "I guess I'm just impressed that you

were willing to go to such lengths to . . . change back. You know, for Walter's sake."

"She means it was good of you to stick yourself with Crispin's Needle," William translated. "By the way, did it hurt much?"

Jane began to reply but was cut off by the sound of the ghost brothers clapping.

"He's come!" they cried. "He's come!"

Jane turned around. Walter was standing at the entrance to the chapel. Byron was beside him.

"Look who I found!" Byron said cheerfully.

Jane walked over to them. "You look very handsome," she said.

"Thank you," said Byron. "I'm quite fond of this suit and—"

"Not you, you idiot," Jane said. "I was speaking to Walter." She smiled. "But you do look handsome too," she said.

"Of course I do," said Byron. "Now I believe we have a wedding to go to."

"Not yet," Walter said.

Jane stiffened, waiting for his next words.

"Can I see you in private for a minute?" Walter said.

Jane nodded, afraid to speak. Walter took her hand and led her out of the chapel.

They returned five minutes later. When they entered, both had clearly been crying. But they also had smiles on their faces, and when Lucy looked at Jane and silently mouthed, "Are you okay?" Jane nodded.

Once more Jane found herself standing in front of Ben.

"Dearly beloved," he began. "We are gathered here—again— to celebrate the marriage of Walter Aaron Fletcher and Elizabeth Jane Fairfax." He paused and Jane tensed, knowing what was coming next. "If anyone can show just cause as to why these two should not be joined together in holy matrimony, let him speak now," Ben said.

"Well, since you asked—" Byron began.

"Shut up!" Jane, Lucy, Miriam, and William said as one.

"I was only joking," Byron muttered, then yelped as Lucy pinched the back of his arm.

"Walter and Jane will now exchange vows," Ben said.

Walter turned and, holding Jane's hands, began to speak. "I, Walter, take you, Jane, to be my wife. To have and to hold. To love and to cherish. In sick—"

"Wait a minute!" Byron said.

Jane and Walter looked at him.

"Those are your vows? Really?" He huffed and rolled his eyes. "And you call yourself a writer," he said to Jane.

"They're traditional," Jane said defensively.

"They're *dull*," said Byron. "Just a moment. Who has a pen?"

Miriam produced a pen from her bag and handed it to him. Byron removed a train ticket stub from his coat pocket and began to write on it. He paused a moment, closing his eyes and tapping the pen against his forehead.

"What *are* you doing?" Jane asked, growing annoyed.

"Quiet!" Byron ordered. "I'm trying to think."

He scribbled some more on the ticket and set it aside. Then he searched his pockets and came up with another piece of paper, this one a crumpled sales receipt for a box of cough drops. He smoothed it out and once more set to writing. When he was done he handed the train ticket to Walter and the receipt to Jane.

"There you are," he said. "Now proceed."

Walter peered closely at the train ticket. "I, Walter, take you, Jane, as my beloved wife and friend. As we walk this world together I promise to guard your heart from despair and worry. I will be your champion and rejoice in your accomplishments as if they are my own. When you laugh I will laugh with you, and when you cry I will kiss away your tears. Something about a white-winged dove."

"Not that bit," Byron called out. "It was just an idea. Sorry. Should have excised it."

"I will be your constant companion until the end of this world and the beginning of the next," Walter concluded.

Jane, who was trying very hard not to cry, sniffed. "I, Jane, take you, Walter, as my beloved husband and friend. I promise to make our journey together one of adventure and discovery. Every morning I will wake beside you, and every night I will go to sleep in your arms. My dreams will be yours, and yours mine." She choked up a little, and Walter squeezed her hand. "I will be your true love and heart's east—"

"Ease!" Byron shouted. "His heart's *ease!*" He shook his head. "I give up!"

"Your true love and your heart's ease until the end of this world and the beginning of the next," she concluded.

"I believe there are rings to be exchanged," said Ben.

"Yes, there are," said Lucy. "Sorry. I forgot all about them."

She got up and came forward. She handed one ring to Walter and one to Jane. Walter held Jane's hand as he slid his ring onto her finger, and then Jane did the same with her ring.

"Now that you have stood before us and exchanged these rings and these vows, it is my great pleasure to pronounce you husband and wife," Ben said.

To much applause, Walter kissed Jane. Then, not knowing what else to do, he kissed her again. Moments later they were surrounded by their friends, being hugged and kissed all around.

"That was quite nice," Prince Edward said to the First Duke of York.

"But not quite as thrilling as a beheading," said Richard.

"Well, no, not quite *that* nice," agreed his brother.

"I'm not sure what we do now," Jane said after she'd run out of people to hug. "Shall we go to breakfast?"

"I think tradition dictates that you leave for your honeymoon," William suggested.

Jane looked at Walter. "But we haven't really planned any—"

"Actually, I had an idea," Walter said.

Jane looked around her bedroom. "It looks very much the same," she told Walter.

Chawton Cottage was quite crowded. Walter and Jane had arrived at the same time as a tour group from the United States, and as they walked through the rooms of Jane's old home they were constantly competing with ladies dressed in period costumes clutching bags from the gift shop.

"Too bad you're not getting a piece of this action," Walter said.

"I know," said Jane. "Can you imagine what we could make on this pile if we turned it into a bed and breakfast? Everyone would want to sleep in my bed."

"Hey," Walter said. "I'm the only one who gets to sleep in your bed."

Jane laughed. "Let's go out into the garden," she suggested.

It was raining lightly, enough to keep most visitors inside the house but not so heavy that being outdoors was unpleasant. The grass was green, and the yard was coming alive with bluebells and violets. Jane and Walter sat down on a bench and enjoyed the quiet.

"I used to sit here quite a lot," Jane said. "Particularly when something in a plot was vexing me. I'd sit here and look for pictures in the clouds or in the stars. Almost always I would come away with a clear head and my problem solved."

"It must be strange seeing people going through your house," said Walter.

"A bit, yes," Jane agreed. "But it's not my house any longer. It belongs to them, really. They're the reason people still know who I am."

"I can't believe you wrote all of your novels on that little desk,"

Walter said. "And by *hand*. I think most writers today would give up if they didn't have computers."

"It certainly made me think good and hard about what I wanted to say before committing the words to the page," Jane said. "And it was hell on the eyes."

"We'll have a proper honeymoon later," Walter said. "I just thought this would nice to have a few days on our own before we head back."

Jane sighed. "We're going to have to have a wedding all over again," she said. "I don't know if I can take it."

Walter took her hand. "This time we'll let Lucy and my mother handle everything," he said. "We had the wedding we wanted."

"Was it really the wedding you wanted?" Jane asked him.

"You were there," said Walter. "That's all I wanted."

"Byron's rubbing off on you, I see," Jane said, kissing him on the cheek.

"Nope. I came up with that all on my own," said Walter. "Besides, it's true. You're all I ever wanted."

"We'll see if you say that when the honeymoon is over," Jane said.

Walter was quiet for a minute, then said, "Where do you think Char—Our Gloomy Friend went?"

Jane smiled. "You catch on quick," she said. "And I don't know. She has a way of disappearing and then popping up again when it's most inconvenient."

"Do you think she'll try to use the fake Needle?"

"Not before she tricks some other poor sucker into trying it first," Jane answered. "She's many things, but she's no fool. She won't try it on herself until she knows it works."

"Which means someone else will die," Walter said.

"That's if she even bothers," said Jane. "I believe what she said about only wanting it so that no one else could have it. She's a terribly unhappy person. I'm sure that's why her writing is so dreary."

"You just couldn't let that one get by, could you?" Walter said.

"Sorry," said Jane. "I know it's an awful habit."

"And Joshua?" Walter said.

"Oh, I imagine he'll go back to doing whatever it was he was doing in the first place," Jane said. "Something tedious I . . . " She stopped without finishing the thought.

"What?" asked Walter.

Jane turned to him. "It just occurred to me. We never did encounter the Tedious Three, and nobody we know has ever seen them. I wonder if Joshua could be . . . He certainly fits the tedious bit to a tee. But no, that would be too peculiar. Still, odder things have happened."

"How about we leave that mystery for another day?" Walter suggested.

"You're right," said Jane. "This is all about us."

The rain began to fall harder, but still they didn't move. Walter put his arm around Jane's shoulders, and she laid her head against his neck. She closed her eyes and tried to imagine herself being any happier than she was at that moment. And she couldn't.

Epilogue

Brakeston, New York

JANE GRIPPED WALTER'S HAND AND SQUEEZED IT SO HARD THAT HE yelped.

"Suck it up!" she said through gritted teeth. "It's nothing compared to what's taking place down below."

Lucy held the cup of ice chips to Jane's mouth, and Jane sucked a few in. "What I really want is a rare steak," Jane said.

The midwife, peering between Jane's legs, said, "It won't be much longer now."

Jane growled in response as another contraction came.

The bedroom door opened and Byron stuck his head in. He wore a gold cardboard crown with HAPPY NEW YEAR! spelled out in red glitter, and in his hand was a glass of champagne. Behind him, William looked over his shoulder.

"Are we too late?" Byron asked.

"No," said Walter. "She hasn't popped yet."

"This is so exciting," said Byron, coming into the already crowded room. "I've never been to a birth before."

"Probably because you always left the women when they became pregnant," Jane snarled.

"There's no need to be insulting," said Byron, lifting the sheet and looking beneath it.

"Do you mind?" the midwife said, giving him a disapproving look.

Byron made a face. "I'd forgotten what they look like," he said. He turned to William. "It just occurred to me—you're going to be a grandfather!"

"And you a fairy godfather," he said.

The door opened again and Miriam appeared. She pushed between Byron and William. "Is it a boy or a girl?" she asked.

Jane replied by groaning loudly and uttering some not entirely pleasant words.

"The great reveal has yet to occur," Byron informed Miriam, who rolled her eyes.

The midwife stood up. "I'm going to go get some more towels," she said. She pointed at Jane. "Don't have this baby until I get back."

"Don't worry," Byron told her. "If she does, we'll just pop it back in and she'll do it all over again so you don't miss anything."

The midwife shook her head and left the room. As the contractions had stopped for the moment, Jane lay back against the pillows and breathed in short, even bursts.

"How is the party?" she heard Lucy ask.

"Wonderful," Byron answered. "When you're done here you should all come over."

Jane opened one eye and fixed him with a stare. "By all means," she said. "There's nothing I would like more right now than to jump about with a noisemaker and toast the new year."

"Oh, do you want some?" Byron asked, holding out the champagne flute.

"No, I do not want any!" Jane bellowed. She followed this with a wild yell. "What I want is for this child to come out now!"

The midwife returned, her arms loaded with towels.

"It's still in there," Byron assured her.

"Not for much longer," said the midwife, assessing the situation. "Jane, are you ready?"

"No," Jane said. "I've changed my mind. I think we'll just wait a bit if nobody minds."

"Push!" the midwife commanded as a contraction hit.

Jane obliged, nearly cracking the fingers of Walter's hand in the process.

"Again!" said the midwife.

Jane heard Walter's voice in her ear. "You're about to be a mother," he said gently.

Jane pushed.

The room was silent for what seemed an eternity. Then a baby's cry filled the air, followed by cheering.

"It's a girl," Jane heard the midwife say.

Walter kissed Jane's forehead as everyone else crowded around the midwife and the baby.

"She's beautiful," Lucy said. "Just beautiful."

"Looks a bit like Churchill," Byron added. "Without the cigar."

"Hello, little one," said William.

"I'm a grandmother," Miriam announced. "Finally!"

"Excuse me," Jane said. "I know this is terribly thrilling for everyone, but might I have a look at my daughter?"

The midwife brought the baby over and handed her to Jane. Jane was almost afraid to take her, but her instincts overcame her nervousness and she accepted the child into her arms.

"Hello, baby," she said, looking into her daughter's eyes. "It's lovely to make your acquaintance."

The baby wrinkled her nose and squirmed, her tiny arms waving. Her mouth opened and closed, making a popping sound.

"You should feed her as soon as possible," the midwife said to Jane.

Jane looked at all of the faces staring at her. "This isn't a girlie show!" she said. "Everybody out. You can come back in a bit."

"We'll be right outside," Lucy said as she herded the others out of the room. "I'll call Ben and tell him and Sarah the good news."

Alone with Walter and their child, Jane held the baby to her breast. At first the little girl pushed away, twisting her face up and mewling like a kitten. But Jane kept bringing her back, and finally her lips closed around Jane's nipple and she began sucking.

"Can you believe it?" Walter said. "We're parents."

"And ten minutes ago we were just people," said Jane.

Walter laughed. He stroked Jane's hair and watched the baby feed. "When do you think we'll know?" he asked Jane.

Jane shook her head. "I don't know," she said. "This is new for me too."

In the days since the wedding, the question of whether or not Jane had used Crispin's Needle had come up several times. Each time she had deflected the question and it had gone unanswered, until finally people had stopped asking her.

The truth was, she had not used the Needle. But she still had it, sitting in its black velvet box in the top drawer of her bureau. Like Walter and Jane, it was waiting for the birth of the baby.

Before getting married, Jane and Walter had made a deal. Although both of them were willing to change for the other, neither was willing to ask the other to do so. And so they had compromised—when they had their first child, they would make the decision based on whether the baby was a vampire or not. If she was, then Walter would turn. If she wasn't, Jane would use the Needle. That way they would all three be the same. They would then announce the results to their loved ones.

Now that the moment had arrived, though, Jane had no idea how to tell. Perhaps it wasn't even something that *could* be discerned until a certain age. As she watched her daughter suckle, it occurred to Jane that once again she had failed to ask the proper questions. *We always seem to be making it up as we go along,* she thought.

"It doesn't really matter," Walter said. "Not right now."

"No," Jane agreed. "It doesn't."

The baby opened her mouth and burped.

"Now, Cassie," Jane said. "Is that any way for a little lady to behave?"

Cassandra Austen Fletcher opened her eyes very wide and stared at her mother and father. Deciding they would do, she then yawned, kicked her tiny feet, and went to sleep. It had, after all, been a very eventful day.

About the Author

MICHAEL THOMAS FORD is the author of numerous books, including the novels *Jane Goes Batty, Jane Bites Back, Z, The Road Home, What We Remember, Suicide Notes, Changing Tides, Full Circle, Looking for It,* and *Last Summer.*

www.michaelthomasford.com